Cash frowned at her. "I can't pay you a compliment?"

"You won't win me over with flattery."

"Flattery implies I'm lying."

He had moved closer to her. "Aren't you always?" She wasn't threatened by the closeness. She would stand her ground and make him move first.

"I wasn't lying. You know you're gorgeous. Every man and woman on the team thinks so. I'm the only one bold enough to say it to your face."

She scoffed. "You can't possibly know what everyone else is thinking about me."

"Again, I have a talent for reading people. When people look at you, they have the same interest in their eyes that I have. You're so beautiful they need to look for an extra few seconds to take it all in. But unlike most of the people on our team, I plan to do something about it."

"What is it you're planning to do?" she asked, unable to help herself.

"I'll win you over and make you forget how much you dislike me. Once that's out of the way, you'll see that I have a great many talents you may enjoy."

***

Dear Reader,

This book was inspired by the concept of a gray character, a man who has a speckled past, who is neither good nor bad, who means well, but who makes questionable decisions.

Cash is a criminal with a heart of gold, a con man with a good cause. Recently released from prison, he's been given the opportunity to work for the FBI. He's a man who desperately needs this second chance, and despite his cavalier attitude, he is determined not to let it slip away.

Lucia first appeared in *Under the Sheik's Protection*. She's thorough, smart and savvy. The straitlaced FBI agent is rankled that she has been assigned to be Cash's partner. But like Cash, she is also looking to escape her past and be taken seriously in the Bureau. But Cash being his charming self won't make it easy for Lucia to stay on the straight and narrow.

I love stories that celebrate new beginnings, leaving behind the mistakes of the past and moving forward into a brighter future. Everyone deserves a shot at happily ever after.

Best,

C.J. Miller

CJ-Miller.com

TAKEN BY
THE CON

———

C.J. Miller

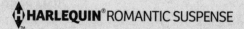
HARLEQUIN®ROMANTIC SUSPENSE

Recycling programs
for this product may
not exist in your area.

ISBN-13: 978-0-373-27908-1

Taken by the Con

Copyright © 2015 by C.J. Miller

Printed in U.S.A.

www.Harlequin.com

C.J. Miller loves to hear from her readers and can be contacted through her website, cj-miller.com. She lives in Maryland with her husband, son and daughter. C.J. believes in first loves, second chances and happily ever after.

Books by C.J. Miller

HARLEQUIN ROMANTIC SUSPENSE

Hiding His Witness

Shielding the Suspect

Protecting His Princess

Traitorous Attraction

Under the Sheik's Protection

Colton Holiday Lockdown

Taken by the Con

Visit the Author Profile page at Harlequin.com for more titles

To my big brother Shawn. Master of the art of persuasion, the definition of grace under pressure and loyal to a fault. I'm glad you're on my side.

Chapter 1

Lucia Huntington peeled off her blue-and-white-pinstriped blouse and dropped it in her dry-cleaning bag. She'd spilled coffee down the front of her shirt at her morning meeting, the first in a series of bungles that had lined her day.

At least the day was over, paperwork filed and everyone's notes reviewed and approved. After she returned her mother's phone call, she'd have a few hours to sleep before she did it all again tomorrow.

A knock sounded on her door. Lucia hadn't buzzed anyone into the building, but her neighbor Audrey from across the hall periodically stopped by before she went out for the night. Audrey had a great sense of humor and would provide some comic relief after Lucia's dreadful day. On her way to the door, Lucia took another sip from the glass of wine she had been drinking.

Looking through the peephole and seeing David

"Cash" Stone's face stirred several emotions, primary among them anxiety. Ever since he strode into her morning meeting with his cocky swagger and dark hair, captivating sapphire eyes and buff shoulders, Lucia had been controlling her libido's overreaction. Sexy with a hint of danger, everything about him screamed warnings. He was a take-no-prisoners kind of man. If she gave him an inch, he would take a mile.

Her workday was over and that meant she didn't have to deal with him. This was her turf.

Another tap sounded on the door. "Come on, Lucia. I know you're home."

Not willing to hide in her condo like a coward and wait for him to leave, Lucia grabbed a coat off the coatrack and pulled it on over her bra. She wasn't a lovestruck teenager and she was in control of her hormones. Composing herself, she pulled open the door and met Cash's steely stare. It was as if he was seeing right through her cool facade to the part of her that was panting and restless just looking at him.

"Can I help you?" she asked. She had other questions, like "How do you know where I live?" and "How did you get past my building's security?" but she'd stick with the one that would get rid of him fast. The less time she had to spend with Cash Stone the better.

He leaned against the doorjamb. "Aren't you going to ask me in?"

His visit was inappropriate at best, but Cash played by his own rules. He radiated charisma and self-assurance on top of his playboy good looks, and most women found the combination irresistible. Lucia wasn't most women. She had hard-won, carefully exercised control.

Since knowing about his criminal past didn't put a damper on her lust, she needed to find something physically wrong with him and latch on to it. The one physical flaw she could find was that his secondhand clothes lacked style. She needed to mentally harp on that point and banish any sensual ideas of him. He wasn't someone she was planning to date. He wasn't part of her personal life. He was the con man skilled in fraud, counterfeiting and high-tech crimes, brought in to help in an important investigation. He had an abundance of confidence and he was an untrustworthy criminal, a dangerous combination.

"I am not asking you in," she said. "I don't fraternize with my coworkers in my home."

He laughed. The gun at her hip tingled against her skin. Were her instincts sending her a warning? Cash was remarkably bold and she was tempted to close the door in his face. She clamped down on the urge. She wouldn't have an emotional outburst and let him know he'd gotten to her. Unacceptable.

"Benjamin wants us to make nice," Cash said.

Lucia gritted her teeth. She didn't want to make nice with Cash Stone. She wanted him gone. "Benjamin has not advised me of that." She was out of the loop on matters concerning her team. With Cash joining today, she was the second newest member, but she was supposed to be Benjamin's right hand. As the assistant special agent in charge, or ASAC, she should be consulted on matters affecting the team. In reality, her new job duties were paperwork and spending extralong hours at the office.

"Check your phone," Cash said.

Lucia left the door and grabbed her phone from the

counter. Sure enough, there was a text from her boss: Cash on his way over. Make it work. We need him.

Annoyance caused a rush of heat to flame up her neck. Lucia set the phone on the counter and shook the irritation off her face. When she turned around, she smiled. "We don't have a problem. As long as you don't break the law or run a con on me, we'll be fine."

"I think you're forgetting that Benjamin hired me because I can read people and I know you're lying. I piss you off and I need to know why." Cash was darkly good-looking and maybe he was accustomed to every woman falling at his feet. He'd have to learn she wasn't every woman and she didn't throw herself at men.

"Benjamin cut a deal with you because you have connections to a criminal we're hunting, and catching that criminal will make him look good for a promotion he wants." There. That should set Cash straight. He had skills they could use, but she wasn't giving his ego a boost by acknowledging them.

Broad shoulders lifted. "He hired me for both reasons. Tell me why you can't stand me. No one else on the team has a problem with me."

That her team had welcomed and embraced him added to her agitation. They hadn't been nearly as warm with her. Lucia shouldn't have a problem with Cash. She didn't know why he got under her skin. She dealt with criminals on a weekly basis. She'd been on stakeouts and watched scumbags commit crimes. She'd been undercover and lived with the lowest of the low. It hadn't taken a personal toll.

But Cash Stone grated on her. "You shouldn't have been released from prison. You need to serve your time.

With you at my back, I'll be waiting for you to put a bullet in it."

What she'd said was blunt, but that was how she rolled these days.

His eyes sparkled with amusement. Was he enjoying this? If she'd hoped to get a rise out of him, she'd failed.

"I am serving my time. For the remaining three years of my sentence, I'll be chained to you." He lifted his pant leg to show her the ankle monitor. "You can trust me to do my job. If I don't, I'll earn myself seven more years in prison."

"Unless you skip town before you've worked your three years," she said.

"Won't happen," he said. "I want you to give me a real chance and treat me like everyone else on the team."

Lucia rolled her eyes. He would run the first chance he had. Men like Cash didn't change. He was a con man and a felon. He was probably conning her now, saying what he thought she'd want to hear. She wouldn't mince words with a known liar. "You can count on me to behave professionally."

"I don't know what it's like at the FBI, but in my world, professionally doesn't include showing your colleagues you hit the gym six days a week."

"What are you—"

He gestured at her and she looked down. In her anger, she'd set her hands on her hips, which had opened her jacket and given him a view of her white lace bra and bare stomach. Fantastic. She'd flashed a convict.

She refused to show remorse or embarrassment. "You came to my home. Deal with it."

His eyes were wide and a smirk played across his lips. "Gladly."

Lucia pulled together the jacket. He was infuriating. "How did you get in here, anyway?"

Cash tipped his head to the side. "Do you want me to point out the security weaknesses in your building? It won't help you sleep better at night."

"I sleep fine at night next to my gun," Lucia said. The words weren't intended as a threat. They were the truth. Lucia worked hard to practice constant vigilance. In her line of work, she made enemies. She wouldn't be someone's victim.

"Benjamin wants us to move past the hostility."

It wouldn't happen. At least, not until she'd had time to figure how to get Cash kicked off the team. They didn't need him to crack this case. She could find Clifton Anderson and the hundreds of millions he'd embezzled. She'd return the money to the people it belonged to, people who were counting on that money. She didn't need a felon to help her.

"Stay out of my way in the field and we won't have a problem," she said.

"Then you won't mind if I join you for happy hour tomorrow after work?"

Lucia felt the familiar sting of rejection. Someone had already invited him to the weekly happy hour. Lucia hadn't been invited to it, although she'd overheard others talking about it. She was an outsider on her own team. Again.

Cash was too charming for his own good, but she pegged his laid-back, easy demeanor as hiding something dark and dangerous. "You should do whatever you want," Lucia said.

"What's that scent?" he asked.

She didn't smell anything, but her condo was over that of a gourmet chef and she had grown accustomed to the tantalizing smells that wafted to her place. "Maybe it's trash." She might as well dump on the conversation. She didn't want to have a gourmet-food discussion with Cash.

"It's not trash. It's something delicious. Earthy. Sexy." He leaned forward and inhaled. "There it is."

Outrage jolted her at the same time her legs tightened and heat pooled between them. "You cannot speak to me like that." Boundaries. They desperately needed boundaries.

Cash frowned at her. "I can't pay you a compliment?"

"You won't win me over with flattery."

"Flattery implies I'm lying."

He had moved closer to her. He smelled like a fresh shower and spices, a scent she enjoyed but ignored. The kitchen breakfast bar was at her back and Cash was standing a few inches from her. He was six inches taller, but when he looked at her she felt as if they were eye to eye. "Aren't you always?" She wasn't threatened by the closeness, but he'd view it as weakness if she asked him to back away. She would stand her ground and make him move first.

"I wasn't lying," he said. "You know you're gorgeous. Every man and woman on the team thinks so. I'm the only one bold enough to say it to your face."

She scoffed. "You can't possibly know what everyone else is thinking about me." If Cash didn't already know it, she wouldn't point out that most people thought first about her family's wealth, not how she looked. Or, if they weren't thinking about her family money, they were wondering about her time with the violent-crime division and why she'd been transferred.

"Again, I have a talent for reading people. When people look at you, they have the same interest in their eyes that I have. You're so beautiful they need to look for an extra few seconds to take it all in. But unlike most of the people on our team, I plan to do something about it."

"What is it you're planning to do?" she asked, unable to help herself.

"I'll win you over and make you forget how much you dislike me. Once that's out of the way, you'll see that I have a great many talents you may enjoy." Sexual innuendo laced every syllable.

She had never been spoken to this way and it turned her blood hot. She had no doubt some of Cash's *talents* related to his bedroom activities. Heat rushed low in her belly and her thighs tingled. "Does anyone buy that crap you're selling?"

Cash smiled. He had to know it was his ace card with most women, but it didn't work with her. Seeing a handsome man didn't make Lucia giggly and weak in the knees. Considering his past, he was front and center on her "men to avoid" list.

"I can read you. You're turned on. You want to kiss me and you hate that."

Lucia inhaled slowly to calm herself. Lust was quickly overtaking the anger she'd felt. Interrogation techniques. Hiding her emotions. She called on the skills she'd learned as a special agent, but felt them failing. Cash was rattling her and Lucia didn't rattle easily. She fought for composure and clear thinking. Was something in her face or posture giving away that she was attracted to him?

He was tall, handsome and confident. She could acknowledge he had certain attractive traits. That didn't mean she wanted him in her bed. "You can't read me as well as you think."

"Kiss me and prove it."

She laughed. He was contemptible. "I'm not kissing you."

"I'll go on believing the reason is that you're afraid of what might happen."

Afraid? Never. She feared nothing. Not even a player with thick brown hair that skimmed the tops of his ears. A strand had fallen over his forehead as if he'd styled it to draw her attention to his too-perfect face.

A surface-level attraction held no sway over her. It would pass. A kiss would change nothing, but a kiss would happen on her terms.

One hand cinching her coat together, Lucia grabbed the back of his head with her free hand and brought his mouth to hers in a hot, fierce kiss. She was unaffected by anything he could dish out. She could take it and not let it break her stride.

Except the kiss was like none she'd ever had. It sizzled and scorched her. She should stop it and throw him out, but her libido urged her for a few more seconds to taste him, a little more, a little longer. His tongue moved in sync with hers, his mouth brushing over hers with the right pressure and the right speed. The man had skills. She wondered what he was like in bed.

"How much have you had to drink?" he asked in breathless pants between kisses.

He must have tasted the wine on her lips. His question gave her a moment to think. She'd drunk half a glass of wine, but more importantly, she was standing in her condo kissing Cash Stone.

He had manipulated her so easily. Her guard hitched up and she broke away. She slid to the right, away from the counter and straightened her coat around her, ensuring everything was covered. He wasn't getting another peep show.

She folded her arms. "See? Nothing between us but air. Now write this down as a rule so you don't forget it. None of my other colleagues come to my home uninvited and unannounced. If you need something, you can tell me at work. Or better yet, don't tell me. Tell Benjamin and he'll pass it along to me."

Cash studied her and Lucia refused to shift under his blue-eyed gaze. She tipped her chin up proudly. The master of reading people wouldn't know how much he'd excited her. Thrills of pleasure still danced over her. Her knees felt weak and her thighs were quivering. She blamed the length of time she'd been alone.

"Benjamin will ask how our meeting went," Cash said.

Would Cash tell him about the kiss? Would it matter? How her boss and colleagues saw her was important to her. Her reputation had been tarnished when she was moved from the high-profile violent-crime division to the lower visibility of the white-collar division. She had so much riding on this case. She had to prove she was a good agent. A great agent. "I'll tell him it went fine and we won't have any issues working together."

"I think we might have an issue," Cash said. "You'll have to keep your hands off me."

She sputtered.

"Come on, Lucy, I was joking. Lighten up."

"Don't call me Lucy. It's Lucia."

"Can't we be friendly, Lucia?" he asked.

"If saying yes will get you out of my home, then yes."

"That's not very friendly," Cash said. He looked around the condo. "Do you mind if I go out on the balcony?"

And invade her space further? "I'd prefer that you leave."

"I spent the last four years in a cage and the last thirty seconds having my mind blown by a topless FBI agent. Let me grab some fresh air and cool down." He strode to the balcony and opened the double doors leading outside.

"Fresh air is also available on your walk home," she said.

"Come here a minute," Cash said. "Please."

The word *please* surprised her. Until now, he had been bold and confident. He hadn't seemed like the type to ask, but rather that he would expect she do as he requested.

She walked to the balcony. He was a difficult man to say no to. His eyes and voice beckoned like a siren song—a very hot, very male siren.

"Look up," he said, pointing to the sky.

She did and the sight took her breath away. The moon was bright and full, and stars filled the sky. How long had it been since she took a moment to enjoy her view? "The full moon explains that kiss."

Cash put his arm around her shoulders. "Whatever story you want to tell, I'm game."

She shrugged off his arm. "We can't be friends. I don't make friends at work." Easier to define her role in clear terms and not wonder why no one looped her into their personal lives.

Cash took a deep breath. "Whatever you say, boss."

He sounded sad and a touch of compassion brushed her. He seemed to be enjoying the view. What harm would it do to stand out on the balcony for a few minutes?

"I guess you aren't married," Cash said.

Prying, but she allowed the question. "I'm not married." She had once been close to being someone's wife, but it had been years since she'd dated or had much of a social life. Since the heartbreak of her broken engagement, she'd changed focus and had sacrificed a private life for her career. She now enjoyed being alone. She liked her space and preferred to do whatever she wanted with her free time and not feel guilty about working late.

"I was married once," Cash said.

A personal conversation was unnecessary. She didn't want to share details of her own misadventures in love. "Why are you telling me this?"

"You said you're worried you can't trust me. I'm giving you a reason to trust me."

"That reason is what?" Lucia asked. "That you convinced some woman to marry you and now she has to live as your ex?"

"Not ex-wife. My late wife. She died in a car accident."

She was a jerk of the worst kind. She'd gotten prickly and snarky and run her mouth. "I'm sorry. I didn't mean—"

Cash held up his hand. "Please don't apologize. It was years ago and I'm okay now. But we have a son."

Benjamin hadn't said anything about Cash's personal

life and Lucia found herself riveted by what Cash was sharing with her, even as traces of doubt slipped through her thoughts. "Where's your son?" she asked, scared of the answer. Cash had been in prison. His wife was dead. What had happened to the little boy?

"He lives with my wife's mom. If I stay out of trouble and make a life for him, the court may let him live with me. That's how you know I won't betray you. My son is my life and getting him back means everything to me. Next time you worry about me running away, know that I have everything that matters riding on making this job work."

Cash hated being chained to the FBI office in Washington, DC, and he hated the place where he was living. He hated being a free man in name only. He hated his crappy motel room where he was forced to live. He hated the tiny stipend the FBI paid him that kept him from enjoying any part of life. But most of all, Cash hated being away from his son. Adrian lived in Seattle, Washington. He was ten years old, a fifth grader, and he loved soccer and martial arts. Thank God Helen had written Cash weekly, sending along pictures of Adrian while Cash had served his time in jail. Those letters and photos were the only possessions Cash cared about. Adrian had visited him once in prison, but the visit had given the little boy nightmares for weeks after, and Cash and Helen had agreed it was healthier not to bring Adrian again.

Since learning he'd be turned out on the FBI's release-and-reform program, Cash had been begging Helen to bring Adrian to DC to see him. Without money for the trip, and while he was living in a fleabag motel room, Helen thought Adrian was better off in Seattle. Helen had a life in Seattle and she didn't have the resources or desire to pick up and move across the country, even temporarily.

At least Adrian's cancer hadn't returned, making the jail time well worth it. The experimental surgery and treatments had saved his life. Cash had broken the law and he'd made a deal with the devil, but his son was healthy. To his way of thinking, the end had justified the means.

He'd purchased a phone card from a nearby gas station and used the pay-per-call landline in his room to call Helen in Washington.

"Hi, Helen. It's Cash. Is Adrian around?" Cash asked.

"Cash, honey, are you safe? I've been praying for you."

He was as safe as he could be living in a motel that advertised hourly rates. "I'm fine. I'm hoping to have a better place by the end of the month. I'm saving every penny and as soon as I can, I'll send a plane ticket to Adrian so he can visit."

There was a heavy pause and then the sound of a door creaking open and crickets chirping. Helen had stepped onto her porch and out of Adrian's earshot. "Cash, I've cared for and loved this boy for the last four years. I don't feel right sending him across the country without me."

Cash's heart squeezed hard in his chest. She had legal rights to Adrian, but Cash had to have his son back in his life. He was tied to DC for three more years. Three more years lost of his son's childhood. He couldn't stand that. "Please, Helen. Don't keep my boy from me." He couldn't keep his voice from breaking.

"I'm not keeping him from you. I'm trying to do what's best for Adrian. He's finally doing better in school and making friends. I can't tear him away from that."

Adrian was best with him. "Tell me what I need to do and I'll do it."

"We've discussed that. It's not only your living situation and the money. It's how he'll feel about seeing you. You remember the nightmares he had after the last time. He doesn't know you. You're a stranger to him."

He was a stranger to his son. It was a knife hit to the heart. "I'll buy plane fare for both of you. Put you up in a hotel. Whatever you need for you both to be comfortable." He was desperate and he knew he sounded it.

"Let's start with a talk. Let me get him."

Cash waited, feeling dizzy and sick. He had missed Adrian every minute he was in prison. It was torture being away from his son. If there had been any other way to save his son's life and not break the law, he would have taken it.

Helen came back on the phone. "I'm sorry, Cash. He's tired and doesn't want to talk now."

Cash squeezed his eyes shut. His throat was tight. "Thanks for asking. Please tell Adrian I love him and I miss him. I'm working on things here. I really am."

"I know you are, Cash. I know you're trying."

He said his goodbyes and disconnected the phone. Looking around his room, he didn't feel defeat. He would find a way. All that stood between him and his son was money and 2,700 miles. He'd close the gap. He had to.

He had a few hours until his 11:00 p.m. curfew, and Cash fled his room to walk alone on the dark street. He refused to think of the motel as home. The drug dealers that hung out in the parking lot made it unlikely that he could rest easy. The noise and constant fights in other rooms were disturbing. But, he'd been in prison for four years. Outside was good. Outside was the most wonderful place with fresh air and endless sky.

Cash didn't have money for a cab and he didn't have a car. The rules of his release prevented him from traveling unescorted farther than ten miles away and his movements were tracked by the FBI via the GPS tracking device he wore around his ankle. Benjamin would have a report emailed to him the next morning detailing every step Cash had taken.

He kept his pace brisk, loving the openness of the sidewalk. He saw a help-wanted sign in the window of a deli. Maybe a second job could help with his money problems.

His old contacts could increase his cash flow by sending some jobs his way, but Cash was finished with that life. He didn't want money from running cons. Every penny he earned for his new life with his son would be earned legally.

Turning down a familiar street, he realized he'd been walking in the direction of the house where he'd grown up. The house where he believed his father still lived. Not looking to dredge up buried memories or walk in old footsteps, he changed directions.

This was a fresh start. Another one. When he'd married Britney and talked her into moving to DC, he'd promised to leave behind contact with the criminal world. His single foray back into that world had been to save Adrian's life.

Benjamin knew about Adrian, but he'd said he

needed Cash in DC, working to find Clifton Anderson. The faster they closed the case, the sooner Cash had more options. At least, that was what Cash was telling himself.

To ease some of the hurt in his chest, he forced his thoughts away from his son and they turned instead to Lucia Huntington. He'd find out why she had a chip on her shoulder. From what he'd gathered from the others, she carried power in the organization, although she was quiet and didn't seem close to anyone in the office.

He'd win her over. Having an enemy in Lucia could mean his return to prison. Having a friend in her could mean a transfer to an FBI field office closer to Adrian after the case was closed and maybe even a raise. The more money he could sock away, the faster his son was back in his life.

As attracted to her as he was, Lucia seemed equally put off by him. She was the first woman he'd met since his late wife who got him hot under the collar. She was smart, sophisticated and articulate. It didn't hurt that she was gorgeous. Brown hair and deep brown eyes, delicate features and lips that on some women might look too big. On her, it worked, drawing his attention, making him think about the things she could do with her mouth. She was put together and in control, but he sensed that, if she allowed it, passion and heat would come roaring out. He'd gotten a peek at her bare midriff, which showed him enough to say she had a body to match her face. It was rare to cross paths with a woman who was the complete package. He wondered why she was distant from the team. A professional code of conduct or was something else at play?

He crossed the street and walked past a man and his

dog sleeping on the cement steps outside a church, both curled near the railing. Cash reached into his pocket and pulled out the rest of the cash Benjamin had given him that morning. It wasn't much, about thirteen dollars and some change. He tucked it under the man's hand.

"Thank you," the man muttered. His dog whimpered.

"You're welcome," Cash said.

He'd been there. He'd been that down and out. He hadn't had anyone to help him. But he was resourceful. He would find a way to make a good life for himself and Adrian.

Chapter 2

"We may have more success if you don't flash your badge at everyone we pass," Cash said, after Lucia had shown her identification to the guards working the security desk at Holmes and White, the company Clifton Anderson had defrauded into near ruin.

Lucia whirled to look at him. Though he'd been quiet on the ride from headquarters, she didn't appreciate his criticism. She was irritated enough that Benjamin had assigned her and Cash as teammates for the day's assignments.

"I'm not here to con anyone," she said, keeping her voice low. "I'm here to speak to Clifton Anderson's victims. I'm identifying myself because I'm on their side." She had interviewed dozens of victims. She knew what she was doing.

Cash lifted a brow at her.

"Do you find this funny? Because nothing about

this is funny. People lost their homes, their pensions, their savings and their college funds over this. Regular people. Teachers. Nurses. Police officers. Everyone who trusted this place lost everything. We have to find this money for them."

Cash frowned. "I take this seriously. I know what was lost. I have a way I do things. Getting upset changes nothing."

Lucia took a deep breath. She'd been told she could be a stickler for the rules and policies and procedures. If she and Cash were going to survive this, she needed to give him some latitude. It was one afternoon. She could do anything for one afternoon.

Cash folded his arms over his chest. "Did you see the security guard's reaction when you told him you were with the FBI? He got nervous. He was worried."

Lucia was accustomed to people having a reaction to her badge. "I got what I wanted. I was let through without any fanfare."

"He's no doubt calling ahead to give warning we're on our way to the top floor."

"It's not a secret that we're investigating the embezzlement. There's nothing to give warning about." The FBI was working under the assumption that the C-level managers at Holmes and White wanted the culprits found and the stolen money recovered.

Cash took her elbow and moved her to the side of the hallway, out of the way of a passing group of employees. "Let's not leave time for preparations. The most telling reactions are the most impromptu."

Benjamin's voice rang in her head. He wanted her and Cash to get along. Benjamin seemed set on the idea that their skill sets complemented each other. Lucia had the sense they'd been partnered for today's interviews as a test. If they made it through the two interviews Benjamin had assigned them without killing each other, it was a success. Lucia wouldn't let Cash make her lose her cool or fail in Benjamin's eyes.

"I will hold back on showing my badge to too many people. Happy?" She pulled her elbow away from him. Touching was off-limits, especially after the kiss last night. She didn't know how he'd convinced her it was a good idea, but it wouldn't happen again.

"Thank you. Has anyone else mentioned you look hot when you're fired up about something?"

She gave him a cutting glower. "My colleagues don't talk to me that way."

"I wasn't asking about your colleagues. I was asking about people in your personal life."

Sad to admit, even if it was only to herself, she wasn't sure any man besides Cash had ever called her "hot."

"That's not a conversation we'll have right now." Or ever.

They stepped onto the elevator and Lucia pressed the button for the top floor, where Holmes and White's CEO, Leonard Young, had his office. Her arm brushed Cash's and Lucia increased the distance between them.

Every time the elevator stopped at a floor and people entered and exited, Cash seemed to flirt and smile at every woman, especially the pretty, young, well-dressed ones. It bothered Lucia to watch. Given the long over-the-shoulder looks they shot his way, these women would be all over him if given the chance.

Lucia and Cash got off the elevator. Young's office was directly ahead. The cube farm around them was empty. Layoffs had been an immediate fallout of Holmes and White's recent financial problems.

Young's assistant stopped them in front of his office's beveled glass doors.

"Mr. Young had to step away from his desk. Do you mind waiting here until he returns?" She gestured to the cluster of leather chairs along the wall.

"No problem," Cash said and flashed her a smile. "I'm David Stone." They had agreed Cash would use his real name while working with Lucia to avoid rumors floating on the street about Cash Stone being employed by the FBI. Cash Stone, son of the notorious con man and who'd become a con man himself, was well-known. To her knowledge, Cash hadn't ripped off anyone on the same scale that Clifton Anderson had, but the con that had landed him in jail had stolen fifty thousand dollars from a senator's real estate company. The company bought run-down foreclosures, made repairs and flipped the houses for big profits. The senator had been friends with the judge on Cash's case, so he'd had the book thrown at him. Hard.

"I'm Georgiana," Young's assistant said. She blushed and lowered her face, looking up at Cash from under her eyelashes. Overselling it a bit, wasn't she? Hot pink blouse with a tight, dark gray skirt suit and four-inch heels wrapped a neat, prim package. Lucia despised the pang of jealousy that struck her. Emotions didn't belong in the field. She didn't know if she was jealous because she wanted to be on the receiving end of Cash's attention or because the woman looked like the delicate, polished lady Lucia couldn't be.

Neither one was a thought to harp on.

For a moment, Lucia regretted the simple black pants

and blue blouse she'd chosen that morning. She hadn't bothered with jewelry or makeup, and her one-inch black heels weren't anything that screamed *sexy vixen*.

"Could I have a cup of coffee? I didn't sleep well last night and I'm feeling foggy," Cash said.

Georgiana straightened and grinned at him as if he was a genie granting her a wish. "Oh, of course. How would you like it?" She said the last two words while giving Cash a long, lingering look. Cash had Georgiana eating out of his hand after ten seconds. Then again, Cash's charisma and charm were legendary. Even Lucia had fallen for it, however momentarily, the night before.

Georgiana was behaving as if Lucia wasn't standing there or her presence didn't matter. If Young's assistant represented Holmes and White's employee base, no wonder they'd been snowed. Lucia chastised herself for the nasty thought. What had happened at Holmes and White could have happened to anyone Clifton Anderson selected as his target.

"Sugar and a little creamer. Thanks," Cash said.

Georgiana hurried off, not asking Lucia if she'd like something, as well.

"Was that necessary?" Lucia asked.

"Was what necessary?" He took a seat behind the woman's desk and started looking around.

"Flirting with her. And you can't do that," Lucia said, setting her hand over Cash's to stop him from searching Georgiana's desk.

The heat that burned between them had Lucia stepping back. She had to keep these strong reactions to him in check.

"Come on, boss. This stuff is in plain view," Cash said. "What's the harm if I take a look?"

"Gray area," Lucia said. Even if Georgiana were involved in the fraud, she wouldn't have evidence that she'd leave on top of her desk with the FBI sniffing around.

"Relax. I'm not looking to get anything entered into evidence. I want a little more insider knowledge and to get a sense of the people we're dealing with," Cash said.

"The people we're dealing with are the victims," Lucia said.

"Anderson could have had people on the inside. A well-placed assistant with a lower-paying job who could be bought off," Cash said.

Since Cash had worked with Clifton Anderson in the past, Lucia took note of the theory to explore later, though she had considered it herself. Many of the employees at Holmes and White had been questioned. Lucia would see if Georgiana was one of them.

Cash removed a small pen from his pocket. She recognized it as one of the FBI's camera pens.

"Where did you get that?" she asked.

"Renee in IT gave it to me. She heard I was doing some interviews today and thought it might come in handy. Which it does," Cash said.

No one in IT had ever given her a device to use in the field, at least, not without her prompting.

After snapping some pictures, Cash took a seat in a chair outside Young's office. "Is this what it's like to be an FBI agent? Running around the city and interviewing people?"

He made it sound easy. "Sometimes." The work could be challenging and dangerous. Days like today were among the easier ones.

"Come on, I'm being friendly."

"You're making me hate that word," Lucia said.

"Then give me a chance to get on your good side," Cash said.

Everything he said sounded light and good-natured. It was almost harder to keep her dislike of him than to give in to his charm. "You don't need to be on any of my sides," Lucia said.

"There's one side of you in particular I've seen and really like," Cash said, looking at her mouth.

Her lips prickled and burned and she remembered how amazing kissing him had been. "You are something else," Lucia said, trying to diffuse the blistering desire spreading down her body. She would not let down her defenses.

"I think she would agree with you," Cash said under his breath, rising to his feet and taking the coffee from Georgiana's outstretched hands.

Cash talked with Georgiana, leaning in and laughing at her lame jokes. Lucia pretended not to notice. Georgiana returned to her desk, wrote something on a piece of paper and handed it to Cash.

"Call me," Georgiana said. She ran her hand down his pale green tie, fisting it at the end and pulling him a little closer to her.

Cash looked at the paper and then slipped it into his suit jacket pocket. He looked pleased and interested in the cute redhead.

Annoyance burned through Lucia. Why was it so easy for some men to win over a woman?

Lucia could think of a dozen snappy remarks to make about the exchange, but she kept her mouth shut. Saying anything would make her sound jealous and juvenile.

"Tell me. I can hear you fuming," Cash said, taking a seat next to her.

"I'm not fuming," Lucia said. "I'm observing."

"I'm establishing a rapport," Cash said, the light-heartedness gone. "If she knows something about Young or the theft, I want to know it, too."

They waited in silence for twenty minutes before Leonard Young returned to his office. Twenty minutes of thinking about Cash when she should be thinking about the case. Twenty minutes of replaying that kiss. Twenty minutes of every nerve in her body being aware he was next to her and dancing excitedly about it.

When Young returned, he had another man in tow.

"I thought it would be a good idea to have our in-house attorney present for this conversation. He's worried about lawsuits," Young said, ushering them into his office. "Nothing's been finalized with our clients and we have a lot of angry people waiting for a settlement."

Lucia's bull-crap meter went off. A month ago, when the story went public, Holmes and White had publicly asked the FBI to assist and had reassured their team they'd be cooperative and open. A lawyer in attendance seemed like a defensive measure.

Holmes and White were likely conducting their own internal investigation. If they'd stumbled on a mistake, they'd want to keep that under wraps. It was Lucia's job to bring everything on the level.

Young took a seat behind his large desk. His lawyer sat next to him, quiet and with a notepad poised on his lap.

Sensing this interview would be a waste of time, Lucia introduced herself and Cash and then launched into her questions. She had not conducted the initial interviews with Young, but she had read them. To this point Young had been helpful but cautious. That hadn't changed.

Cash said nothing and his face was impossible to read. He appeared both indifferent and slightly amused.

"How is your investigation progressing?" Young asked.

Not as well as Lucia would have liked. Their team had tracked two percent of the stolen money to accounts within the United States. Those accounts had been frozen pending the FBI's investigation. The rest of the money had disappeared. "We're following every lead we have available."

"I'll tell you whatever I can," Young said.

His lawyer shook his head and Young glanced at him. "I will tell you anything I can within reason."

Cash didn't write anything. He didn't fiddle. He didn't look around the office or sneak another look at Georgiana. His eyes stayed riveted on Leonard Young and his lawyer.

As Lucia expected, Young's answer was "I don't know" to almost every question. When he did answer, he gave disappointingly little information. For someone who wanted the money found, he was stingy with details. His behavior earned him a slot in Lucia's "look into this much deeper" folder.

"Thank you for your time, Mr. Young," Lucia said after forty-five minutes of questions had yielded nothing new. "We'll be in touch."

Lucia would need to find another way to approach Young or some other angle to use. Maybe she could get in touch with someone else in the company, perhaps someone lower on the food chain. Starting at the top wouldn't have been her preferred technique, but Benjamin had suggested Young and had warned her to keep things friendly. This case had many victims, and the public and media were watching closely.

Once they were outside the Holmes and White building, Cash spoke for the first time since before the interview.

"You know he's lying, right?" Cash asked.

"What makes you think that?" Lucia asked. She suspected Young was withholding information, but Cash was along to lend his insights.

"He has a tell. It took a few questions for me to notice. He looks at his left ring finger and then he lies. Interestingly, his ring finger is bare. Is he married?" Cash asked.

"According to the file we have on him, yes," Lucia said.

"He's cheating on her," Cash said.

"How do you know that?" Lucia asked.

"Gut feeling. He had this way of answering the questions. He thinks he's in control and he thinks he can do whatever he wants."

Interesting observation. Arrogance and control went with the territory. "We'll follow up."

"Do you want me to call Georgiana? I could take her to dinner and see if I can learn anything from her."

Imagining Cash on a dinner date with the beautiful, younger woman annoyed her and Lucia couldn't answer that question objectively. "Talk to Benjamin about it."

"Is that how this partnership will work? You'll pass me off when you don't want to discuss something?" Cash asked.

Lucia continued toward the car. "It's not a partnership. Benjamin sent us out together to handle these interviews. In future tasks, hopefully you'll be assigned to work with someone else."

"I like working with you," he said.

"Why?" Lucia asked, drawing to a stop and looking at him. Few others did. Either she was accused of going by the book or being too impulsive.

"Why do I like working with you?" he asked.

At her nod, he rubbed his chin. "You're smart. You're strong. You're spunky."

"Spunky?" she asked.

"Yes," he said. "You're making this fun."

She sensed something unsaid. "I guess that's something. I think you're angling for something from me and I need to be up-front with you. I feel badly about your son and I appreciate that you were honest about your situation, but I won't interfere in a domestic matter."

He blinked at her and held up his hands. "Understood."

"Let's finish these interviews. Don't you have a happy hour to attend?"

Preston Hammer's Georgetown townhouse was located in a small community where ten million was the going price for houses. Hammer's was four townhomes gutted and converted into one large, stately unit. Lucia knocked on the door, surprised when Hammer answered the door himself.

Lucia showed him her badge. "We spoke on the phone, Mr. Hammer." She introduced herself and Cash.

Hammer stepped back from the door and gestured for them to come inside. The interior wasn't what Lucia was expecting. The foyer was stacked with brown moving boxes, each labeled in precise printing.

"Relocating?" Lucia asked.

Hammer gestured at the grand Juliette staircase, oak handrails, the shiny hardwood floors and the insets along the wall containing artwork illuminated with custom lighting. "Do you think I can afford to live here? After what Holmes and White did to me, I'm lucky I have food to eat." He mumbled something else under his breath Lucia didn't catch. "Come into the kitchen. We can talk there."

Cash wandered over to one of the pieces on the wall. "Is this a Monet?"

"Interested? It's headed to auction in a few days," he said. Hammer started down the hall and Lucia and Cash followed.

"That artwork is probably worth more than this place," Cash whispered to Lucia.

One of Cash's areas of expertise was art forgeries. If Hammer was liquidating his assets, he hadn't saved much of his eight-figure salary for a rainy day.

The kitchen was large, extending almost the length of the houses. Butler's pantry, gleaming granite countertops and maple cabinets indicated luxury living.

"Your former employer tells us you were let go because Clifton Anderson reported to you," Lucia said. Leonard Young had also implied that Hammer should have caught the accounting fraud before it reached massive proportions. She dangled the information to garner his reaction.

"Anderson did report to me. He also reported to ten other managers between his level and me. No one caught him. I was the scapegoat. Highest paid non-executive. Holmes and White wants me to take the fall."

Lucia didn't want Hammer to become so mired in anger that he couldn't answer her questions. "Clifton Anderson is good at what he does. Holmes and White isn't the first firm he's duped during the course of his career," Lucia said.

Hammer walked to the wet bar and opened the top cabinet. "Doesn't change anything. They needed some-one near the top to take the heat. The press has been all over me. Do you know how many death threats I receive every day? Angry people want their money back." He threw a glass against the wall and it shattered. "News flash! I don't have the money. I don't have a dime to my name. Where do these people think I invested my money? The same place they did. Anderson robbed me right along with everyone else."

That explained where Hammer's money had gone. "I'm sorry to hear that," Lucia said. Hammer had been through an ordeal, but his reactions were overly volatile. Was he under the care of a psychiatrist? On medication?

"What about you two?" Hammer pointed at Cash. "Are you working this or did your boyfriend tag along in case I went crazy?" Hammer took another glass and set it on the counter.

Denials about Cash's relationship with her sprang to mind. Remembering her training, Lucia checked her words before she spoke. Defensiveness would make her look like a liar. "I already explained that this is my colleague."

"He didn't show me a badge," Hammer said, pour-ing a large amount of scotch into the glass.

"I'm not an FBI agent. I'm a consultant," Cash said.

Hammer took a long swig from his drink. If it wasn't his first of the day it would explain his strange, erratic behavior. Most people didn't think it was wise to question the FBI while they were investigating a crime in which they were involved. "Right. You can call him a consultant if you want." Hammer took another swallow of his drink. "You two are sleeping together."

If he hoped making accusations would throw her off the reason she'd come, he was wrong. "I'm here to learn more about Anderson and what it was like to work with him. If you're planning to make incorrect guesses about people, then we can finish this interview at headquarters." No one liked making the trip to the FBI's interrogation room.

Hammer set his glass down hard. "I'll tell you what I know, but there's nothing new that I haven't already told you people a dozen times."

Lucia walked Hammer through what he knew about Anderson and how the scheme had unfolded. He didn't reveal anything she hadn't read in the case file. While she spoke, Cash wandered to the sliding glass door and looked out into the yard. She didn't blame him for being drawn to sunlight and the outdoors.

"Tell me more about being in the upper echelon at Holmes and White," Cash said, turning away from the door as the conversation lagged.

Hammer poured himself another drink. He wasn't pouring more than a finger or two at a time, but he was drinking steadily. "Imagine being the king of your own domain with a personal assistant to take care of your every need. You hire people and you fire them at will. You're available around the clock, but when you have down time, it's spectacular. Five star hotels and the best restaurants in town. Wine and women and parties. I lived the life and I loved it."

Lucia let Cash continue to engage with Hammer. She sensed this could be a topic Hammer was more comfortable discussing with Cash.

"What happened to your personal assistant?" Cash asked.

Hammer stiffened. He let out a long breath before answering. "She was fired the same day I was."

Hammer slid his drink back and forth between his hands. "Keep her out of this. She didn't do anything wrong. She signed the nondisclosures and the confidentiality agreements. She left town and is living with her parents while she puts her life back together." He sounded like a heartbroken teenager.

Lucia would follow up on Hammer's personal assistant. She remembered reading about her in previous interviews and her instincts tingled that the FBI hadn't heard her whole story. What was her name? Kresley? Katie?

"It must be hard to have lost so much so quickly," Cash said.

Hammer looked at the table and then lifted his head slowly. His eyes were rimmed with unshed tears. Compassion tugged at Lucia's chest. Was Hammer a hapless victim of Clifton Anderson or had he been involved in the fraud? Neither the media nor the FBI could directly connect him to any legal wrongdoing. Unless he was hiding the money well, Hammer hadn't been paid for any assistance he'd given Clifton Anderson.

"You have no idea. People lost their retirement accounts and their savings, but I've lost everything. Everything."

Was his former personal assistant included in "everything"?

"We're doing our best to find Anderson," Lucia said.

"I'll be long gone before you find him," Hammer said.

Lucia didn't like the sound of that. Was he planning a suicide? To run? "We'll need you around throughout the course of our investigation."

"Yeah, yeah, right."

"Do you have a forwarding address?" Lucia asked.

Hammer ran his hands through his hair. "To add to my nightmare, I'll be moving in with my brother and sister-in-law. She's a shrew who hates me." Bitterness touched every word.

She sensed his cry for help. Lucia would ask Benjamin to provide Hammer with any counseling resources they may have. "We'll be in touch if we find anything or have more questions," Lucia said.

"Great, you do that," Hammer said. "If I never see another FBI agent again, it will be too soon." Then he mumbled something about how useless the FBI were. Lucia ignored the comment. Hammer was a man on the edge and she wasn't looking to push him over it.

Hammer walked them to the door. Lucia handed Hammer her business card, which he threw to the floor. Again ignoring the rudeness, Lucia and Cash took the marble stairs to the sidewalk.

Hammer slammed his front door.

"He picked up on something between us," Cash said as they walked. "Do you want to talk about that?"

"He's half drunk and out of his mind with bitterness," Lucia said. "What is there to talk about?"

"If you want to ignore it, then fine."

"Yes, I want to ignore it."

"We need to go back and check on him," Cash said, turning back toward to the townhouse.

Lucia held up her hand and stepped in front of him. "Check on him? He will not let us back into his place."

"He could be a danger to himself or others."

Not in the immediate. "Cash, what are you playing at?"

A mischievous look danced across Cash's face. "Let's see if round two helps us."

Cash circled around to the back of the group of townhouses, cutting down the alleyway between the sections. The alley behind the townhouses was narrow, passable by no more than a single car. The yards behind each home were beautifully landscaped.

Cash hopped the white chain-link fence into Hammer's backyard.

"You're trespassing," Lucia said.

Cash extended his hand to help her over. "Come on. I have a feeling."

They couldn't waltz into someone's backyard. Anything they heard or saw would be obtained illegally and inadmissible in court. Add to it how furious Benjamin would be, and it had the makings of a bad plan.

"Have courage, Lucia."

Courage? She had courage in spades. Was he calling her a wimp? Knowing she was being baited into complying and unable to help herself, Lucia took his hand and climbed the fence. At least this way, she could keep an eye on Cash and if he learned something, she would be in the know. Cash took the steps to the deck, pulled opened the sliding glass door and stepped inside.

He had unlocked the door while he had been pretending to admire the view. She should have found his gall appalling, but Lucia was impressed by his planning.

They stepped inside and Lucia's heart beat faster. If they were caught entering Hammer's home without a warrant, they could be arrested. If they were arrested, she'd lose her job and Cash would go back to prison.

"Cash," she whispered. She needed to warn him. To make sure he understood what he was risking by doing this.

He pressed a finger over his lips. Hammer's voice floated into the kitchen. It sounded as if he was on the phone. To make out what he was saying, Cash crept across the floor. Then he was still.

"I know, but I have the FBI crawling all over me and that makes me nervous."

A pause.

"I lost everything. My home. My career. Kinsley, what more do you want from me? I don't have anything left to give."

Kinsley. As soon as Lucia heard the name she remembered Kinsley had been his personal assistant at Holmes and White. Another pause.

"Don't be ridiculous. I told them nothing. What more do you need me to do? I've done everything you've asked."

Cash closed his eyes, perhaps concentrating on what Hammer was saying.

"She asked about me? When can I see her?" Hammer asked.

A growl. Cash's eyes snapped open and Lucia whirled to see a black dog standing between them and the sliding glass door. The dog locked his legs and bared his teeth. He barked.

"Hold on a minute," Hammer said into the phone. "Slasher! Quiet!"

Slasher. What a wonderful name for a dog. Based on the dog's demeanor, it fit. They were intruders in his home.

Cash stood and advanced on the dog. He looked as though he was planning to charge at the dog, but when he was close he laid his hands on the dog's flank and whispered something into his ear. At the same time, Cash motioned for Lucia to leave. The dog visibly relaxed.

Lucia did as Cash directed, looking over her shoulder at the pair. Cash seemed to have the situation under control, but it could escalate quickly if the dog decided Cash was an enemy. Slasher barked again.

"Slasher! Shut up!" Hammer yelled from another room. "Let me see what that lunatic dog's problem is now."

Cash didn't panic. He remained facing the dog and slipped away, following Lucia outside. He slid the glass door closed behind him and leaped over the deck, falling to the ground. Lucia followed him.

"Are you okay?" she mouthed.

He nodded.

They crouched under the deck. If Hammer looked outside, he wouldn't see them. If he let his dog into the gated yard, they could have a problem.

"You even charm dogs?" Lucia asked.

"Dogs are pack animals. I love them and they sense that. They want to be friends and please me," he said.

He made it sound easy. Her respect for him increased.

They waited a few minutes before leaving the yard the same way they'd come.

"How did you know Hammer would call someone?" Lucia asked.

"He was sweating when we were talking to him. We rattled him and he'd need to vent about it. He's not a leader. He's a follower. He needs someone to tell him what to do. That's why he was easy for Anderson to use, knowingly or unknowingly, in the con and for Young to use as a scapegoat," Cash said.

"We can't use anything we overheard as evidence," she said.

"Doesn't matter. We have something more to go on," Cash said. "Hammer knows something but he's being instructed to shut his mouth. Someone is dangling the woman he loves, Kinsley, in front of him like a prize if he does."

It shouldn't be hard to find out more about Kinsley from employment records at Holmes and White. Getting a warrant for those records could prove challenging, given that Lucia couldn't explain how and why they wanted Kinsley's records. "Do you think that he would lie about what he knows for a woman? He's taking all the heat."

"Haven't you ever been in love?" Cash asked.

She'd once thought she was and had been terribly wrong. "No."

Cash frowned. "Then as a man who has, I'll tell you. When a woman wins a man's heart, deserved or not, he will do anything to be with her and to make her happy."

How would it feel to be on the receiving end of Cash's devotion? Exploring those thoughts felt too intimate and were, at best, inappropriate. She brushed them away. She'd been a fool for love before and it had ended badly. "We have to build a strong case. Not prop it up with flimsy evidence and theories."

Cash leaned closer. "I'm not asking you to do it my way. But don't ask me to do it yours. I never did learn how to color inside the lines."

Cash walked a step behind Lucia, giving her space to think. Even though it hadn't been Cash's call to work with Lucia, she'd been annoyed to be assigned the Young and Hammer interviews with him and hadn't hidden it.

Cash's plan to win her over at the first opportunity wasn't going well. She was prickly, standoffish and immune to his charm. When he thought he'd made headway, she backed off and shut down.

His one remaining ray of hope was in her words. Lucia had said clearly she *wouldn't* help him, not that she *couldn't*. If he could convince Lucia he had good intentions and planned to serve his time, but that being close to Adrian was crucial, perhaps she would change her mind and pull the strings he knew she held.

"Hey, man."

It was a voice from the past that Cash recognized immediately. He considered pretending it was a case of mistaken identity, but he had to face his new reality. Hiding and lying were habits he'd left in prison. In this life, if he wanted to live with Adrian as a family, he had to be completely honest. One sniff of a lie, and Lucia would never trust him. Trust was the key to winning her over.

"Hey," Cash said, turning around, extending his arm and clasping his former associate's hand.

"I heard you got sprung," Boots said. Boots was a petty criminal with more brawn than brains. But he had good connections and knew how to keep his mouth shut.

"I'm a free man," Cash said. It was the story the FBI had told him to use if he encountered anyone from his criminal past. If the FBI had any chance of using him to locate Clifton Anderson, he couldn't broadcast he was working for the Feds to every member of the criminal underworld. He'd be shunned and mark himself for a hit.

"Who's your lady?" Boots asked, putting his hands in his pockets.

"This is my friend Lucy."

"Are you working?" Boots asked, looking between the two of them.

Lucia's eyes widened slightly, perhaps wondering if they'd had a breach in their cover. Cash knew Boots was referring to them working a con.

"Not at the moment," Cash said, darting his eyes over his shoulder at Lucia and subtly shaking his head at Boots. Let Boots think Lucia was a woman he was dating. He didn't want Boots propositioning him with a job offer, especially in front of Lucia.

"Where you staying?" Boots asked, taking a cigarette from one pocket and putting it between his lips while drawing a lighter from another pocket.

"The Hideaway."

Boots winced and lit the end of his cigarette. "How the mighty have fallen. I'll be in touch. I have some work that might interest you and help you get some nicer digs."

"Appreciate it, man." They nodded and went their separate ways. Boots continued down the street at a slow lope as he smoked his cigarette and flicked the ashes on the ground.

"That was close," Lucia said, once they were in the car, a company sedan with its boring, fabric interior and no luxuries.

"Would it have mattered if he'd pegged you for a Fed?" Cash asked.

"Of course it would. I don't want your cover blown. We've just started," Lucia said.

He took it a step further. "If my cover is blown, then I'm no use to you and I'd go back to prison."

Lucia turned and looked at him, keeping her hands gripped on the steering wheel. He was pressing her emotionally without much effort. "I don't want you back in prison."

That was an improvement from the initial hostility he'd encountered. "Then take the anger down a notch," Cash said. "You're making me nervous."

Lucia blew out her breath. "You have nothing to be nervous about. You're working with me on this case. When it's over, we'll part ways as former colleagues."

"We'll be working in the same building for the three years I've been given in this program. Tell me how to pretend there is nothing between us. I've already slipped once. I kissed you."

Could he use their physical attraction to convince her to use her influence to transfer him closer to his son? She couldn't deny the powerful chemistry between them forever and she may prefer he work farther away from her to avoid any temptation.

Lucia stared at him, panic registering on her face as if she hadn't considered how long they would be trapped together with that kiss haunting them. "I won't ask for a transfer. I've been with white collar for a few months and I plan on staying much longer."

He'd wait for her to realize that transferring *him* at the end of this case was the better option. He sensed something she wasn't saying about her short time with white collar. "I don't want you to walk away from your job. Maybe they'll move me to another office," Cash said, planting the idea.

Lucia stared ahead at the road. "If you're as good as Benjamin seems to believe, you'll crack the case, bring in Clifton Anderson and we'll recover some of the money. We'll wrap the case up in a few months. Benjamin will get his promotion and you can spend the rest of your time filing paperwork at headquarters."

Cash hated paperwork and office work, which were about the same to his way of thinking. Being stuck at headquarters away from Adrian doing both was near the worst-case scenario. "Sounds abysmal." But not as bad as jail. Not nearly as good as being closer to Adrian. A commutable distance. Maybe he could get special privileges to drive to see his son, nights and weekends. As long as he showed up to work on time and did what he needed to do, what boss would begrudge him time with his son?

But any allowances required trust and worthiness. He needed to find Clifton Anderson and the money he'd stolen first.

"Aren't you looking for anything out of the deal?" Cash asked.

"The money returned to the people who need it," Lucia said, stating it like it was obviously her goal.

"No promotion?"

Lucia tensed. "I've already been given a promotion."

She sounded defensive.

"Do you want me to drop you at the Hideaway?" Lucia asked.

He'd rather go anywhere but there. "No, thanks. Even when I take a shower there I feel dirtier. I'll head back to the office." Which was where he had taken a number of showers. Their onsite gym facilities were clean and free of pests—unlike the bathroom at the motel.

Lucia pulled into traffic. "That's where I'm headed. I have paperwork to do."

"How'd you get stuck with that job?"

"I wasn't stuck with it. Benjamin wanted me to handle that part of the job."

The administrative part? Benjamin had mentioned to him that Lucia was in charge of filing reports and documents for the team. Why would Benjamin waste a good field agent's time with that? "You can pass the torch to me, I guess, when this is over."

The idea seemed to cheer her up a little. "The time will be over before you know it. Then you can be with your son."

Which was exactly what he didn't want. For the time to pass and Adrian to grow while Cash never had the opportunity to have a relationship with him. It was a small measure of comfort that Lucia hadn't forgotten about Adrian. "The four years in prison went by at a crawl."

Prison had robbed him of time with his son, but it had also been difficult, challenging and stressful to constantly watch his back, be on guard and anticipate someone trying to harm or kill him. Six men had died on his cell block while he had been incarcerated. Cash considered himself lucky that he'd survived relatively

untouched. At least physically. Thinking about his cell
and the rules and restrictions and food made him sick
to his stomach. Jail was emotionally and psychologi-
cally draining. It was no wonder some repeat offenders
were hardened beyond reach.

The car felt cramped, and a rush of frustration and
anxiety bubbled up in him. He needed space and air.
"I've changed my mind. Drop me off here."

Lucia looked at him, her brows knit together. "Here?
In the middle of the street?" She stopped for a red light
and he climbed out of the car. "See you, Luc." He shut
the door behind him. He needed to walk and breathe
fresh air.

So little stood between him and that cage. Disgust
and anxiety clawed at him. Prison. He could go back
if he made a mistake. The FBI would only keep him
out as long as they could use him to bring in Clifton
Anderson. What if Cash couldn't lead them to him?
What if something went wrong and Clifton Anderson
was picked up by another agency? Would the FBI return him to jail? He could lose his chance of a reunion
with his son.

Lucia called after him and he ignored her. Embarrassed about his behavior and unwilling to explain it, he
stuck his hands in his pockets and kept his head down.
He didn't want to risk being recognized again by anyone from his former life. He didn't want to talk to anyone. He wanted to disappear, but with the GPS tracker
monitoring him, he couldn't do that. He was trapped in
the confines of the city under the careful watch of the
FBI. It was hard to feel truly free. He was still impris-
oned, just in a different way.

The pounding of footsteps and Lucia calling his

name had him glancing over his shoulder. The persistent woman didn't know when to give up. She caught up to him, out of breath. Strands of her brown hair had broken free of the ponytail she had it tied in. He had the urge to pull the elastic from it and let it loose around her face. He kept his hands pressed to his sides.

"I need space," he said, feeling a combination of weak and whiny. He hated weak and whiny.

Concern touched her face. "Tell me what that was about because normal people don't jump out of a car," she said.

"I didn't jump out of the car. I stepped out," Cash said.

"Going from being locked in a cell to walking around on the street is a big change. But it's a good change."

He realized she knew where his thoughts had gone. He added intuitive and considerate to his list of her good attributes. He'd liked Lucia from day one, even if she was strung a little tight, but the more time he spent with her the more he saw her best qualities were buried beneath her icy facade. "I'm not free and not much has changed. I'm monitored around the clock. I live in a dump. I eat crappy food." Benjamin had made it clear he wanted to know if Cash was in touch with anyone from his past. Cash half expected him to demand Cash keep a log of everyone he spoke to.

"Living in a motel isn't ideal and I know your budget is tight." She pressed her lips together. She was uncomfortable talking about money.

Was it because she had financial problems, too? The place where she lived was at least three thousand square feet and she had a number of decorative items he'd price high on the open market. She was either living above her means, on the take or the FBI was paying better than he'd thought.

"I'm grateful to Benjamin for what he did for me." Even if the other man had a lot to gain by capturing Clifton Anderson, like a huge promotion and a raise, he'd put himself out to help Cash.

"You don't sound ungrateful, but you sound like you're coming unhinged. I'm supposed to keep an eye on you while we're together," Lucia said.

That's what he needed to dissolve the anxiety, someone else watching him. "I have the tracker. You don't have to worry about me skipping town."

"I'm not worried about you skipping town. At the moment, I'm just worried about you."

Compassion and an olive branch. Cash hadn't realized how isolated he'd felt until she spoke the words. He had the urge to reach back, to connect with someone in a real way. Not to manipulate her or get on her good side for any other reason than needing a friend. "I can't go back there."

Empathy touched the corners of her eyes. "I know," she whispered. "We'll get this guy, and as long as you keep your head down and work hard, prison stays off the table. Now, please come back to the car. We'll head to the office and sit on the rooftop and review our case notes, okay? And then you have the team's happy hour."

"Aren't you going?" he asked.

"I have paperwork to finish up," she said.

He let her lead him to the car. Lucia was looking left and right.

"What's the matter?" he asked, sensing her unease.

"I have the strangest feeling we're being watched."

Not one to ignore instincts, Cash looked around. He

didn't notice anyone watching. They were surrounded by tall buildings. Anyone could be watching from those windows. Someone on the street? Another driver? He'd made a scene. He could have drawn the curiosity of a passerby or a people watcher with nothing better to do.

Or someone from his past had already caught up to him.

As people brushed past on the busy sidewalk, Lucia reached for her gun, unsnapping her holster. The atmosphere had tensed and shifted. If someone approached her or Cash, she would defend them.

Before her transfer to Benjamin's white-collar crime team, Lucia had worked in the violent-crime division on a complex murder-for-hire case. Her contributions to breaking up a ring of Egyptian nationals selling their services as assassins had led to fifteen arrests and fourteen convictions. Unfortunately, several of the well-known assassins who were part of the ring remained out of reach.

Her old team leader had let her know that the assassins still at large could seek revenge and target the team who had broken up their lucrative business. A few months had passed without any whisper of a threat. Lucia had been lulled into a sense of security that shattered the moment her instincts pricked that something was wrong.

Her instincts had served her well at the Bureau. She couldn't have explained why or how she knew trouble was near. Just as she had known by their treatment of her as the only female member of the violent-crime division that they were looking for a reason to kick her off the team.

In the end, it hadn't been something she'd done or hadn't done. It had been her success that gave her boss a reason to request a promotion for her. A promotion to a better-paying, higher-ranking open position in another unit.

She and Cash returned to her vehicle. They got in and she turned the key. The eerie sensation of being watched wouldn't subside.

The car didn't start. She paused a moment and heard the sound of the battery whining. "Get out of the car! Run!" she yelled.

Lucia opened the driver's-side door and rolled, covering her face and head. Car horns blared at her and she narrowly avoided being struck by oncoming traffic. Cash had heeded her warning and was standing on the street looking at her strangely. Maybe the car was old and needed a new ignition. Maybe the engine needed a tune-up. Maybe that first faulty turn was driver error.

Then Cash was next to her, lifting her to her feet. "Lucia, what is—"

The car exploded, the boom echoing against the tall buildings around her, a blast of heat hitting them and knocking them to the ground. Heat burned up Lucia's side. Cash covered her, shielding her. Something hit her leg hard enough to send pain radiating up her body.

Lucia had been in the line of fire before, but she hadn't experienced the impersonal coldness of an assassination attempt. Her follow-up thought was just as terrifying. It hadn't blown the first or second time she had started the car that day. Either someone had put the bomb in the car while she had been on the sidewalk talking to Cash or someone had been watching her and waiting to detonate the bomb. Either way, a killer was close.

Chapter 3

A moment of stillness, and Lucia only saw darkness and heard silence. In a flash, the world around her came into focus. People crying and screaming, and car horns honking assaulted her ears. She forced open her eyes. Around her, complete panic ensued. People were running and cars were smashed into each other and run up on the sidewalk.

She had to help. Lucia pushed Cash away.

Cash grabbed her arm, dragging her to her feet. "Lucia, we need to take cover."

Cash hauled her to the sidewalk, shoving her behind a row of metal newspaper dispensers.

She peered around the corner. The car was consumed by flames. Traffic around her had stopped and several vehicles had veered into each other and into the curb trying to avoid the flaming ball.

If an assassin had a bull's-eye pinned on her, she was dead.

"Give me your badge," Cash said.

"What? No!"

He ripped it from her pants. "Stay here. Do not get up."

Cash charged into the street, holding up her badge. People were running and screaming, but some pass-ersby were staring open-mouthed. "I'm with the FBI. Stay away from the car. Help is coming. Clear this area."

"Ma'am? Ma'am?" A delivery woman on a bicycle was staring at Lucia. "Are you okay?"

Lightheaded, Lucia struggled to focus. The pain in her leg was intense. "Can I use your phone?" She needed to call for help.

"You're bleeding. I'm calling 911," the woman said.

Lucia nodded her agreement and another wave of dizziness hit her. She couldn't lose consciousness. Cash was in the open. If the bomber was watching, he knew they'd escaped the blast. He could have a backup plan.

"Cash!" She called his name, needing to warn him. He couldn't hear her over the chaos. She tried to get up, but her leg wasn't working. She slammed against the ground.

"Cash!" He was moving people away from the scene and helping people out of their cars. He was in the line of fire.

Was this the man she had judged as selfish, manip-ulative and a bold-faced liar? Shame hit her. Actions were far more telling than words. Seeing his response to a crisis, she was in awe.

She waved at him and, finally, he turned in her direction. He jogged to her and squatted next to her. "Help is coming."

He swore.

"What's wrong?" she asked.

"Nothing. Stay calm and stay with me." He removed his suit jacket and pressed it over her leg hard. "Lucia? Lucia!"

Her vision blurred and then darkness again swallowed her.

"When you didn't show up for happy hour, I thought you might have killed each other. I didn't think someone had tried to kill both of you," Benjamin said, sitting between Lucia's hospital bed and Cash.

Cash had called Benjamin when he'd borrowed a phone, after he was sure Lucia had received medical attention.

Lucia's leg injury had required twenty stitches and she was being monitored for a concussion. Cash had a few scratches and had been admitted to the hospital for observation.

Benjamin appeared frayed, his hair a mess, his tie loose around his neck and his pants rumpled. "If you want off this case while we figure out who's targeting you, I understand."

Benjamin hadn't made the same offer to Cash. Cash was tied in regardless of the danger.

Lucia's expression turned stony. "If this is about the Holmes and White case, I won't let someone scare me off. I know people who lost money at Holmes and White. They're counting on me and I won't let them down."

"I understand," Benjamin said sounding relieved she

hadn't accepted his offer. "I have my best guys trying to track down what happened. But I don't want you worrying about the investigation. I want you to rest and heal. I've briefed hospital security on the situation and they're keeping an eye on your rooms," Benjamin said. "You have my cell phone number. Call me if you need anything."

They said their goodbyes and Benjamin left the room. Cash had a semiprivate room across the hall, but he wanted to stay and watch over Lucia. The bombing wasn't an isolated incident. Something about it spoke to professionalism. A bomb was more complex than other forms of murder.

"You heard the man," Lucia said. "Get some rest. I'm fine. My whole leg is numb. I'm not in any pain."

That also meant she couldn't run or defend herself. Cash came to her bedside. "Are you sure you're okay? Do you need anything?"

Lucia pointed to the nurse call button. "If I need anything, I have this. Thanks, though, Cash. You were a hero today." She set her hand over his and gave him a light squeeze.

He had never been called a hero. He had never felt like a hero. But hearing her say the words, he suddenly felt as if anything was possible.

Cash got up from his hospital bed several times and paced the hallway, keeping an eye on Lucia's room. He stretched. He watched. He couldn't stay in his bed and have a good view of her room, so he took up a post in the visitor's lounge, a small, bright space on the hospital floor. Bright he liked. Small bothered him immensely.

He concentrated on his objective: keeping Lucia safe. He could sleep later.

Around 3:00 a.m., the door marked Staff Only on the far end of the floor opened, squeaking on its hinges. A man in dark clothes slipped out. Cash rose to his feet, adrenaline firing and chasing off exhaustion. The man moved closer to Lucia's room, circling around the nurses' station.

The man kept his head down. Cash stepped forward, placing himself in front of Lucia's room. The man jumped as if startled.

"Can I help you?" Cash asked.

"Going to see my sister," the man mumbled, keeping his head down, pulling his red ball cap low over his eyes.

"At three in the morning?" Cash asked. Cash didn't move. The man stepped toward Lucia's room. Cash saw a flash of silver under his coat. A gun? A knife? Cash was unarmed, but that wouldn't stop him from protecting Lucia.

The man froze, then lunged for a desk chair outside the empty nurses' station and hurled it in Cash's direction. Cash dodged the chair, taking several steps back. The man ran, throwing anything behind him to slow Cash down: paperwork, a wheelchair and a rolling TV tray. He whipped a hypodermic needle disposal bin at Cash. Cash ducked. The plastic can hit the floor, and needles broke and skidded in every direction.

Cash chased after him down the hallway to the stairwell on the far side of the building.

The man slammed the metal door behind him. Cash pursued. Entering the stairwell, he heard sneakers squeaking against the floor and then a metal door closing.

Cash looked up and then down over the bannister. Where had the man gone? He'd been a second, maybe two behind him. He couldn't have dropped over the side of the bannister. It was a five-story fall to the ground.

He'd gotten a good look at the side of the man's face. It wasn't enough to make a positive ID, but maybe Cash could catch him.

The man seemed to have disappeared, but he couldn't have gotten far.

If Cash pursued, the man could loop around and return to Lucia's room via the elevator or other stairwell. As much as he wanted to find the man, Cash couldn't track anyone through a hospital on his own. He needed to call Benjamin and the police for help.

The man stalking Lucia wouldn't give up. He'd attempted to hurt her twice in one day and he'd try again.

That the man hadn't come after him told Cash that he wasn't necessarily the target of the attack as he'd initially feared. He had skeletons in his closet, but Lucia must have some powerful enemies, as well.

"Why don't you tell me what you need and I'll get it?" Cash asked.

Lucia walked through her place feeling as though her leg muscles were cramped. Her eyes were heavy with fatigue. She had slept little in the hospital. The monitors beeping and bright lights and interruptions had been bad enough. Someone trying to kill her had made sleep impossible.

The extra security precautions were a small comfort. A uniformed police officer was keeping watch over her place. She had enabled her rarely used home-security system. How determined was her would-be murderer?

Benjamin was assuming the bombing had to do with the Clifton Anderson case and she'd let him believe it. Until she did some investigating on her own, she wouldn't sound a false alarm.

"I don't need you to do anything. I have it covered. You're here because you saved my life and I owe you at least a hot shower. I promise my shower isn't disgusting," Lucia said. Based on his reaction any time someone mentioned it, Cash hated the Hideaway and she didn't blame him. She wanted to do something, anything, however small, to help him and thank him for what he'd done for her at the scene of the bombing and at the hospital.

She walked to the linen closet and pulled out a pink towel. She handed it to him. "Go ahead. One hot shower, as long as you'd like it. Use whatever you need."

She had seen a different side of Cash, a protective side, a warm side, and it had melted some of her resentment and irritation with him. It was hard to imagine him being the same person who had run a con to defraud a senator.

Cash took the towel. Their fingers brushed and Lucia ignored the shower of sparks between them. She was on medication. She was imagining things.

"Thank you, Lucia. I appreciate it."

Cash was in her bathroom, in her shower, all bare broad shoulders and sinewy arms, tight abdominals and muscular legs. Lucia refused to fixate on what he might look like naked.

He was proving to be loyal and an asset to the team.

He'd looked out for her after the car bombing. He'd saved her life then and again in the hospital.

She had been bent on seeing him as an interloper on the Anderson case. Now, she didn't know what to make of him.

Her gratitude for what he'd done was mixed with anxiety. She wanted to stay far, far away from Cash. It had only been a few days and already he was naked in her condo. Cash was a difficult man to say no to. Would he break down her resistance totally? She reassured herself she wouldn't get into bed with a colleague, even a temporary one. If anyone found out, it would damage her reputation and her career, which had suffered enough in the past year. Besides, she wasn't looking for a quick screw and Cash wasn't a man she wanted to spend her life with. A felon and an FBI agent didn't mix at work, much less in a relationship.

A relationship her parents would have to approve of and they would not approve of Cash. If she brought home one more unsuitable man, one more man who her family found inappropriate, she wouldn't hear the end of it. She'd made it clear to her family she wanted to pick who she dated. The problem was that she had the hardest time finding the right person. She wasn't looking to actively rebel against her parents' wishes. She wanted her parents to understand she needed something more than an Ivy League degree and a six-figure salary to fall in love.

She wanted passion and heat. She wanted excitement. Qualities she'd found in Cash.

She hadn't been able to find everything she wanted in one man. Something important was always missing. Bradley, her former fiancé, had been missing fidelity.

Every relationship before and since had been much of the same.

Her pain medication was wearing off so Lucia took another pill with half a glass of water. Her muscles were sore from tensing before the explosion and the injury to her leg throbbed. Planning to return to work on Monday, she needed to rest now.

Lucia closed a shade in her bedroom, leaving the other four open. It was too much effort to close them. She lay on her bed and propped a pillow under her foot to elevate her leg. A list of who might have been targeting her ran through her head.

Among the first suspects were criminals she had caught followed by anyone from her personal life who had a problem with her. The first list was far longer than the second.

When the shower shut off, Lucia heard Cash moving around the bathroom. She imagined him towel drying his hair and it standing on end. He'd rub the towel over his big body and pull on his clothes.

Lucia concentrated on the low hum of the shower fan. When it clicked off and the door to the bathroom opened, she waited. She was lying stock-still on her bed, her muscles aching and a mild headache pulsing at her temples. If Cash went into the living room and crashed on the couch, that would be enough distance between them.

Her toes curled thinking of another option. What if he came into her bedroom? Would he say anything to her? Would he lie on her bed with her?

She forced her mind back to the case and off the sexy man in her place. She thought of her friends who needed the money from their plundered pension accounts at

Holmes and White. One of Anderson's victims was a retired police chief who had taken her under his wing early in her life, guided her through her education and written a glowing recommendation for her application to the FBI. He was counting on her to find the money or he'd need to return to work. Since he had a permanent hip injury that limited his movements, he couldn't return to the force and instead of enjoying his retirement, he'd be forced into a low-paying job he'd likely hate.

Lucia had sent his wife some money to make ends meet, but she couldn't supplement everyone who needed their funds returned.

Mentally reviewing the case facts, she searched for an important detail she may have missed.

Her phone rang, pulling her away from her thoughts. Taking her phone from her bedside table, she winced when she saw her father's name on the screen.

"Hey, Dad," she said, clearing her throat, trying to inject some energy into her voice.

"How are you feeling? I called the hospital and asked to be transferred to your room. They said you had been discharged. Is everything okay? That seems like a short stay for a bombing victim."

"I was only hit by some debris. I'm fine. Admitting me was routine. They wanted to monitor me."

"They admitted you to the hospital. That's serious. Doctors don't give away a bed unless they have a medical concern."

Her parents didn't approve of her career choice and this latest incident highlighted the reasons.

"It was a precaution. I have the best doctors looking after me." She even had follow-up appointments with specialists, most of which she planned to keep.

"I hope this proves that the fears your mother and I have for your health and safety are not in our heads. When your boss called and told me you'd been injured, it was the most panicked I've been in years. Quit that job. Give your resignation immediately. You don't need the money. You don't need that job."

She did need her job. Try as she might, she could not get her parents to understand that. It wasn't about the money. "I'm sorry you were scared. I was scared, too. But it's okay. I'm okay." She wouldn't delve into the details of the bombing. It was an active investigation and the FBI was controlling what was released to the public.

Her father wasn't ready to let it go. She gave him another five minutes and then interjected.

"Could we talk about this later? I'm tired." She wouldn't tell her father about the man who'd tried to get into her room at the hospital. Lucia could practically hear her father's teeth grating together. "Please don't worry about me. I'll call you later."

"Are you coming to brunch Sunday?" her father asked gruffly.

"Yes, Dad. I'll see you then." She said goodbye and disconnected the phone, setting it on her bedside table. Huntington family brunch was something she tried to attend at least twice a month, once if her schedule was crammed. She loved her family but sometimes they drove her crazy. They had expectations she couldn't meet and they didn't understand her life choices. They almost seemed more willing to her accept her sisters' lack of direction over Lucia's career.

And yet their approval meant something to her. Not fitting in at work was one thing. But being rejected by her parents was even harder to live with.

Cash appeared in the entryway to Lucia's room. A strand of hair hung over his forehead. He was wearing a pressed pair of gray pants and a white T-shirt. It looked great on him.

"Did I wake you?" he asked.

"I wasn't sleeping. Too much to think about," Lucia said. As her suspect list faded, Cash's presence came into sharp focus.

"Can I ask you a personal question?" he asked.

She tensed. When she was alone with Cash, their relationship slid from professional to personal too quickly. "You can ask. I may not answer it."

"What does your father do?"

Red flags went up. "Why are you asking?"

"He was in the ER for two minutes and he had you moved to a private room. And this place is too expensive for an FBI agent's salary."

Lucia took a deep breath and sat up, wincing as the pain in her leg renewed. Her father's identity wasn't a secret. Everyone on the team knew she came from money. It didn't hurt for Cash to know it, as well. Since she knew what his father did, inquiring about hers was fair play. "My father is a partner in a successful legal practice. He gave me this condo because he wanted me to have a safe place to live." She waited for a look of disgust. Some people begrudged that she'd had an easy life, at least financially. From the outside, it seemed like greener pastures. Sometimes it was, sometimes it wasn't.

"I picked up some dinner," he said.

"That's it? No follow-up questions?" she asked. Usually people wanted to know more about her family or had some negative comment about her lifestyle, sometimes implying she'd been handed everything she had or that she hadn't worked for her position in the FBI. Her career was the one thing in life she had earned herself. It was part of why she became so prickly when it wasn't going well. It made her feel like a failure.

"I get the picture," he said.

He said it as if knowing she came from money explained everything about who she was. Old insecurities rose up. "What picture is that?" Her being a brat? Spoiled? Out of touch with the world?

"Your family has money and consequently you have nice things."

It didn't sound like judgment. Just a statement. "Why does that matter?" she asked.

"It doesn't," Cash said. "But based on how annoyed you're getting with me about it, I'm guessing you're accustomed to a certain reaction that I'm not giving you. What is my reaction supposed to be?"

She didn't know what it was supposed to be, only that she was surprised he seemed not to care. Lucia was careful not to overreact. "I've worked hard to get where I am with the Bureau. My father doesn't have any influence on my job. My career is my own."

Cash regarded her with curiosity in his eyes. "That's why you're uptight at work."

Outrage struck her. "I am not uptight at work."

"You've taken on the paperwork for the team. You look for missed dots on i's and crosses on t's."

"That wasn't my choice. I was assigned that responsibility," Lucia said. It grated that he thought she enjoyed looking for mistakes on bureaucratic waste-of-time paperwork. Her "promotion" to white collar was hardly that.

"You have a list of rules and you follow it. It's black and white to you because shades of gray scare you."

She had professional standards. What successful person didn't? His assessment that she was uptight stung. "I play by the rules."

"But the criminals you're trying to take down don't. That puts you at a disadvantage."

"But I have you. You'll break the rules. That puts me back on an even playing field." Too bad she hadn't had Cash around when she worked in violent crime. She had been so careful not to make mistakes, but they'd kicked her out another way. Cash would have been slicker.

Cash laughed. "I bend the rules. I don't break them."

He lay next to her on the bed. It was a bold move, but she knew he hadn't done it to take advantage of her. He was being a friend.

"Let me sleep here with you," Cash said.

Not possible. How could he suggest it? "No. I have a rule about that." She threw his words back at him. "You can crash on the couch tonight if you want." She wouldn't send him back to the crappy motel. She could call Benjamin and explain.

"It means a lot to me that you're letting me stay here, even temporarily. It's much nicer than the Hideaway."

The frank admission struck her. Her bull-crap meter was well honed from years of listening to suspects and criminals lie. It wasn't going off now. Cash was a really good liar. Was he telling her the truth now?

Her stomach growled when she caught a whiff of the food Cash had brought. "How did you disable and re-enable the alarm?"

"Don't pick such an obvious access code," he said.

He'd guessed the number: the date she had been

made an FBI agent. Was she that obvious? Cash must have done his homework on her. "Nice guess," she said.

He didn't ask why she had picked that date. "Come on. Let's eat while it's hot."

"Is eating here okay?" she asked. Her leg hurt too much to move around.

"Whatever you prefer," Cash said. He left the room and returned with two bottles of water from the kitchen. He set them on her bedside table. He placed the brown paper bags of food on her bedspread. "I stopped by the security office. I pointed out a few security flaws in the building and he promised to address them. I'll make sure that he follows through on it."

Lucia rearranged her pillows as an ache spread across her leg. She tried to find a more comfortable position to take the strain off it.

Cash twisted the top off her water and handed it to her. "How can I make you more comfortable?"

"I'm not sure. Everything hurts," she said.

"Do you need another pain pill?" he asked.

Lucia shook her head. "I don't want too many meds in my system. I'm returning to work Monday."

Cash dimmed the lights and turned on the wireless speakers connected to her music player. Soft instrumental music piped through the room. "Did you make an appointment with the Bureau's shrink?"

"I sent him an email," she said. "How about you?" They were both required to be assessed by the Bureau's psychologist before returning to work.

"I'll talk to him Monday," Cash said.

"You like this music?" she asked. She wouldn't have guessed he was a fan of orchestral music.

"It relaxes you. You need to relax. It will make your leg hurt less." He handed her a plate.

She reached for the food and flinched when the movement pulled at her stitches.

"Let me help you get more comfortable." He wrapped his right arm around her waist and shifted her. Intimacy zinged between them and Lucia turned her head at the same moment he looked down at her. Their gazes connected and Lucia felt her body melting into Cash's. Heat burned a path where their bodies touched. The ache in her leg was a dim sensation compared to the sultry hum of anticipation that pricked at her.

"Lucia—"

"I don't think—"

They'd both started speaking at the same time. Cash nodded at her to continue. When he said her name, it had communicated he had feelings for her. Either that or he was manipulating her and doing it well.

He said nothing and watched her with soulful eyes.

"I don't think we should do this." She pulled away from him and felt the immediate loss of pleasure.

"Ignoring what's happening between us won't make it go away," Cash said.

"I'm not ignoring it," Lucia said. "I'm just hungry."

"Then you feel it, too?" Cash asked.

Lucia took a long drink of her water. What should she say? Being blunt could diffuse some of the sensations or could open the door to others. Playing relationship games weren't her strong suit. "I didn't say that." She'd hedged and she was disappointed in herself. Being blunt and honest were traits she admired.

"I'm looking for a new place to live," Cash said.

Glad he had changed the subject, Lucia relaxed.

"That's great." She was happy to hear he was moving out of that dump.

Events of the past couple of days had forced her to reevaluate her initial impression of Cash. Though she hadn't once seen it in other ex-cons, maybe Cash was reformed. Maybe he wouldn't return to his old ways. Most felons found it too easy to return to their lives of crime. Operating in the legal world required skills and sacrifice and some offenders couldn't understand how to assimilate.

"Hard to believe, but I won't spend any more time in the place I'm living than I have to. I'll move as soon as possible. Maybe by the end of the month."

Lucia shifted away. Being close to him was like being too close to a fire. Beautiful and bright and captivating, but she'd be burned if she wasn't careful. "I wanted to thank you for what you did at the scene and at the hospital."

His brow pleated. "I did what any partner would do."

He had a sense of commitment and dependability she hadn't expected. For the first time in a long time, she felt like someone had her back.

Cash put some food on his plate. "I hope you don't mind. I called Benjamin to check in. He thinks it might be a good idea for me to call Georgiana and see if I can pull anything more out of her about Hammer's assistant, Kinsley. They reviewed the interview with Georgiana and it wasn't helpful."

Imagining Cash with Georgiana bothered her immensely. "Are you sure that's a good idea? We don't know how she's involved with this."

"You think Georgiana set the bomb?" Cash asked, appearing to consider it.

The woman didn't seem like the type who could wire a bomb. She barely seemed capable of performing her duties as a glorified secretary. They hadn't heard from the bomb squad so they didn't know the details of how it had detonated, but Lucia couldn't picture Georgiana planting it. She could be protecting her employers or working for Anderson, but it seemed like a stretch.

Then again, looks could be misleading. "Unlikely. But we have to be careful."

Cash grinned and pulled her tight against him. She didn't pull away. She didn't want to. He was a criminal working on the side of the law, he was gorgeous and silver tongued, and yet he was loyal and decent and had layers she had only begun to discover.

"Lucia?"

"What?" She turned her head toward him.

"I find it sexy that you're jealous." Cash brought his mouth down on hers before giving her a chance to respond.

"I am not jealous," she said against his mouth.

Cash laughed again and turned his full attention to a fierce, demanding kiss. Lucia slumped against him, giving in to it and giving in to him. Cash's hands were strong and firm, and having them at her sides was both frustrating and arousing. This shouldn't be happening, especially not in her bed.

A knock on her front door made Lucia spring apart from Cash.

"Lucia?"

It was Audrey's voice.

Cash groaned. "If we're quiet, she'll leave."

Lucia climbed to her feet with Cash's help. She smoothed her shirt and ran her fingers through her hair though neither was out of place. Audrey was a genius at intuiting when a man and woman were sleeping together and Lucia didn't want her to get the wrong idea about her and Cash.

They hadn't slept together. Not even close. Cash had kissed her. Twice. That was the end of it.

Lucia hobbled to the door, peered through the peephole, disabled her security system and opened her front door. Almost feeling guilty, she turned on more lights.

Audrey looked over Lucia's shoulder and smiled conspiratorially. "Am I interrupting something?"

Audrey was the closest person to a friend Lucia had in DC. It was hard not to like Audrey. She was warm and outgoing. Lucia opened the door wider. "No, please come in. Audrey this is—"

"We've met. On the stairs a few days ago," Audrey said, giving Cash a once-over, her gaze lingering.

Did every woman feel compelled to stare at or flirt with Cash? It was a wonder he had any moves. Lucia guessed women just took off their clothes and climbed into his bed, making it easy.

Audrey faced Lucia. "I wanted to be sure you were okay and to check if you needed anything before I head out for the night."

Like Lucia, Audrey was a trust-fund baby, but unlike Lucia, Audrey didn't have a full-time job. She sometimes joked her full-time job was to avoid the media whenever possible because every time her picture appeared in a gossip rag, her dad took away one of her credit cards. He almost always gave them back.

Audrey gave Lucia a long look. "My mom saw yours today and your mom mentioned you weren't feeling well."

Lucia wished her mother wouldn't talk about her to her friends. She was concerned, but Lucia hadn't been comfortable in her parents' social world where everyone seemed to know everyone else's business. A little privacy in her line of work was preferred. "I'm doing fine. I had a little accident at work. Thanks for checking. Where are you headed tonight?" she asked, not wanting to linger on the details of her "accident."

Audrey smiled. "A friend is taking me to the opening night at a club. Invite-only, but that could mean half the city was invited." She laughed. It was something Lucia liked about Audrey. Though she was from money and part of DC's elite crowd, she wasn't pretentious.

"It looks like you two have a super-exclusive party already going on," Audrey said.

"No, no, nothing here," Lucia said. Audrey wasn't a gossip, but Lucia didn't want word floating back to her parents that she'd had dinner with a man. They'd question her endlessly about him and his family and his work. Those answers would only lead to disaster. "If it's all the same to you, please don't mention this to your mom."

Audrey waved her hand dismissively. "No problem. The information channel is one way, anyway. My mom talks my ear off once a week and I listen while I catch up on my mail. I'll have my cell phone on me. Call if you need anything."

They said their goodbyes and Audrey left. Lucia shut the door and re-enabled the alarm. The interruption had given her time to process what had happened with Cash in her bedroom. She had been at the mercy of her hormones.

Cash crossed the room. "I should be leaving, too," he said. "It's almost curfew."

"I thought you were planning to sleep here," she said. She could call Benjamin and let him know Cash was staying at her place. Benjamin was aware of how crappy the Hideaway was and wouldn't read into Cash staying with her.

"That might not be a good idea. I have the sense that you're not comfortable with what's going on between us and staying here will make it harder."

She wasn't comfortable, but she didn't want him to leave. "You didn't eat," she said.

"The food was mainly for you," he said.

He had an hour until curfew. "Please stay and eat."

He blew out his breath. "Lucia, this is hard for me. Being around you and seeing you and not being able to touch you is driving me crazy. I want to kiss you. I want to put my hands all over you. I want to taste you and find out what you like best and how you like it."

His words heated her entire body. She could almost feel Cash's tongue on her. A shudder rippled over her.

He groaned and closed his eyes. "You're going to kill me, Lucia. I'm trying to be good and follow your rules and you're standing in front of me, tempting me, taunting me and I am not supposed to do anything. Are you even wearing a bra?"

She crossed her arms over her chest. She had been planning to sleep and had nothing on under her shirt. "I am not taunting you," she said, her voice quiet.

"Yes, you are. You have no idea how good you look to me."

"That's because you haven't slept with a woman in four years," she said, trying to diffuse the tension she felt. His intensity was shockingly honest and scary. Intensity directed at her.

He cupped her cheek briefly before letting his hand drop. "Tell it like it is. But Lucia, if there is one thing we have, it's chemistry. That doesn't happen with every woman I meet, four years of celibacy or not."

"I see you with women. They practically crawl into your lap," Lucia said.

Cash watched her for a long moment and she waited for him to deny it. "It's always been easy for me to get along with women. But having a real connection with someone is rarer than you might think. It's about the intellect and emotions and how easily she makes me laugh."

"Physical attraction doesn't play a part?"

He chuckled. "It does. A very big part. But a connection that's more than about what happens between the sheets isn't something to be dismissed easily. Even if it's temporary or it doesn't make sense to anyone else, those moments are exceptional."

How did he do that? He made her feel special and feminine and powerful. Her nerves jittered, and excess energy escaped in a laugh. "We seem to end up lip-locked when we're together, but anything more happening could jeopardize our jobs."

"I know that. Even with jail time waving like a flag, my libido doesn't care." He stepped close to her, pulling her hips to his, and she felt his arousal pressing at her core.

His voice was filled with empathy and she wavered. Being in his arms felt good. He'd worked her up and she was finding it impossible to cool down and untwist the desire corded around her. "We have to work together." The more she said it, it mattered less and less.

"I know."

"We need boundaries." The current ones were fading into the distance.

"My life is filled with them."

Sympathy pricked at her. He lived with someone else's rules. She had once lived like that and had hated it. "I'll call Benjamin and tell him you're staying on my couch so you don't have to sleep at the Hideaway again."

"You don't owe me anything," he said.

She did. "I guess I put more worth on my life than a few gallons of hot water and a few hours on the couch."

"After the places I've been, both were heavenly. Didn't have to wear flip-flops in the shower stall or worry about being jumped while I slept."

She shuddered. "That's a charming picture."

"I could tell you stories that would blow your mind," Cash said.

Her mind was already blown from that kiss. "I'm an FBI agent. I have heard horror stories. I don't want to hear more."

Her work took most of her time and until she was in this moment, she hadn't realized how much she wanted something else in her life. She found herself confronting a strange new desire for romance and companionship.

"Then I could tell you some good stories that would make you laugh."

"You have a way with words," she said. But he already knew that.

"Aren't you afraid if I stay here something will happen?" Cash asked.

She was almost sure something would happen if she

let it. But she also trusted Cash not to do anything she didn't want. "I'm in control of myself," Lucia said, not confident in her words.

"If you can handle it, so can I," Cash said. "I won't pass up a night in a clean, safe place."

When her alarm went off at seven, Lucia didn't feel groggy despite her sleep being erratic over the last several days. Her body felt primed and tingled in the places where the Cash in her dreams had touched her. Would it be as good in real life? Based on the preview he'd given her, she guessed it would be better.

Her all-too-vivid dreams replayed through her mind. She had forgotten how it felt to be in a man's arms and touching Cash had triggered an avalanche of sensations. Her skin acutely remembered the feel of his hard, lean body pressed to hers and wanted more.

The man's words turned her on. His voice—the low, smooth timbre. The caress of his hand. The graze of his lips. It was as if everything he did was part of the seduction, a days-long foreplay that had her body on the edge of completion. Even when she knew this couldn't lead anywhere good, those thoughts didn't cool her down.

Freefalling into a relationship with him would be an even worse mess than she'd made in previous relationships. Sex, no matter how good, would not make it any easier to explain to Benjamin why she was sleeping with a teammate.

The longer she was awake, the more the dream faded, leaving a dull ache where her body was unsatisfied with the mental foreplay and no action, and her brain took over, putting her back into her unsexy state of mind.

It took her longer than usual to dress as she was careful how she moved her leg. Though she was tempted to make an excuse and skip it, brunch with her family and then attending church service was a priority. Proving to her family she was fine and recovered was top on her list.

She opened the door to her bedroom and jolted when she came face-to-face with Cash. Had she been talking aloud? Had she called out his name? Moaned in her sleep? She was loud during sex. Was she loud during sex dreams?

He held out a cup of coffee. "I heard you were up and I thought you could use this."

She accepted the coffee and took a sip. "You don't have to serve me." Though it was thoughtful that he had.

"Like it?" he asked.

The scent of the coffee woke her body and the scent of Cash woke her senses. "It's good. Thank you. Did you sleep okay?" she asked, glancing at the couch. He'd folded the blanket and laid it on the pillow like the perfect houseguest.

"Very well. What about you?"

The glimmer in his eye had her nervous that she had called out his name. She rushed to get out of the condo and away from his gaze. "Yes. Good. Thanks. Right." She scuffed past him. "I hate to be rude, but I'm in a hurry this morning. My family's weekly brunch is Sunday morning, nine a.m. sharp."

"I'll come with you and make sure you arrive safely," Cash said.

If her family saw Cash, it would bring a world of questions slamming into her. She would have enough questions to answer about her injury. "The squad car outside will follow me."

Cash pressed his lips together. "I embarrass you."

That wasn't true at all. "No, my parents are relentless about digging into my personal life. I won't give them fuel for that fire."

His shoulders had lowered. "Thanks for the place to crash."

"Please, don't mention it." She wanted to explain more, but guessed it wouldn't help. Had she hurt his feelings or was she misreading him? It was the last night they would spend together. Maybe if she put some distance between them, their attraction would flitter away. She could talk to Benjamin about sending her into the field with another agent.

Lucia drove the forty-five minutes to her parents' home in suburban Maryland, followed by the police cruiser assigned to watch over her. By the end of the drive, her leg was aching and she'd had too much time to think, mostly about Cash, but also about who could be targeting her.

She could imagine her parents' neighbors now, gossiping about a police cruiser parked outside the Huntington home. Lucia shook off the thoughts. She'd given up caring about being the subject of gossip and the butt of jokes long ago. She parked behind the cars belonging to her sisters and brothers-in-law. Her heart clenched at the sight of Bradley's red sport car.

Bradley had been married to her sister for seven years. Lucia hadn't even dated him that long, but he'd cheated on her with her sister and that was a bitter pill to swallow. Embarrassment, hurt, betrayal and a touch of anger nipped at her even when she tried to pretend it didn't matter.

She used her key to open the front door and walked inside, working to hide her limp.

She met her family in the morning room, where they had brunch laid out buffet style. Her mother brightened when she saw her, and her sisters Chloe and Meg, appeared surprised. Alistair and Bradley, their husbands, appeared bored. Typical family meal.

"We were beginning to think you wouldn't make it," her mother said.

She'd told her father she would. "I'm sorry I'm late." Ten minutes wasn't a big deal, but her parents preferred her to be punctual. It was another unwritten Huntington family rule and one that Lucia couldn't always follow.

"We've invited some friends to join us this morning. I hope you don't mind. They'll be here soon," her mother said.

Her parents often asked her father's business partners and friends to join their Sunday gatherings. Sometimes, they turned into bigger events than brunch and a church service.

When she was a girl, Lucia had hated Sunday social visits. She'd often felt awkward, as if she couldn't say or do the right thing. As a teenager, once she was a dateable age, she had despised the gatherings. Every week was a chance for her to meet someone's son or worry about wearing the latest fashion and keeping up with the trends of her peers, something she hadn't been good at doing. She didn't fit in. When she was old enough, her parents had been bent on introducing her to the right men and that hadn't worked out, either.

None of them, not even Bradley, had gotten Lucia half as excited as Cash had the night before. Her parents wouldn't approve, even though, unlike her, Cash was a social chameleon and would fit in as long as no one asked him about his past. He had a way of setting people at ease, of creating camaraderie with other men and casually flirting with women. Conversation flowed with him. He got along with every member of their FBI team in a way she hadn't mastered.

He had even made her feel special, as though they had a bond. Thinking about Cash made her feel as if she had a secret, something special that only she knew. Her "secret" would carry her through this meal.

Lucia took a seat and poured herself a cup of tea. She listened to the conversation, but didn't have much to say. Her parents' butler ushered in three people at 9:30.

Lucia's heart fell when she laid eyes her family's invited guests, one of her father's partners at his law firm, his wife and their son. Their thirty-something son had the look of an investment banker. He wore a perfectly fitting custom-made suit, smiling as his gaze lingered on her.

A setup. If she hadn't been in an accident recently, she might have smelled it before it was in front of her. She blamed the lingering effects of the pain medication for dulling her senses. It made it doubly embarrassing when a setup played out in front of Bradley. It was as if her entire family, Bradley and her sister included, thought she was too much of a loser to find her own dates.

It wasn't that she was a loser. She hadn't put much effort into finding a man. She didn't have time. The men she had brought to family occasions were met with disapproval, so she stopped bothering.

"Lucia, you remember the Bradshaws, Blair and Tom and their son Camden."

She didn't remember them, but she was too polite to contradict her mother. Lucia tamped down her frustration. It wasn't Camden's fault he'd walked into one of her parents' traps. Though it stung, she kept a smile on her face.

After making a round of introductions, Camden was escorted to the empty seat next to her. Subtle.

"Lucia, it's been a number of years since you've seen Camden," Blair said.

She felt like everyone was expecting her to say something. "How is work, Camden?"

It was a boring question that deserved a boring answer, but Lucia couldn't think of what else to ask. Her parents would be mortified if she was rude, and she was trying to smooth things over with them after the car bombing. They were on the edge of riding her case again about being an FBI agent. Given the problems she'd had in her career, she didn't know how much more energy she had to defend her job.

"I've recently made partner at my uncle's law firm," Camden said.

She'd been wrong. He wasn't an investment banker. He was a lawyer. Both career paths amounted to the same thing to her. School ties, Ivy League education, a master's degree, a house in an exclusive part of town and season tickets to the opera and symphony. "Congratulations." She put effort into sounding sincere.

"What about you, Lucia? Your mother tells me you've moved to a new condominium," Blair said.

The question and follow-up comment grated her. True to form, her mother likely glossed over her working for the FBI and had spun the situation to sound as if Lucia was spending her days tending to an herb garden or redecorating her home.

"My place is close to work. Great commute. I've gotten a new position at the FBI," she said. She might as well put it out in the open that she wasn't like her mother or her sisters. She had career ambitions that didn't include managing a household and arranging parties.

Blair inclined her head in confusion. "Are you a secretary?"

The question was blatantly sexist and spoke to a different way of thinking. Could a woman only be a secretary or housewife in her parents' world? "I'm assistant special agent in charge." She trotted out her title for impact and worked to keep the censure out of her voice.

Camden leaned in. "I didn't realize you worked for the FBI." Genuine interest thickened his voice and it voided her irritation with him. "Do you like working there?"

Around the table, her family cringed. They preferred it when she didn't talk about her job.

Lately, she hadn't liked it. It was long hours, no recognition and it felt as if she was being sidelined with administrative duties as a punishment for succeeding in violent crime as a woman. Because she refused to miss out on field work, she saved the admin work for nights and weekends. "Most days, it's interesting. Of course, it's scary when someone puts a bomb in my car or tries to smother me in my sleep." Her mother and sister's jaw slackened and her brothers-in-law appeared amused. The comment about being a secretary had annoyed her and she had lashed out.

Bradley rolled his eyes. Lucia was feeling smug at having annoyed him until she saw the anger on her father's face. Why had she let her mouth run off? She wasn't like this at work. Her family brought out the impulsive teenager in her.

"Sounds…interesting," Blair said.

Lucia's mother skillfully turned the conversation to other topics and Lucia's work wasn't mentioned again. When they left for church, it was clear that Lucia had earned the silent treatment from her father.

It wasn't the flippant comment. Her father disapproved of every decision she had made in the last seven years, and now that something bad had happened he wanted to use it to twist her arm and force her to quit.

Lucia wasn't a quitter. Not bothering to explain the uniformed police officer who followed them to the church, Lucia sat through the service and made a flimsy excuse about needing to return home to rest. In deference to her father, she didn't mention that her leg was throbbing. She said goodbye to her family, shook Camden's hand and returned to her car.

"Lucia," her father called out as he jogged over to her. "Why are you in a hurry to leave?"

They were the first words he'd spoken to her since she'd mentioned the car bomb. "My leg hurts. I want to go home." Why did he want her to stay? So he could ignore her?

Her father's irritated look saddened her. She had tried to be a daughter who made him proud. She'd failed.

"Camden is a good man. He could provide a nice life for you."

This conversation again. "I don't need a man to provide a life for me. I provide a life for myself."

Her father looked at her car and then at her. "I've been waiting for you to give this up."

How could she make her parents understand? They weren't listening. Her career wasn't launched in rebellion. "I'm not giving it up. I've worked hard to get where I am." If no one else recognized it, at least she did.

Her father's face turned cold. "I see."

He was disappointed in her. Again. "If I were a woman who could cook and clean and garden and find that interesting and fulfilling, we wouldn't have this problem. I'm sorry to disappoint you, but I am not good at those things and I don't like them."

She couldn't be who her parents wanted. She wouldn't have their approval, no matter how much she wanted it.

One day, she'd accept that and move on, but until then a part of her would always wish it could be different. That she could have a soft place to land, a secure place where she fit in and someone she could count on when the chips were down.

Chapter 4

The moment Lucia walked in the door of her condo, she smelled Cash. The scent of soap and spice hit her and she swooned. Not actual falling-to-the-ground swooning, but enough that she grabbed the table next to the door to steady herself. He affected her that much.

Lucia crept inside and set her keys on the counter. Walking into the living room, she found Cash asleep on the couch. He was lying on his back and had one foot on the floor and the other hung over the arm of the couch.

She watched his steady, even breathing as his chest rose and fell. He was a beautiful man, with strong features, a perfect mouth and a brush of a beard across his face. His appearance was almost playful. It spoke nothing of the emotion she'd glimpsed beneath. What had it been like for him in prison? Had his charisma and charm kept him out of trouble?

His eyes snapped open with a look of alarm on his face. Lucia had wandered closer, too close and she took a step back. "It's okay. It's me. Lucia."

Watching an ex-con sleep wasn't wise. Actually, watching anyone sleep wasn't a good idea and was borderline creepy. For Cash, it had to be unsettling on a whole other level.

"Lucia?" As his eyes cleared, she searched for an excuse for why she had been standing over him. He sat up and ran a hand through his messy hair, perhaps trying to smooth it. It looked more tousled and gave him an overall sexy appearance. "How was breakfast?" he asked, his voice gravelly.

It had been a disaster. Could she confide in him? She was the black sheep who couldn't blend with the flock. She bleated out of turn and she ran amok. But he hadn't been judgmental when she'd confided about her family's money.

Going into the kitchen, she poured him some juice. "It was brunch, church and a setup."

"A setup?" Cash asked.

Lucia handed him the juice glass. "A family friend's son they wanted me to meet."

He took a swig of the juice. "Oh. That kind of setup. Financial advisor?"

"Lawyer," she said.

He straightened. "Did you like him?"

No hint of jealousy, just curiosity. "He was probably better than the lawyer I almost married."

"You almost married a lawyer?" Cash asked. "What happened? You realized marrying a lawyer was a horrible mistake?"

She chuckled. "Although in retrospect it would have

been a mistake. He would have suffocated me. He decided to marry my sister, instead. She is much better for him than I could have ever been." It was the first time she had spoken those words and not felt shame, as if she had done something wrong. She didn't miss the stifling emotion.

Cash's eyebrows knit together. "Your ex-boyfriend married your sister? Guess I'm not the only one with family problems."

"Ex-fiancé, but yes, he married my sister." This was more than she had said about her sister and Bradley's relationship since it had happened. It was easy to tell Cash the details. She didn't feel he had an invisible bar she had to measure up to or that she had to hide how she felt for the sake of decorum.

"Pretty hard to believe you sat down to eat with them and kept your food down," Cash said. "I don't have a brother, but I thought there was a sibling code of honor not to share boyfriends and girlfriends."

Bradley was part of her family's tight-knit social circle, giving him elevated status despite his two-timing behavior. Lucia wondered if her parents sided with Bradley, believing Lucia had chased him away. "It was a long time ago," she said. It's what she told herself whenever insecurities and anger rose up over the past.

"For some betrayals, there's not enough time in ten human lives to make those hurts disappear," Cash said.

"They haven't disappeared," she admitted. "But at least no one expected me to be in the wedding."

"Did you attend the wedding?" he asked.

It had been a pretty dark day in her life. "I went and I'm not proud to say I got raucously drunk and Audrey drove me home to keep me from making a total fool of myself." It was one of the first times she had gotten to know Audrey. Audrey had told her that she respected her for not pretending she was cool with Bradley and her sister getting married.

"A little drunken madness sounds in order."

"You don't know my family. Drunken and madness are not states they approve of under any circumstances."

Cash whistled. "You never let loose on your sister?"

"No."

"That's a lot to keep bottled up."

Maybe it was. "Having a hissy fit over something that happened years ago over someone I don't want is a waste of time."

"Sometimes a tantrum can be fun," Cash said.

Lucia chuckled. "I'll keep that in mind next time I get screwed over."

"Your family wants to set you up with someone else? Maybe that's the perfect time for a tantrum."

"I didn't need to have a fit to put anyone off. I mentioned the bombing and I was immediately put into the column with other social pariahs by the guy's parents."

"I'm sure it wasn't that bad," Cash said.

It was over. If she saw Camden and his family again, it would be at a large social gathering and she could be distantly polite. "I'm the oldest unmarried woman in my family. The pressure is on. That I'm not married is a stain on our family name."

"I'm sorry to hear that."

"It's nothing I can't handle," she said. It didn't bother her as much as it used to.

"What are your plans for the rest of the day?" he asked.

"I need to review old case files and trace who might

have set the bomb in my car and who might have snuck into the hospital to finish the job they bungled," Lucia said. "I've been thinking more about Kinsley and Georgiana, too."

"You keep FBI files in your condo?" he asked.

Lucia shook her head. "I can access my case files remotely from my secure computer. What's on your agenda for the day?"

"I got a lead on a new apartment," he said. "The current tenant is moving out in two weeks. Then it's mine. Gives me time to acquire some furniture."

"You can crash on my couch for a few more nights," she said. Two weeks wasn't long and he wouldn't cramp her style. Having him around made her feel safer and he was fun to talk to.

"You don't have to take care of me," Cash said, sounding wary.

"This place is big enough for both of us. Besides, I'm working this case around the clock."

Cash smiled. "Thank you, Lucia. I'll stay out of your way."

Lucia was aware of him. She was attracted to him. And having him in her personal space was a test. Logic over emotion. Reality over fantasy. Even if he stayed at the opposite end of the condo from her, she would know he was there.

After setting her laptop on her dining room table, she paged to the case files from the beginning of her career. Cash strolled into the room and sat next to her. "Need help? Something to drink?"

"You don't have to wait on me. We're colleagues." If she said it enough times, maybe it would penetrate her thinking and her dreams. "Talking through some of this might help. I'm looking for anyone I could have pissed off who likes playing with explosives and who isn't afraid of direct confrontation. Those modus operandi are dissimilar. Bombers hide in the shadows and watch from a distance. This person is taking a front-row view."

"Maybe it's more than one person," Cash said. "A group targeting you."

It was a chilling possibility. "That's not out of the question."

Cash narrowed his gaze on her. "You have an idea who could be behind this."

Lucia weighed how much to disclose. "The case I worked before moving to white collar involved a murder-for-hire ring. The group was well organized, skilled and ruthless." Thinking of what they'd done to their victims terrified her. The killings were precise and cruel. "But I could be wrong. It doesn't fit, not exactly. The members of the group were well trained, but the attacks on me had miscalculations and errors."

"Is there anyone outside work you've pissed off?" Cash asked.

Her social life was practically nonexistent. Her personal life involved her family, their friends and a handful of former classmates, colleagues and neighbors. "No one I've pissed off enough to want to kill me."

She looked through her cases, talking over some theories with Cash.

After several hours, Cash moved closer. "I want to ask you a favor that I've been debating asking."

He appeared uncomfortable and she immediately went on alert. She couldn't break the rules for him. She couldn't even bend them.

"I need to make a long-distance phone call to Seattle," he said. "I don't have a cell phone. May I use yours?"

It would cost her nothing to allow him to make the call. "Who are you calling?" She wouldn't provide him with the means to make contact with other felons and violate the terms of his release.

"My son," Cash said.

The words came out in a thick voice and sympathy washed over her. Lucia should have offered sooner. "Of course you may."

She handed him her phone. She could verify later if the call had gone to Washington state, but Cash wasn't stupid enough to use an FBI agent's phone to transact illegal business.

A few minutes later, Cash was standing on the balcony, staring out over the city. The phone was clasped in his hand.

She opened the door. "Everything okay?"

Cash looked over his shoulder at her. "He won't speak to me."

The hurt in his voice was plain. "I'm sorry."

"He doesn't understand and he's angry at me for going to prison."

"Is there someone who can speak with him?" she asked. Family relations weren't her forte. She couldn't offer advice to Cash.

"His grandmother tries," he said.

"You're welcome to call someone else if you need to talk," she said. She wasn't pawning him off on someone else, but she didn't have the expertise in this situation to help.

"I don't have anyone to call."

No one? A man like Cash seemed to make friends easily. How could he not have people to call? "What about other family?"

"My father's a con man too. He didn't come to see me in prison. I spoke to him once on the phone from prison during the trial. He said it messed with his head to come anywhere near me."

Her heart ached for him. Though her family wasn't perfect, at least her parents didn't cut her out because of her choices and the consequences of those decisions.

"What about friends?" she asked.

"I've cut ties with my old life. I had to."

If he was conning her, he was doing a good job, making her sympathies swell to an almost insurmountable point.

"It's almost dinner. What do you want to eat?" Cash asked.

A pointed change in the subject and Lucia let it slide. It had to cut deep to have his son refuse to talk to him, and given the other things in his life that had gone wrong, Cash might be barely holding everything together. She wouldn't apply pressure. "I'll check the pantry. I probably have something we can throw together."

Cash joined her in the kitchen. The food in her refrigerator was half-spoiled and her pantry contained several boxes and canned items that wouldn't make a meal.

"I'll run to the market and pick up something," Cash said.

"We can order carryout," Lucia said.

"Let me earn my keep. I fed you carryout once. I can cook for you," Cash said.

"I'll grab my food bags and come with you," Lucia

said. Though he wasn't openly devastated, she sensed he was still down and leaving him alone didn't sit right.

Con man or not, he wasn't hiding his emotions well. His pain was palpable.

She wanted to give him some encouragement. What could she say? Lucia grabbed his elbow. "Cash, I want you to know that I think you're doing a good job. I know this is hard for you."

Cash watched her with his perceptive eyes. Why did it always seem as if so much was going on inside his head? He had layers she couldn't fully understand. "That's nice of you to say. Most days, I feel like the world's biggest screw-up."

When they left her building, Lucia noted the police cruiser that had been watching her house earlier was no longer parked outside. It wasn't across the street, either. Strapped for resources, monitoring her place could have been rotated to the occasional drive-by.

The market where Lucia preferred to shop was five blocks away. Grabbing a cart, she strolled up and down the narrow aisles letting Cash toss items into the basket. She didn't make comments, although preparation of many of the items he'd selected was foreign to her.

"Why do you keep wrinkling your nose?" Cash asked. "These are fresh ingredients. I've missed them."

She realized that she took the ability to buy fresh food for granted. "I'm confused about what you're picking. How do you know how to fix avocado?"

Cash laughed. "Slice, knock out the seed and remove the skin. Easy and delicious."

Lucia could have fumbled her way through it, but wouldn't have attempted it if she were alone. "Learning to cook is on my to-do list."

"You don't need to learn to cook. Cook and see where it takes you," Cash said.

His suggestion highlighted a big difference between their personalities. He was intuitive and she went by the book. When she needed to do something new, she studied it. She'd wager Cash just did it.

They paid for their groceries and Cash carried the bulk of the items in her fabric food bags. Lucia held one. Her leg was feeling much better and she would have made more of an issue about each of them carrying the same number of bags, but it seemed as though he needed to be in control for a while. She gave him some leeway.

The sun was beginning to dip low in the sky and the streets were less crowded. Turning down a side street, she sensed someone behind them. She glanced over her shoulder and saw a man with his hands in his pockets and his head down. He could be traveling in the same direction, but his posture and proximity made her nervous. On the heels of the bombing, was she overreacting to nothing?

"I think we're being followed," she said.

"Advise," he said.

Cash's immediate willingness to defer to her surprised her. Lucia looked around for their next move. "When we reach that Dumpster, I'll pull my gun and turn around. Duck behind the Dumpster and protect your head."

"You need to take cover, too," he said. "We should turn around and let him know we see him."

If he was following her with the intent to approach, that might scare him off and Lucia wanted to put an end to this. "I want to catch him. I can take care of myself," she said. "Do as I said."

She didn't want their follower to know she'd made him, so she was careful to conceal her movements, reaching for her gun, unsnapping the strap over the handle and removing it from the holster. As many times as she had practiced using it, she hadn't fired her gun with a lethal result. She'd been trained to do so and she could protect herself.

When they reached the Dumpster, Cash moved behind it, pulling her with him.

Lucia shook him off and peeked around the corner. The street was empty. "Cash, that was not the plan. I lost him. There's no one there now."

Cash didn't move. "I heard the footsteps, too. Someone was behind us. I didn't want you hurt."

Lucia looked up. No stairwell leading up from the ground level. A metal door halfway down the street could have been the exit point. "I'll look for him."

"Don't be insane. Call the police and let's get out of here," Cash said.

She hated backing down from a fight. Whoever was stalking her had to know he couldn't intimidate her. As persistent as her follower had been, would he duck away that easily? Lucia lowered herself to the ground and peered under the Dumpster. She could see a pair of dirty worn sneakers on the other side. Her nerves tightened and her mouth went dry.

Someone was waiting for her to leave the safety of the metal box. She signaled to Cash to stay and handed him her phone and pressed a finger over her lips. He dialed 911.

"I must be hearing things. Let's go home," she said.

As she'd hoped, the man stepped out from behind the Dumpster and Lucia leveled her gun at him. His hooded sweatshirt covered most of his face. "FBI. Hands where I can see them or I'll put a bullet in your head."

"Lucia, for crying out loud. Don't get trigger-happy on me."

Surprise had her lowering her gun. Jonathan Wolfe, her partner from her former team, lifted his head and knocked back the hood of his sweatshirt.

"Why are you following me? Are you trying to get yourself killed?" Lucia asked.

Jonathan shook out his arms. "No, but I almost crapped myself. I was told to follow you and keep an eye out for whoever might be stalking you."

"The Bureau sent you to stalk my stalker?" Lucia asked, not amused by the FBI's plan and why she was left out of it. "Why didn't Benjamin tell me?"

Jonathan rolled his shoulders. "You weren't supposed to know. The section chief's assembled a task force. We're trying to trace the bombing to someone and we don't have any decent leads. From what was left of the bomb, we know it was triggered remotely. We suspect someone was watching and waiting to trigger it."

To hear her remote bombing theory confirmed did not make her feel better.

"Benjamin didn't want you to change your routine, which you would if you knew we were watching you."

"You were stuck with me, then?" she asked.

"I wouldn't call it stuck with you. We all want this guy found. If we let someone attack one agent and get away with it, it sets an ugly precedent."

Cash extended his hand and introduced himself to Jonathan.

"Don't tell Benjamin you made me. I'm supposed to be good at this. It's been a long time since I had to follow someone on the street," Jonathan said.

"You're good at this. I'm better," Lucia said. She turned to pick up her groceries.

"Hey, Luc," Jonathan said. Something in his voice had her turning slowly and meeting his stare.

"I think it was crappy what happened to you."

Meaning her promotion to white collar to push her off the team. "Thanks."

"I wasn't part of that decision."

His words made her feel a little better. She had more to say, but not in front of Cash. What had happened was embarrassing and the past, no matter how rotten, was over.

"How'd it go with Dr. Granger?" Benjamin asked from three desks away. He strode to Lucia's desk and leaned against it.

Lucia was eager for some normalcy, like checking her email and catching up on any case notes that had been added. "He was thorough." She'd had pelvic exams that had been more comfortable. "I told him about my concerns about Preston Hammer. He said he would follow up."

"Then you're cleared for work?" Benjamin asked.

"I'm here, aren't I?" Lucia asked, typing her password into her computer. Her words were sharp, but she didn't want to sit through another interrogation.

"While you were gone, we drew straws. You drew the short one," Benjamin said.

Lucia rolled her eyes. "Shocking. What do we have?

An overnight stakeout?" Copies of files to be made? Paperwork from the seventies to be sorted?

Cash was watching her and hadn't said anything. Her senses tingled. Something big had happened.

"What did I miss?" she asked.

"We got a hot lead on Clifton Anderson. He wasn't working one con job in the city. He had two going. The one at Holmes and White may be over, but he's running an underground gambling ring in the city."

Excitement coursed through her. It was the lead they'd been waiting for. "That's the short straw? Going to one of his underground casinos?" She considered that great luck. She needed to be in the action. The closer she got to Anderson, the closer she was to finding the stolen money.

Benjamin laughed. Cash rubbed his jaw.

"The casino Anderson is running is invitation-only. He's lying low, but he's definitely still involved in it. We hear it's too much money to walk away from."

Something didn't sit well with what Benjamin said. "He stole hundreds of millions from Holmes and White. How much does he want?"

Cash tapped a pen against his palm. "He's greedy, so it could be that he's looking for his final big score and then he'll slip away."

Slip away out of their reach and take the money with him. Lucia wouldn't let that happen.

"Maybe something went wrong with the Holmes and White deal and he either can't access the money or he's worried he can't get away with it clean," Lucia said. If the money was tied up, that made it more likely they could put their hands on it before Anderson did. "Who gave you the lead?"

Cash raised a finger. Of course. Cash had contacts and connections.

"I called Georgiana first thing this morning and got nowhere. I also called a buddy who gave me the info," Cash said.

"Tell me how to find this underground casino." Lucia had a few informants in the city that liked to gamble. Perhaps she could lean on them and find out if they knew anything.

"Cash will work his contacts until he secures an invite. Once he's in, we'll bankroll him at the casino, but we want a couple of people to go with him as backup."

Backup, like security detail? Not as fun, but it could still be a great way to catch a break in the case. "What's my role exactly?" Lucia asked, taking the file folder Benjamin extended to her.

She inwardly groaned when she scanned the mock profile. Lucy Harris, Cash's floozy girlfriend. It wasn't the first time she'd played the part of a girlfriend, but it would be the first time she'd played it alongside someone she wanted to sleep with. Keeping emotional control during undercover ops was critical to their success.

Could she and Cash pull this off?

"Is that a deep enough cover?" Lucia asked. She could go under as a fellow gambler.

"Anderson knows Cash went to prison, but they have a history. Cash's father and Anderson go way, way back. They grew up in the same neighborhood and ran scams from the time they could walk."

Cash didn't appear upset by what Benjamin was saying. No hint of the emotion he'd felt the night before showed.

"Cash was also married to Anderson's estranged daughter."

Lucia hoped she hid her shock. Cash's late wife was Anderson's daughter? Cash's son was Anderson's grandson? Why hadn't he mentioned that to her? It hadn't been in the file Benjamin had given her earlier.

"If you're his son-in-law, what's your relationship now?" Lucia asked Cash.

"My late wife wasn't part of her father's life. She didn't keep me from seeing him, but she made it clear she didn't want him in her life," Cash said.

"Does Anderson carry a grudge about that?" Lucia asked.

"I guess we'll find out," Cash said.

"Did he help you with the con that landed you in prison?" Lucia asked.

Cash said nothing.

"He doesn't have to answer that," Benjamin said.

His silence was an answer. Anderson had been involved but Cash wouldn't sell him out.

"Maybe Cash can approach him looking for a big score," Lucia said, not liking the idea of putting Cash close to the fire, but knowing it could work if Cash could take the heat.

Or as long as he could stand the heat and not get burned.

Anderson was smart. He vetted the people he worked with. It wouldn't take long for Anderson to work his contacts and find out that Cash was working with the FBI. "What will Cash tell Anderson about his release and working with us?"

"A modified truth," Benjamin said.

"I'll tell him the pay is lousy and for the right price, I'll get as dirty as he needs," Cash said.

Lucia didn't like it. "It's dangerous." She didn't want their lead to negate the need for proper preparation.

"Worried about me?" Cash asked, his eyes gleaming with amusement.

"You can handle yourself," Lucia said, worry still nipping at her. At least she would be with Cash as his backup. "Now score us an invitation. I'm in the mood to gamble tonight."

Lucia and Cash rifled through the FBI's costume closet. The outfits were meant to be less cowboys and superheroes and more prostitutes and gangbangers. Lucia found some items that could work for the part she was playing.

"Anderson knows you. Would he really believe you'd be into a woman who dresses like this?" Lucia held up the sparkly purple minidress.

"I think any straight man would be into a woman who dresses like that. Especially when that woman is you," Cash said.

He didn't sound hot and bothered, which was exactly what his words made Lucia feel.

She held up the dress. "It looks like a box of glitter exploded on it."

"Sexy."

"I guess that tells me something about your taste," she said, only half joking and taking another dress off the rack.

"It tells you something about how I feel about you," Cash said.

Lucia stopped. For a moment, the closet felt still and small. "Careful, Cash. People might hear us."

"Just getting into character," he said and winked at her. "Does it bother you that you're attracted to me?" Cash asked, holding up a pair of thigh-high brown boots for her.

She shook her head to the boots.

It did bother her that she was attracted to Cash. Her hormones were overriding common sense. "You're a handsome man. You know how women respond to you. You don't know how to turn it off when you should. Like when you're with me." A feather boa? Did anyone wear feather boas?

"It's not a one-sided thing. Being near you brings out something in me. It's not every woman who responds to me the way you do. How you look at me, how you laugh, how you touch me."

He was implying an intimacy that wasn't, or shouldn't be, there. She wasn't playing an active role in the attraction. "Is this appropriate for your girlfriend to wear to an underground casino?" she asked, holding up a black dress.

"I prefer the purple one," he said.

She returned to the racks. She wouldn't lie to him and deny she found him attractive, but they didn't need to harp on the point.

"Have you slept with Benjamin?" Cash asked.

Lucia whipped her head around to look at Cash. "What?"

"I thought I saw something between you and him."

"You did see something. Respect. I don't know whether to be insulted or angry you asked me that," Lucia said.

"You don't have a boyfriend and you should. I want to know why," Cash said.

She hated that question enough at family gatherings. She didn't need it from him. "You're the king of figuring people out. You tell me."

Cash looked her up and down, his gaze traveling slowly over her. "You find reasons to reject people, like using your rules to keep them away. It's easier for you to reject them, than give them the opportunity to reject you. Giving someone a chance to get to know you is hard because you could be hurt."

He'd struck a nerve and she felt it. Cash was good at digging around and finding information about someone. She wasn't giving him the chance to dissect her psyche. The staff psychologist had done a thorough enough job of that earlier in the day. "I don't reject people." And yet she didn't have many friends or any long-lasting romantic relationships. She pulled a pink dress from the rack.

"You're not impulsive because you don't want to make a mistake again. You want to be in your father's good graces without sacrificing who you are and what you want. You want to be with a good man, but you fear he'll let you down. You end it before he gets the chance to."

His words hurt, giving away how close he hit to the truth. "Maybe you have a future as a relationship counselor," she said.

"It matters what your parents think because they've never given you approval for anything you've done," Cash said.

Was it wrong to want their approval? "I would like a relationship with someone my parents approve of and who I enjoy being with," Lucia said. She could have both, though it hadn't been the case to date.

"Guess that takes me out of the running."

He'd spoken so plainly to her, it stung. When it came to relationships, she was a failure with a capital *F*. Lately, her career had been in the D range. Not much to be proud of. "Now that's where you're mistaken. You were never in the running, Cash."

"Ouch," he said.

She'd intended the words to hurt. She wanted him to stop analyzing her and stop trying to force a conversation she hated. "You can console yourself with any of the dozens of women who fall at your feet."

"No one falls at my feet," Cash said.

Lucia rolled her eyes. "Maybe I don't know anything about your personal life, but you don't know much about mine, either."

She wouldn't tell Cash the most difficult secret she harbored. Her career was rocky and her time with the FBI marred by her transfer. On paper, it looked fine, but everyone knew the chief of the violent crime unit had wanted her out.

Now, she had to play by the rules. One screw-up or even a hint of one, and she could be relegated to permanent administrative duty or fired.

Chapter 5

Frustration was burning a white-hot hole in Cash's chest. Adrian was still refusing to speak to him and Helen had asked Cash not to call for another week. She promised she would talk to Adrian and help him understand what had happened. His son was a tough little boy, but he was fragile, too, and he'd been hurt, surviving cancer and then losing his parents. It wasn't fair, but then life wasn't. It was a lesson Cash knew Adrian had learned too young.

Cash needed some space from Lucia. He'd been staying with her and believing that he could somehow make it work as a regular guy, an FBI consultant with a checkered past, but he was still a man, a man attracted to a woman who seemed to want to keep boundaries.

Since he wasn't certain of where those boundaries were, he'd best not go anywhere close to them. If he made a mistake with Lucia, if he got on her bad side, he was endangering his future with Adrian.

It was yet another way that being a felon would follow him for the rest of his life. He'd need to keep his distance from people.

The time he'd spent in prison should have hardened him. Sadly, he hadn't shaken off the need for a real connection. He missed his son. He couldn't call his father, not out of the blue when they hadn't spoken in years. He had to be careful around old friends, since he was working them for an invite to one of Anderson's exclusive casinos.

Lonely. It was the best word to describe what he was feeling.

He stopped at Lucia's place, grabbed a few essentials he'd left and fled. Taking the stairs down, he passed Audrey and a group of her friends who were on their way to Audrey's condo.

One of the women stopped and grabbed his tie. "Where are you going?" she asked.

He could smell liquor on her breath. He removed her hand from his clothes. "Out." He looked at Audrey. "Nice seeing you."

"You know Audrey?" the woman asked.

Audrey stopped on the stairs and gave him an assessing look through narrowed eyes. "Where's Lucia?"

"At work."

She'd stayed late at the office to review Clifton Anderson's case file and catch up on some paperwork. Cash told her he planned to stop by her condo. To avoid unnecessary drama, he hadn't mentioned returning to the Hideaway that night.

"Come party with us," the other woman said to him.

She was leaning on the bannister, letting her hair fall across her face.

In another life, he'd be up for a party to blow off some steam. But lingering meant possibly running into Lucia. He didn't want to face her again until he'd had time to clear his dark thoughts. "Not tonight. Thank you for the invite."

"You're welcome to come over and have a few drinks," Audrey said. "We went to a club opening and there were entirely too many people for our liking." She stepped down to the stair he was on and smiled up at him. "You look like you could use a friend."

Friend. Cash missed having one around. Returning to the depressing Hideaway was the last thing he wanted. He didn't have anywhere else to go except a bar and he didn't have money to drink. His curfew was a couple of hours away. "For a few minutes." Maybe listening to someone else's conversation would take his mind off his problems and shake off his bad mood.

A few minutes in Audrey's condo turned into twenty. With a drink in one hand, Cash lounged on the comfortable furniture. Her style—abstract, modern designs, clean lines, black and white floor to ceiling—was different than Lucia's.

Audrey and her friends reeked of money. Fifteen years ago, he would have been enjoying every moment of this and trying to edge himself into their crowd.

For a few hours he could forget he was a felon, out of touch with his son and the people who mattered. The people in this room didn't know he was a convict or that he was being used by the FBI to track a con man. He was surrounded by four beautiful women. They'd drawn him into the conversation and were hanging on to his every word.

One of them had to be more attractive than Lucia. One of them had to hold his attention. One of them had to make him forget about Lucia.

But no one held a candle to her. Instead of enjoying the women around him, he made comparisons. He thought about how Lucia would look wearing similar outfits. How she would have something interesting to say. How much he'd want to sit close to her and kiss her.

Audrey strode over to him. "A minute of your time, please?"

Cash rose to his feet, murmured his apologies to the women and followed Audrey to her balcony.

"What's going on with you and Lucia?" she asked, setting her hand on her hip.

He chose to explain it the easiest way he knew how. "She doesn't want me in her life. We're working together, but she's drawn a line in the sand."

Audrey frowned. "She said that? She doesn't want you around?"

"In so many words," he said.

"She's a complicated woman."

"All women are complicated. If I think they aren't, then I haven't gotten to know them well enough yet," Cash said.

Audrey smirked. "Fair enough. I've known Lucia a long time and I know she's a good person who's had some rotten luck. I don't want to be part of anything that would hurt her. Have fun, but don't do anything you'll regret. These women are fierce. They'll strip you, ride you and kick you out before you have time to get dressed."

Her frankness was unexpected. His interactions with Audrey's friends wouldn't go that far. Understanding the warning, Cash returned to the group. As the night wore on, the alcohol flowed more freely and Cash had the urge to walk across the hall and lay it on the table for Lucia. To tell her everything he felt and why he felt it and force her to listen. She had to be home by now and if she understood the extent of his feelings, she might change her mind about keeping him away.

Pride, coupled with the knowledge that he'd been drinking and might not be thinking clearly, stopped him. He wouldn't throw himself at her feet in a drunken, pathetic stupor. Lucia had some control over his time with the FBI and therefore he couldn't screw up and put his future with his son in jeopardy.

Cash took another swig of his drink. Audrey was serving some strong stuff. No fifty-cent bottles of beer in this place. It had been a long time since he'd had much to drink and the alcohol hit him hard, leaving him feeling as though his head was being held underwater.

He needed to get back to the motel. He stood and one of the women, Lexie, set her hand over his chest to stop him. "Where are you going?"

"I have to go. It's late." If he missed curfew, he was in violation of his agreement with the FBI and they could throw him in prison.

She pouted. "Please stay. A few more minutes."

"I can't. It's a long walk." He needed fresh air and exercise. At least the alcohol dulled his senses, enough that he could make it through a night at the Hideaway without being as aware of the stink, the loudness and the general unpleasantness.

"Stay and I'll drive you."

Lexie didn't belong on that side of town even if Audrey had implied her friends could handle themselves. "I live in a rough area."

She giggled and moved closer to him. "Sounds dangerous. You can keep me safe."

Lexie was probably interested in him because he was different from the men in her social circle, the same men Lucia's parents wanted her to marry. He was poor, he had no lucrative job prospects and he didn't come from a long line of well-bred men.

Lexie was flirting with him and beckoning to him to kiss her. Cash wanted to prove that he wasn't wrapped up in Lucia. He could forget about her and kiss other women and be happy about it. He had no reason to feel guilty. Lucia wasn't his girlfriend. She had made it clear she wouldn't be. Maybe this was a distraction he needed. Audrey had said her friends were looking for a night of fun.

How long had it been since he'd behaved like a carefree bachelor?

Her lips were hovering near his and she was leaning against him, but nothing about this felt right and it highlighted the fact he'd been attempting to disprove. Lucia made his blood run hot. Another woman couldn't replace her.

A surge of nausea hit him. He hadn't drunk like this in a long time. His tolerance was nil. He closed his eyes to center himself and Lucia's voice screamed into his mind.

When he opened them, Lucia was standing over him looking royally peeved. She pointed over his head. "Forget something?"

Lexie grabbed his shirt territorially, pressing her hands into his chest. "Who are you?"

He'd made a mess. Again. He wasn't sure how to clean it up. Why was Lucia screaming at him?

Lucia ignored Lexie and stared at him. "Benjamin called. You're past curfew and he traced you to my building. I told him you were with me. I covered for you only to find you here partying with Audrey's friends." She bit her lip and folded her arms.

Cash stood and reached for Lucia. She stepped away from him.

"You don't understand." He had been thinking of her all night. Why did it feel as if he'd betrayed her?

Lucia looked around the room. "We're not doing this here."

"Doing what? Having a conversation?" he asked. "You never want to have a conversation. You're always running away."

"Are you drunk?" she asked, sounding outraged.

His head was swimming. "I had some to drink, first drink I've had since prison."

Lucia spun on her heel and left the condo. Cash followed her across the hall to hers. He hated that he'd upset her and hated even more that his brain wasn't working fast enough to diffuse her anger. This was one of the reasons he hadn't drank much.

When they got inside, she whirled on him. "I can't believe you decided to get drunk."

It hadn't been his intention. "I didn't decide to do anything."

"What were you doing with that woman?" she asked.

"Talking," he said, sticking to few words. If he let

his mouth run, he would say something he regretted. His tongue felt slow and heavy.

"You said you were stopping by my condo to pick up your things. I assumed that meant you were going home," Lucia said.

Was she mad that he'd missed his curfew? That was his price to pay, not hers. "That place is not my home. Imagine not wanting to return to the dump where I live. I was invited somewhere and I went."

Lucia glared at him.

Anger and frustration took hold of him. "Why do you care?" He wanted her to care, to say she had been worried about him or that she was having second thoughts about shutting down their relationship. She hadn't even given it a chance, either being too scared to risk being hurt or because she knew how it would end.

"I care because I covered for you with Benjamin so you wouldn't get into trouble. If you do something stupid while you're drunk, I'm liable for that."

She'd put herself on the line for him. "I didn't ask you to cover for me. I'm a big boy. I'll take whatever knocks come my way."

"Like you did by going to prison?" she asked.

Was she implying he'd wormed out of his sentence? Anger filled him. "My prison time is your favorite whip. Yes, Lucia, I went to prison. I accepted responsibility for running a con. I didn't rat anyone else out. I kept my mouth shut and took the punishment I was given." Anderson had helped set him up with the con. He'd introduced Cash to the senator Cash had defrauded and to the crew involved in the embezzlement.

Lucia stared at him. "You were working with someone else on the con."

No point in lying about it now. "Yes."

"Who?"

"I can't discuss that." Wouldn't.

"Why not?"

Because it didn't matter if others were involved. "It doesn't make a difference. What someone else did doesn't change that I committed a crime. I have criminal connections. I'm using those connections to help you now." Thanks to his father, he'd been born into a world of lying and deceit where trickery and games were part of the lifestyle.

"You were with another woman," Lucia said.

Lucia's thoughts ricocheted and she was hard to follow, harder in his current state. "Why do you care who I'm with?" She had no right to demand an explanation from him. He wasn't in prison anymore.

Lucia folded her arms over her chest and glared at him. "I don't know what's going on with you, but pull it together. I won't cover for you again. You can sleep off your drunkenness, but tomorrow, find another place to stay. I knew you couldn't be trusted."

Lucia couldn't sleep. She couldn't scrub the image of Cash and Lexie from her thoughts. Lexie was a good friend of Audrey's. She was sophisticated and cultured and beautiful and fun. She didn't have a full-time job taking up her time and she spent her nights and weekends staying out and partying. Lexie was a woman who'd show Cash a good time and he deserved to have a good time.

Lucia had no hold over Cash. She shouldn't have unloaded on him. Lucia kicked at her sheets in frustration, wincing when pain shot across her leg. She shifted, trying to stretch her leg and find a more comfortable position.

Nothing about her current situation was comfortable.

She let out a grunt of frustration. Why Cash? Of all the men for Benjamin to spring from prison and use to help in the investigation, why did it have to be someone Lucia felt a blazing-hot attraction to?

Cash appeared in the doorway, his big body filling the space. "You okay? I'm hearing some moaning." His voice had lost the slurring from earlier in the night. He was more sober.

"I'm stretching," she said.

"In the middle of the night?"

"My leg hurts. I'm trying to resolve that without medication."

He stepped into the room and her heart shot to her throat. She grabbed her sheet, feeling exposed.

"Let me rub your leg. It might help. When I was in high school, a buddy and I took a massage class. We thought it would impress girls."

"Did it?" she asked.

"No. We were too young and stupid to have any moves," Cash said.

She hadn't decided if she would agree. If he touched her, she knew how her body would react and her emotions were still in upheaval. Her emotional state and Cash in her bedroom were a potent and potentially volatile combination. Cash crossed the room and sat on the edge of the bed. He reached for her and used his powerful hands to rub her muscles.

"You feel tense," he said.

No mystery why. "Rough day."

"I'm sorry about what happened at Audrey's," he said.

"We don't have to talk about it," she said. Cash wasn't her boyfriend. They weren't even dating.

"I was trying to forget you," he said.

He had flirted with Lexie to forget her? "Hard to do when we work together," she said.

"Sometimes I want to forget everything."

"You don't mean that," Lucia said. "What about your son?"

Cash froze and he pulled his hands away. "I didn't mean him. He's impossible to forget. But it's not going as well as I'd hoped. Maybe it would be better for him if I wasn't around."

She hadn't seen Cash this low. To suggest that his son was better off without him spoke to the depth of his sadness. "Do you want to talk about it?"

"No."

"I'm sorry you're hurting."

Cash stood from the bed. "I'm fine. I'm taking steps to improve my life." He let out a short, bitter laugh. "Tonight being the exception."

"You didn't do anything wrong except miss your curfew and make me jealous."

"Jealous of a felon?"

"Of Lexie," Lucia said.

"Why? She can't measure up to you."

Insecurities she'd been clinging to drifted out of reach. "She's everything I was supposed to be."

"You are who you are. 'Supposed to be' is for people who don't have direction or dreams."

"Try telling my family that. Why can't I go along with what they want? It would make things easier."

"Because when it comes to matters of the heart, it's hard to make a compromise."

He had that right. "Maybe I'm also a little jealous of you. You seem to know what you want. You open up to people easily. You connect."

"I have to connect to people or they won't talk to me. If I don't get the information, I'm useless to the FBI."

The words shook her. "You are not useless."

His eyes narrowed. "Why did you cover for me tonight?"

Why? It had been an impulse. Confusion about where Cash had been had mixed with worry. The lie had slipped out of her mouth. "I knew what was at stake." His son. Jail time. Her shaky status with the Bureau had seemed secondary to that.

"Thank you," he said.

She couldn't leave him like this and she wasn't good with words. A tremble rose through her accompanied by a rush of emotion. She knelt on the bed and reached for him. He took two steps and she grabbed the sides of Cash's shirt and drew him to her.

"I don't like being wrong, but I was wrong to think you were nothing more than a felon," she said.

Then she kissed him. Hard. He opened his mouth and returned the kiss. Ignoring her leg, she pulled him onto the bed beside her. She crawled into his lap, straddling him, pressing her body against his. His arms wrapped around her.

"Don't jerk me around, Lucia, and don't do this if you're trying to cheer me up," Cash said, breathing hard.

Lucia rose up on her knees over him. This man, this sensitive, sweet man who had been through so much and remained loyal to the people around him was better than most men in her life. "I am not jerking you around." She wasn't doing this to cheer him up. It was more than that. Much more.

He touched her hair at her temples and ran his fingers through it. "What is this about? You said this afternoon we had nothing."

She had been wrong then, on the defensive. "I shouldn't have said something I didn't mean." Her impulsiveness was a trait her family had ruthlessly criticized while she was growing up and that she'd worked hard to control. Too hard.

He shifted away and moved her off his lap.

"What's wrong?" she asked.

His flirtation had led her to believe he'd wanted to sleep with her. Had she thoroughly misread the signs? Was he rejecting her?

"I'm preventing you from making a mistake you'll regret in the morning."

"I won't have regrets."

Cash kissed the top of her head. "This is one of the hardest things I've walked away from, but I won't let you hate me in the morning. I'm a man women regret being with. I know you'll never trust me, but you can trust me on that."

For someone who'd slept off a night of drinking, Cash appeared rested and together. His suit was crisp and he worked at his desk, head down, talking with his criminal contacts or doing research or whatever Benjamin had assigned him.

Lucia caught him looking at her several times, but she avoided making direct eye contact. Everyone on the team would know something had happened between them if she turned red. Much to her sexual frustration,

Cash seemed fine with the unconsummated state of their relationship.

Lucia wondered about Cash. He'd rejected her. Lucia had been rejected before, so it wasn't new, but she'd been sure Cash was feeling the chemistry between them. What was it about him that made her instincts perpetually off-kilter?

Her internal instant messenger flashed on her screen. She had a message from Cash.

I'm meeting a contact at the Smithsonian American Art Museum at noon. Come with me as backup and we'll have lunch. My treat.

An olive branch to smooth over some of the awkwardness between them? He didn't have to treat her to lunch. She could buy her own meal. When they had work to do, what had happened—or hadn't happened—in her bedroom was irrelevant.

I'll work backup. We'll buy our own lunches. I'll let Benjamin know.

Whatever you say, boss.

Lucia tried not to read too much into it. Was he trying to keep their personal and professional lives separate, as she was? Was he finding it easy to not let their chemistry cause trouble for them?

Lucia informed Benjamin of their plans so he could inform museum security that an armed agent would be working on site. She checked her weapon and left the building with enough time to reach the museum ahead of schedule.

Lucia and Cash entered the art museum separately. It was a strange place to meet a contact. Security guards were posted everywhere and video cameras captured visitors coming and going.

Lucia sat on a bench with a sketchpad open on her lap and a fedora pulled over her face, her hair twisted into it. She watched Cash through her phony eyeglasses. He was standing in front of *The Knight of the Holy Grail*, a painting by Frederick J. Waugh of a knight kneeling in a boat before two angels. Cash's hands were in his pockets and he stared at the painting.

The man they'd run into on the street when leaving Preston Hammer's house—the man Cash had called Boots—ambled toward the painting and stood next to Cash, almost shoulder to shoulder. Boots was wider and taller than Cash and his clothes were more casual.

The two men were speaking, but Lucia couldn't hear what they were saying.

She touched the gun at her hip. She was a good shot. No one would hurt him, not while she was watching. Her protective instincts surprised her. Cash was fast becoming her partner on the team and that was a title she was slow to give to anyone.

"How much you think it's worth on the market?" Boots asked, nodding at the Waugh painting in front of Cash.

Forgeries and the sale of stolen artwork had been Cash's father's area of expertise. Growing up, Cash had learned quite a bit about the world's greatest masterpieces. In a high school art class, he'd learned to paint by copying the masters. His father had been proud, but later disappointed when Cash didn't express an interest in marketing his skills to sell fraudulent copies as originals. "Immediately after the theft, without papers and with the authorities looking for it? A couple hundred thousand. With papers, the sale to a legitimate private collector could go for five million."

Boots snorted. "How many legitimate private collectors do you know?"

Not many, but that wasn't part of Cash's world anymore. The distance between him and his father was deliberate and clear. Lucia, Audrey and their friends probably had several priceless, legally obtained works of art in their homes. "I assume you didn't want to meet to discuss an art theft. Because there's zero chance I'm lifting anything from this gallery. Too risky," Cash said.

"I wouldn't be so bold." Boot grinned. He was that bold. "I heard you're looking to make some cash and get back in the game."

That was the word Cash had put out on the street. Associates who knew about his trouble with Adrian would know he needed the cash to make a life for him and his son. Those who didn't probably weren't overly concerned about why Cash was looking for work. Most hustlers on the street were always looking to make a buck. "You heard right."

"How much cash you need?" he asked.

"I've got some debt and some dreams and not enough cash to finance either. I want to parlay what I do have into a livable sum."

"You didn't set up a nest egg before you went in?" Boots asked.

Boots was asking if Cash had an illegal account or a location where he stashed cash or other high-value items to fence. "No time to save much. I used almost everything I had." He'd used every penny for Adrian, but he'd need Boots to believe he had something to gamble with.

Boots didn't bat an eye. "You know your father-in-law is running some games at night."

"I heard," Cash said.

"You want in?" Boots asked.

"Sure do," Cash said.

"Working for him?" Boots asked.

While that could put him closer to Anderson, he needed to bring Lucia inside, as well. "I'd rather take my chances at the table," Cash said. "That's where the real money is."

"Depends on what you're willing to do. Your old buddy has some big dogs on his payroll," Boots said.

Cash shook his head. "You know me. I'm not in the big time. I've got limits."

"If you didn't have limits, as you call them, you could get your payday faster."

His limits, including being unwilling to kill or harm anyone, were set in stone. Even before he'd promised Britney he'd turn his back on their fathers' cons, he had never been okay with violence. "I'll wait for my payday." And so Boots wouldn't become suspicious, he added, "I can't risk going back to prison."

"Why don't you call him yourself?" Boots asked.

"I don't know where he is," Cash said.

"I'll see what I can do," Boots said. "I always thought how you went down was screwed up."

Boots had known about the surgery and treatments that Adrian had needed and how desperate Cash had been to help his son.

When Adrian was sick, Cash had asked Anderson for the money directly, but at the time Anderson had had cash-flow issues. He'd helped Cash by setting up the con instead. Though Anderson hadn't met Adrian,

Anderson told Cash he'd hoped to mend fences with his daughter and meet his grandson. After Cash was caught and his lies exposed, it had made everything worse: worse between Britney and her father and worse for Cash's marriage.

Cash's skills had gotten him the job and his desperation had gotten him caught. That he'd taken the fall alone had maintained his credibility and could be a way back to Anderson.

"I'll be in touch," Boots said and walked away.

"How will I explain this exactly?" Cash asked, lifting his pants leg to highlight his ankle monitor. He would be patted down and scrutinized inside Anderson's casino.

Benjamin's rubbed his jaw. "We're sticking to the modified truth. Tell him you're working for us. He'll expect tracking devices."

The tracking device might make Anderson nervous. "Do you think he will take me anywhere or tell me anything with an electronic device around my ankle?" Cash asked.

Lucia tapped her pen against her notebook. "Anderson is careful and he'll be especially careful if he's close to cashing out and getting away with his money."

Benjamin sighed. "Anderson will have questions about how Cash got out of jail. We don't know if Anderson has people on his payroll at the prison. We're sticking with the cover story that Cash is working for the FBI, but willing to be bought."

"Boots said he'd text me the location tonight," Cash said, giving up the argument for removing the ankle monitor. He wouldn't win. He was stuck with it, even if he thought it would impede the operation.

At least Benjamin had given Cash an untraceable cell phone. Untraceable for criminal enterprises. The FBI had access to every phone call and every message sent and received from the phone.

"Where are you planning to be before then?" Benjamin asked.

"We'll get ready and meet at Lucia's," Cash said. At Lucia's raised eyebrows, Cash deferred to her. "Fine, then come hang out at the Hideaway. I figured you'd prefer a place that isn't filthy and overrun with rats."

"I can meet you at the location."

Since the incident in her condo where they'd almost slept together, she'd been standoffish. She'd need to shake that before they went undercover. "You're supposed to be my girlfriend. We go together. Otherwise, Anderson will sense it's a setup. He'll err on the side of caution and cut me out," Cash said.

Cash knew the man was meticulous and careful. With so much money on the line, he'd be paranoid.

"Stay together. Get into character," Benjamin said. "And work out whatever is going on between you two before you go. I don't want this getting blown because of some bull in your personal lives."

Benjamin left them alone. Lucia sat in silence.

"Tell me what's on your mind," Cash said.

Lucia looked out the window behind him and then she met his stare. "This case is important. It's a big one. High visibility, yes, but also people are counting on us to find their money. They are counting on us to give them back their retirement, their savings and their financial security. There's a lot on the line."

"You perform well under stress," he said.

"You know when I don't perform well?" she asked.

"When I have a distraction. When I'm so busy thinking about you that I'm not thinking about the case. I'm wondering what you'll do next and why you're saying this or that."

She was making excuses. Something else was going on, something she wasn't ready to admit.

"Are you blaming me for your nerves?" he asked, feeling annoyed. He'd tried to be friends with her. He'd tried being a good partner. He'd been careful with her feelings.

"Before you, I didn't have this problem."

"What problem is that? Being attracted to someone? Having chemistry with someone who is interesting and complex and not an exact replica of your father?"

She stood and set her fisted hands on the table. "You think a lot of yourself!"

He stood. "I don't think much of myself at all, Lucia. Most days I wake up in a stinking hellhole, knowing I'm a bad father, knowing I'll never be free of what I've done and knowing I have to work with you, a woman who is hell-bent on following some rulebook she's created. It's a wonder you permit yourself to do anything except sleep, eat and work. The worst part is, you don't tell me the rules. You just get mad when I break one of them."

She folded her arms over her chest. "For example?"

"For example flirting with Audrey's friend. Why do you care who I talk to? You've been pissed off at me since then."

"That is not why I am pissed off at you."

"At least you admit you're pissed. Now if only you'd tell me why instead of having me guess, we'd be on the same page."

"I'm pissed off because you were flirting with Lexie and it would have gone somewhere if I hadn't walked in, and then when I tried to come on to you, you rejected me. And, by the way, if I'm so hell-bent on following the rules, why would I have lied to Benjamin about where you were? I lied because I care about you, you jerk."

Tears sprang to her eyes and she blinked them back.

Cash absorbed the impact of her words. She cared about him. She had broken one of her rules for him. She was hurt that he'd pulled away when she'd made an advance. He thought he'd been protecting her, but she'd taken it as a rejection.

He circled the table and pulled her tightly into his arms. On top of it all, he had made her cry. He felt terrible.

"Lucia, I'm sorry. I didn't reject you. It wasn't about not wanting you, it was about not wanting to make a mess of the relationship I'm trying to build with you. You deserve better than me. I'm not good for you."

Lucia rested her head on his shoulder. "I need for us to stay focused on the case. I need to not have this drama."

He didn't want drama either. He felt at odds with his loneliness and the boundaries that required him to keep people at arm's length. "Thank you for covering for me when I missed curfew. You're a good partner. I won't put you in that position again."

Cash hugged her before releasing her. He liked that she cared about him. It had been a long time since someone had.

"Wow. You look amazing," Cash said.

The bright blue dress was short and tight at the

bottom while the top was loose with sheer sleeves. It draped low in the front, hinting that if she moved in a certain direction she'd flash deep cleavage, but covering enough to maintain class.

Lucia looked down and set her hand on her hip, popping it to the side and looking up. "Does this fit the part?"

"You found that in the FBI's costume closet?" he asked.

Lucia shook her head. "Since I'm not playing the part of a hooker, I needed something more upscale. I borrowed this from Audrey."

"You look great." Heart-stopping. Delicious.

"You look good, too," she said.

He was wearing one of the FBI's suits. "You know earlier when we talked about keeping our relationship purely professional?"

She nodded.

"We're supposed to be together. You should look natural in my arms. We shouldn't feel strange and tense around each other."

Lucia straightened. "I know how to be undercover. Do you think I can't handle this?"

"I think I make you nervous. You tense when I'm near you. Come here," he said.

She walked to him and Cash set his hands on her upper arms. "See? You froze."

She forced her shoulders down and set her hand on his hips. "Better? I needed a moment to get in character."

"Lean into me," he whispered.

Lucia slipped her arm around him, tucking herself

next to him. His heart raced and the scent of her drove him wild.

He slid his hands to the shoulder of her dress and let his fingers brush over the fabric. Lower, he touched her sides and then her hips. He turned her around and ran his hand down her bare back where her dress dipped low, bringing her backside against him.

Was she allowing this to prove a point? He wanted to test her, to be sure she wouldn't snap under the pressure. "Do you know how sexy you are?"

Her breathing increased, but she said nothing.

"Let's forget about the casino. I'd rather peel this dress off you and do things I know you'll love."

She looked over her shoulder at him and for a brief moment, he could imagine what it would feel like to sink his body into hers from behind. To melt with her, panting, breathless with pleasure.

"How will you know what I love?"

"Your body is so responsive to my touch. I can feel how you lean into me. You're moving your hips side to side, tempting me. I know you like to be in charge, and I'll let you be in control. But sometimes, I like to have my way, too. My way is very good."

Her eyes were wide. She spun and braced her legs apart, the dress hitching up her thighs. "You are good. I'll play along with whatever you dish out."

He had met his match in Lucia Huntington.

"The chemistry is an unexpected bonus," he said. "I don't have to pretend to want you. I don't have to pretend that I'll be thinking about getting you home, alone, stripping you naked and making sure you know exactly who you belong with."

Her chest rose and fell. "I know how women talk

to you and I'll make it my personal mission tonight that you don't forget that I don't share. My character is possessive and protective and provocative. It said so in the profile."

Cash gathered his control and stepped back from Lucia. He jammed a hand through his hair. "Is everything you do this intense?"

She winked at him. "I don't believe in doing things halfway."

She may have meant her job, but his mind had its own interpretation and she had succeeded in planting the idea of making frantic love to her all night.

Selling it that she was his girlfriend might be the easiest part of this job. Convincing Anderson to let him inside his circle of trust would be the difficult part.

Cash and Lucia took a taxi to the location Boots had texted. Lucia's skirt was short and when she crossed her legs, it was even shorter. Cash pretended not to notice. If he fixated on her bare legs, he would lose his mind.

The cab dropped them at the address on a quiet street. Cash knew what to look for to locate the casino. They waited until another couple entered an alley along the side of the brick townhouses. Cash and Lucia followed at a stroll.

Cash wrapped his arm around Lucia. "This is an interesting neighborhood."

Lucia fluffed her hair. "You mean, interesting as in too quiet and much too suspicious?"

"Yes, that."

"Do you think it's a trap?"

"Could be. But what kind of trap? Why would Boots tell me to come here?"

"I've studied the lifestyle, but I can't say I understand it. I don't think anyone who commits crimes for a living is especially trustworthy," Lucia said.

"You expect something bad to happen," he said.

"I prepare for the worst. If this goes well, then color me surprised."

"If I sense anything is off, we're leaving. Immediately."

Lucia looked at him sideways. "We're partners. We'll decide together."

Cash took her wrist and pulled her against him. He brought his mouth close to her ear, to a sensitive spot on her neck. He flicked his tongue over the area, eliciting a moan from her. "I know Anderson better than anyone. I've lived my life following my instincts. If this goes wrong, we leave."

He angled his head away so she could meet his gaze.

"Don't be overprotective. I can take care of myself," Lucia said.

He kissed her firmly on the mouth and swatted her bottom. Anderson had eyes and ears everywhere. They were being watched and Cash wanted it to be clear to everyone watching that he was smitten with Lucia.

Cash and Lucia walked around to the side of the building. An orange dot over the door, almost looking like a misguided drop of paint, indicated he'd found the right place.

He waited for the door to open. No knocking. His identity was being confirmed.

The door opened slowly and he took Lucia's hand. They stepped inside together. He said nothing, but followed a man in a suit down a hallway that was in desperate need of a paint job. The floor was made of rusty metal grates and echoed with every footstep.

But the decor was flipped on its head when the man opened a door into an opulent game room, complete with lush cream-colored carpets, attractively dressed dealers and comfortable chairs around the game tables.

Lucia slipped her arms around his, as if he were her life preserver. She wasn't a clingy woman. She was into her part.

Cash looked around the room, both deciding his next move and checking for anyone he recognized. No sign of Anderson. He sauntered to the craps table and withdrew his wallet. He set down ten crisp hundred dollar bills, a gift from the FBI for this mission.

Three hours later, he was up four thousand dollars. Four thousand dollars would change his life. He hadn't had such a lucky streak before. It killed him that none of this money was his. Whatever he lost or won was property of the FBI.

From the corner of his eye, he saw a man approaching. Cash had drawn attention. He was running hot and money was flowing fast.

"Excuse me, sir, a moment of your time?"

The gathered crowd watching the game groaned, but Cash held up his hands. "I'll be back."

"You're new here," the man said.

"Yes," Cash said. The man would know who Cash was. He wouldn't have been allowed inside the casino otherwise.

Lucia was at his side, staring up at him. He knew she was listening to every word and absorbing every detail.

"How about you come with me to the VIP room? I have someone who wants to speak with you."

Anderson? Cash nodded and took Lucia's hand. The man shook his head. "She stays out here."

Lucia pouted. "This is supposed to be a date. What am I supposed to do alone?"

The man waved over their heads and a scantily clad waitress approached. "Come on, ma'am, I'll get you a drink."

Cash didn't like splitting from Lucia. The FBI didn't have eyes or ears inside yet. They'd agreed that any surveillance would be uncovered. He had his GPS tracker, but it had been too risky to modify it and add an audio recorder. "Go ahead, Lucy. I'll catch up with you in a few minutes."

Lucia frowned. "Hurry up. I'll be bored without you." She kissed him, a slow, open-mouthed kiss, and then ran her hand down the front of his pants.

He'd been turned on, but her little maneuver dialed his libido higher.

Cash strolled away and followed the man to the VIP room. The room was locked, the door requiring a badge and a passcode to gain entrance. When the door opened, Cash expected to see Clifton Anderson.

His heart fell when his eyes landed on a familiar and unexpected face. Wyatt Stone, his long-lost father.

Chapter 6

"What are you doing here?" Cash asked his father.

Wyatt Stone stood and strolled over to him, drink in hand. Though the surprise had shaken him, Cash controlled his anger and outward reaction. At least, he hoped he did. This wasn't a joyful reunion. His relationship with his father was difficult on a good day and it was an unwelcome surprise tonight.

"I have the same question for you. You get out of jail and you don't call me?"

Was his father serious? After what they had been through, he expected a call? "You made it clear you didn't want to see me," Cash said. Why was his father mixed up with Anderson again? Though they were long-time friends, his father wasn't into big cons. Unless Anderson had flipped him. Cash didn't like anything about this meeting.

The room had a wall of video monitors, each trained

on a different section of the room and areas outside the casino.

"Of course I want to see you. You're my son. When did you get out?" he asked.

"Little while ago. Work release program," Cash said. His father looked relaxed and happy, and that somehow worried Cash even more. His father was always scrambling for money or working an angle.

"Who's the lady?" his father asked.

His father had been watching him on the cameras. "My girlfriend, Lucy."

"She's pretty."

That was an understatement. Lucia had the kind of beauty that was almost hard to look at for too long. Because she also kept to herself in social situations, and because of her family's wealth, people took it to mean she was snobby or full of herself. Cash knew that interpretation was erroneous. "She's beautiful and she's been good for me." Not a lie. Lucia had been incredible to him. Too incredible.

"Can I meet her?"

He didn't want his father involved with this con or the problems at Holmes and White. He didn't want his father involved with Lucia. "No," Cash said.

His father took a swig of his drink. "Don't be like that. I know you're mad that I didn't help you in prison, but I explained about that."

Cash considered his response. If his father was working with Anderson, Cash needed to stay on his father's good side. But it was hard to balance that against his personal feelings. "I don't want to mess things up with her."

"I won't mess anything up," his father said.

Sure he would. He would lie to her. He lied to everyone. "Next time."

"You're planning on gambling often?" his father asked, less fatherly concern and more curiosity.

"I need cash," Cash said.

"For Adrian."

Defensiveness rose up inside Cash. He didn't want his father or Anderson or anyone from this world near Adrian. "For a new life."

His father nodded. "I heard from Boots you were looking for work."

"That's true."

"I heard you were working for the FBI."

Cash snorted. He lifted the leg of his pants. "They have me on the box."

His father swore. "They'll follow you here."

"Give me more credit. They monitor that I stay in the city. That's it," he said, a lie. Though he'd known undercover work would require lies, he resented his father forcing yet another lie from him.

"Then you can't work any side jobs," his father said.

"Working for the FBI means I have to work side jobs. Do you know what they pay me? Next to nothing. I'm living in a dump. No car. Nothing."

His father clapped him on the shoulder. "Your position gives you a unique strength, if you're willing to use it."

His father was an opportunist. Cash was glad he'd seen the angle. It prevented Cash from speaking the treasonous words and suggesting Anderson use him to spy on the FBI. "I'm willing to do what I need to."

"That's my boy."

Cash grinned, but inside he was mentally distancing himself from his father. He wasn't anything like the man. He'd put that life behind him and it had taken his son's life being at risk for him to run a con again. He wouldn't go back. "You'll put in a good word with Anderson?" he asked.

"I don't need to put in a good word. Anderson knows you're an asset. Now clear out before you get on Anderson's bad side. He likes for the house to win. Next time you come in here, we'll talk business and I'll meet this woman, your Lucy."

She wasn't his Lucy. Cash hated that his father had strong-armed a meeting with her. His father didn't do anything without compensation. If Cash wanted to work for Anderson, he'd have to introduce his father to Lucia.

Cash shook his father's hand and left the room. He found Lucia sitting at the bar, swirling a glass of wine. "How'd it go?" she asked, leaning up and kissing his cheek. This time, she spared his sanity by not touching him any other way.

"My father is here."

Lucia set her wine glass on the bar. Cash would guess she had taken a few small swigs to stay in character. "You okay with that?"

The bartender was lingering close, likely eavesdropping.

"Sure. It will be nice to reconnect." A real family reunion. Anderson, Cash and his father. If his mom, the woman who walked out when he was two weeks old, showed up, it'd be the stuff of childhood nightmares. "It's been a long night. Let's go home and get you out of that dress."

"You don't want to play any more games?" she asked. "You were doing well."

"I'll keep my money here on credit," he said.

Lucia slid her hand down his arm and to his thigh. She lightly touched his inner leg, close to where his erection sprang to life. "Come on. Bed awaits."

They strode toward the exit, almost home free. The first meeting wasn't as bad as he'd expected and in a few minutes, he'd be alone with Lucia.

One of the dealers stopped him. "Sir, don't you want your chips?"

"Put it on my house account," Cash said, keeping his eyes on Lucia. If his money was in the casino, he'd have a reason to return. It would please both his father and Anderson.

Lucia poured them each a glass of wine. She and Cash had reviewed what had happened with his father at the casino, but she sensed more below the surface. He had been shaken by the encounter with his father. Though everything he'd reported had been innocuous enough, Lucia wondered if he was hiding something.

"Do you want to talk about your father?" she asked, sliding her computer to the side. She would send her report detailing the evening to Benjamin later.

"I've told you everything I can remember," Cash said, sounding defensive.

"I know you did, but I was asking about how you felt."

Cash watched her through emotionless eyes and Lucia knew he was holding back. He wasn't telling her something. His facade was masking his hurt.

"Felt about what?" Cash asked, sounding tired.

"What was it like to see your father?"

"Strange. I haven't seen him in a long time. I didn't know he was working for Anderson again."

"Were you angry to find out he was still living in DC and hadn't come to see you?" If she asked enough questions, he might admit the truth.

"He didn't know I was out of jail. I didn't call him."

He hadn't let his father know he'd been released from prison. "Did he seem happy to see you?"

Cash folded his arms. "I guess. He seemed worried about my GPS tracker."

She tried not to think about how that would affect the case. The team could discuss it tomorrow. Right now, she wanted to focus on Cash. "Do you want to send someone else in undercover?" If he didn't feel he could handle seeing his father, she wanted to give him an out.

"If I'm off the case, I'm back in jail."

Lucia ran a hand through her hair. If he wanted off the case, she didn't have the power to change that. "If you don't want to deal with him, then we can find another place for you on the team." Maybe. Did she have enough favors to call in to keep Cash working with the FBI and out of jail? Her time with violent crime hadn't ended well and Lucia wasn't sure any favors would be returned from them. But she'd made good friends at Quantico, and their current teammates liked Cash.

"Getting close to Anderson won't be easy for me, much less someone else. Without my history with him, I doubt I could have talked my way in."

They were running on limited time. Anderson had scored big with the Holmes and White embezzlement and he'd cash out soon. If they lost Cash as part of their undercover team, Anderson could slip away before anyone had time to find the money. "If you catch Anderson and bring him down, his empire could collapse. That means people who work with him are in jeopardy." Like Cash's father.

"I thought of that," he said.

"If it comes down to it, will you let your father be caught?" Lucia asked. Emotions could override logic, especially in the heat of the moment.

"Are you asking if I would sabotage a sting if it meant my father would be caught? I'm in for a penny, in for a pound. I have a lot to prove."

Lucia stood. She wasn't making any emotional progress with Cash. "I need to change. This dress is making me feel twitchy." She could think more analytically if she wasn't tugging the hem of her skirt down every fifteen seconds.

"Feeling twitchy because the dress reminds you of the life you never wanted to lead?" he asked.

It was her turn to be on the receiving end of a loaded question. If she wasn't an FBI agent, if she had done as her family wanted and become a socialite or philanthropist, she'd be spending her days differently, likely wearing designer labels and gowns unaffordable on an FBI agent's salary.

"It's shorter than I'm accustomed to wearing. I feel like when I sit, I'm risking flashing the room."

"It's you and me here," he said, gesturing around.

"You know that's an especially strong reason to change."

"I won't revisit that conversation, but I haven't shut the door on us."

"That's good to know," Lucia said, retreating for her bedroom. A change of clothes would be like armor, keeping Cash away.

* * *

Benjamin tossed a file onto Lucia's desk. "The bomb that detonated inside the car was on a remote. Someone was watching and waiting for the right time."

Jonathan Wolfe had shared the information with her, but Lucia had agreed not to tell Benjamin she'd caught her tail. She hid her annoyance that Benjamin hadn't told her about the tail or given her the bombing information sooner.

"The bomb squad said the device used the car's battery to draw a charge before it exploded. If the Bureau's car wasn't in such poor condition, it would have blown you and Cash to pieces before you had time to get away," Benjamin said.

Comforting to know. "Was the bomb maker an expert?"

"Depends on what you mean by expert. Anyone can build a bomb by reading information online and then visiting their local hardware store for the materials. The remote detonator implies a level of skill, but it could have been a stronger bomb. To go through so much trouble and not make sure you were dead seems strange."

The stronger the bomb, the more people who would be hurt or killed. "I doubt whoever built the bomb was looking to take out an entire city block," Lucia said. She'd worked with criminals who didn't care about the fallout of their actions, but too much force and too many bodies resulted in a proportionally strong law enforcement response. No bomber wanted that.

Lucia opened the file. Pictures of the remains of the bomb, a sketch of what the bomb expert believed the bomb looked like prior to the explosion and photos taken at the scene were laid out in order with descriptions accompanying each. "He'll come after me again."

"He might be waiting for our leads in finding him to go cold."

"Do we have leads?" Lucia asked.

Cash strolled in carrying a bag of pastries from a local bakery and a box of fresh coffee. She hadn't seen him since the night before and she was struck by how good he looked in his crisp white shirt, blue tie and suit.

He dropped the bakery bag on Lucia's desk along with the coffee. The team converged on it. "I bring food, drinks and a lead."

He was showing off now.

"What do you have?" Benjamin asked, opening the bag of pastries, grabbing a napkin and taking one out.

"Kinsley, Hammer's lover and former personal assistant, is Grace Tidings, well-known grifter, known at Holmes and White as Kinsley Adams. She is the fiancée of Matt Mitchell, a close colleague of Anderson. Mitchell has a diverse skill set—money laundering, bank fraud, computer fraud and bribery."

"How did you find this out?" Lucia asked, pouring some coffee and ignoring the tempting pastries. She had willpower and she'd proven it time and again with Cash.

"Kinsley Adams's personnel file was added to our case notes early this morning. I looked at her picture and recognized her," Cash said.

"Where is she now?" Benjamin asked.

Cash shook his head. "I don't know. I can ask around, but I'm guessing somewhere Matt Mitchell can find her."

Benjamin smiled and clapped Cash on the back. "That's great work, Cash."

Lucia was impressed. Cash had gotten an early start to have reviewed new case notes before she had.

"What about Anderson?" Lucia asked.

"I haven't heard from him, but I wasn't expecting to," Cash said. "It's early in the game. He doesn't need me to help him. He runs his empire fine without me. If I look too desperate, he'll keep his distance."

"Then how will we get in?" Lucia asked.

Cash seemed unconcerned. "My father will talk to him about me. We'll keep showing up at the casino. They have my money on a house account. I have a good reason to visit it."

Benjamin took another pastry from the box. "We need something to make Anderson want you."

"Too bad Anderson isn't a woman," Lucia said. The thought popped from her mouth before she could censor it.

The look on Cash's face said he didn't appreciate her comment. Benjamin let out a sharp bark of laughter. "Relax, Cash. It hasn't escaped my notice the ladies enjoy you."

Cash poured himself some coffee. He didn't appear to take pleasure in the statement. "I'm open to doing whatever you think will make Anderson more interested in me."

"Your father was nervous about your GPS tracker," Lucia said.

Cash looked down at his ankle.

Benjamin looked between Lucia and Cash. "Are you suggesting I remove it?"

They'd discussed it once. But if they wanted to close in on Anderson, they needed to be closer to him. "If

Cash's tracker is keeping Anderson from bringing him into the fold, it has to go."

Cash said nothing and Lucia sensed he didn't want to appear too eager. Of course he'd want the tracker off. It would give him freedom from being monitored every moment of the day.

"I could make nice with my father and win some points that way. Get him to take me back into the family business," Cash said.

Lucia heard the reluctance in his voice. "Could you invite him out and bond over beers?" The suggestion was both for the case and for Cash.

"Something like that. Hang around him. He's in Anderson's circle and there's a chance I'll cross paths with him. If I do, I'll alert you."

"Tracker stays on," Benjamin said. "I'm not taking you off it and sending you out with a con man. I'm not even sure I like the idea of you meeting up with your father alone."

Lucia saw the fleeting look of hurt on Cash's face. He'd been trying to change. Trust was easily lost and slowly won. All the doubts she'd harbored about Cash weren't gone, but they were definitely in the margins. "I'll stay on Cash," she said. "I've already presented myself as his clingy girlfriend." If she acted dim enough, she'd be dismissed as a threat.

"You're offering to watch Cash around the clock?" Benjamin said.

Was she? They could close the case faster if Cash worked every angle he had. Lucia nodded and Cash appeared surprised.

Lucia felt she had to explain her position. "It won't be for long. Anderson is planning to move with the stolen money as soon as he can. Cash will get closer to his dad and I'll stay close to Cash. With enough luck, we'll have a shot at capturing Anderson and finding the missing money."

"I like it," Benjamin said. "Get to work."

As the team took their treats and coffee and returned to their desks, Cash remained.

"You didn't have to volunteer to be my babysitter," Cash said.

"I'm not babysitting you. I'm doing what's needed for the case," Lucia said.

"You look good this morning," Cash said.

Lucia glanced around. Had anyone overheard him? "Thank you. But we're at work."

Cash let his gaze traverse her body. "What about yesterday? You were very in character at the casino. Almost too in character."

"How can I be too in character?" Lucia asked. But she knew what he was referring to. Given the opportunity, she had kissed and touched Cash in ways she wouldn't elsewhere.

"Just letting you know that turnabout is fair play," he said.

She nodded. "Bring it, Cash. I can take whatever you dish out." Despite her strong words, she knew she'd melt under his touch. Given the right set of circumstances, she would find herself willingly naked beneath him.

And she knew she would enjoy every moment.

"I'm surprised to hear from you," Wyatt said, shaking Cash's hand and smiling at Lucia.

"I thought it would be better for you to meet Lucy outside the casino," Cash said, taking a seat across the table from his father. Cash knew his father was a regular at this restaurant. Did Anderson frequent this place as well? Old habits died hard. Would they run into Anderson?

Lucia hugged Wyatt and kissed his cheek. "When Cash told me you were at the casino, I figured fate was calling and we had to answer." She giggled. "I've been dying to meet you. Cash is so secretive about his family."

Wyatt took a sip of his drink. "How did you two meet?"

Lucia pushed her chair against Cash's before she sat. She slipped her arms around his right arm and her breasts were pressed to him. Cash shifted, his pants growing tighter.

"It was love at first sight. I was volunteering at the prison teaching a class on writing and Cash was in one of my classes," Lucia said. "I feel like I was meant to meet him, like destiny played a role in our relationship." She smiled again at Cash.

Though it was over the top, Cash liked being on the receiving end of her attention and having her close to him was making this meeting with his father bearable. The distraction of her closeness was good for him. He would otherwise want to spit in the other man's face and walk away.

He and his father had a long history of problems. His father had made his childhood difficult. He'd been against Cash's marriage to Britney, saying she was trouble because she was estranged from her family and older than him. Wyatt hadn't wanted to know Adrian.

The list of his father's failures was long and Cash derailed the downward spiral of his thoughts by imagining what Adrian must think of him. Likely, his son had a long list of grievances.

Lucia was still dressing the part of his fun-loving, partying girlfriend. It was hard to forget she was in character when she was wearing a purple halter top and pair of floral shorts. The sandals on her feet had a thin, tall heel. He wasn't sure how she managed to walk in them, but she made it work.

"How have you been?" Wyatt asked. "What's it like to have your freedom after being inside?"

His father had a paralyzing fear of prison. It had been his excuse for why he hadn't visited. But Cash wasn't cutting him a break. If he was so worried about prison, he should have chosen a different career. "I'm working for the FBI. Consulting. The pay is terrible and the perks are lame. But it's better than being in prison."

"Working for the FBI must be bad, but don't ignore the benefits," his father said. "You have access to information it would take others much more effort to acquire."

Cash nodded. His value to his father and to Anderson was his willingness to work his FBI contacts and exploit the access he had. "That's true."

"Do they keep you on a short leash?" Wyatt asked.

Was his father feeling him out for how useful he could be? "I have the tracker, which they've talked about removing for good behavior," Cash said. "I've won over most of the team."

"I'd expect nothing less from you. I haven't talked to Anderson yet. After you went to prison, he was worried you would sell out everyone else for a shorter sentence."

Cash shook his head. "I didn't say a word about anyone else."

His father beamed with pride. "That's what I told him. My boy isn't a snitch."

The decisions he'd made to save Adrian's life were his and no one else had to pay the penalty for that.

The sound of glass shattering erupted around them and Cash threw himself over Lucia. They hit the floor and rolled.

Gunfire peppered around them.

"Are you hit?" Cash asked Lucia from their spot on the ground.

She looked at her arms and legs. A smear of blood marred her clothes. Her eyes grew wide as she looked over his shoulder. "Your dad."

Cash's father had hit the ground, too, but he wasn't moving. "Dad!" A hundred thoughts stampeded through him at once, most strong among them that his father could not be dead. They had unfinished business. Cash wasn't ready to lose his father from his life, not with the anger that still lingered between them. The realization shocked him. His feelings for his father were buried somewhere underneath the resentment he'd been carrying.

Cash raced to his father and checked for injuries. There was no red swatch of blood across his body. He had a pulse. "Dad!" Cash slapped his father's face, trying to wake him.

Lucia was on the phone and she crawled over to Cash and his father. "Door's locked and help is on the way."

She didn't have her weapon on her. If she did, she would have pulled it. The FBI was monitoring them close by, but storming in could blow their cover. They'd need a reason why the FBI was responding to a 911 call.

Cash's father opened his eyes and winced. "What did you bring to my favorite bar?"

Cash shook his head at his father. "Not me. I was thinking they were after you." Except it was the second time he and Lucia had been targeted. No point in advertising that.

His father closed his eyes again, his chest rising and falling unevenly.

"We've got outside cover," Lucia whispered. Benjamin and the team had been watching outside of the building in case Anderson had shown at the meeting, but likely being careful on the approach.

For the first time in his life, Cash was relieved to hear the sound of sirens.

"You could take the afternoon off," Cash said, dropping into his desk chair.

Lucia took a sip of her coffee. Her nerves were still frayed from the shooting that morning and her energy was waning. She didn't have time for rest and tonight they were planning to return to Anderson's casino.

Ballistics weren't back on the bullets and the CSI team was still working the scene. They didn't know how the drive-by shooting would affect Cash's relationship with Anderson. If Anderson believed the shooters were after Cash, he might not want him as part of his crew.

"Is your dad okay?" she asked. Cash's father hadn't been hit by a bullet, but the hospital reported he'd had a "minor heart event." Lucia didn't know if that meant a heart attack or just a terrible scare, but either one worried her.

Cash had gone with his father to the hospital. "He's

already been discharged. He's fine. Go get some rest. We have a long night ahead of us."

Lucia couldn't slow her thoughts enough to rest. "I need to review the interviews we have from Holmes and White. Benjamin sent another team to talk to Leonard Young about Kinsley Adams. He's still keeping his mouth shut although he did imply they were conducting a thorough internal investigation and would let us know if they found anything." Lucia guessed they would bury anything they found. They wouldn't want any more backlash than they were already getting from the public.

"Have you considered that whoever is trying to kill you, or us, is either lazy or incompetent?" Cash asked.

Lucia had considered it. Several failed attempts spoke to an amateur. "I'm also wondering why he keeps changing techniques. Most killers have a preferred method to dispose of their victims. A bomb, the direct approach at the hospital and a shooting don't fit a pattern."

"It supports the theory that it's a group," Cash said.

That was part of her fear. The assassins' ring she'd broken up had men of many violent talents. They could be pooling their resources to take her out. But why hadn't anyone else from the investigative team been targeted? She was certainly not the highest-profile member of the unit. "None of my theories are making sense."

Cash looked around the office. "Can we take a walk? There's something I need to talk to you about." He spoke in a low voice.

Lucia stood and followed him to the elevators. He said nothing until they were on the ground floor, walking outside.

"Is everything okay?" Lucia asked. Would he tell her if it wasn't?

"I heard from Boots today."

"Okay."

"Anderson wants me in," Cash said.

"That's great." Why had he felt the need to leave the office to tell her this? It was the break they'd been waiting for.

"I won't meet with him directly. Anderson will have someone else talk to me."

"This is what we wanted," Lucia said.

"I want to find Anderson. Not be jerked around by him."

"Why would he jerk you around?" Lucia asked.

"He'll test me. Of course he'll test me. I've got a GPS tracker identifying me as the FBI's errand boy and I've been in prison. He'll want a show of my loyalty."

Now the picture was becoming clearer as to why Cash was anxious about it. Getting into Anderson's crew wasn't a straightforward operation. "What are you afraid he'll ask you to do?" Lucia asked.

"Could be anything. Steal. Lie. Cheat. Whatever it is, he'll collect the evidence I did it and use it to control me," Cash said.

"I am not a fan of you or anyone breaking the law, but depending what he asks, you'll have to use your best judgment."

"I don't have immunity for anything I do for this case," Cash said.

Lucia stopped and faced him. She took his hands. "I won't let you be sucked into Anderson's world. I won't let you go back to prison."

"Are those things you can control?" Cash asked.

Lucia would be watching Cash, helping him make the right decisions, the decisions that would keep him away from breaking the law and she would stand behind him if bad things resulted. "Yes. I can. You can count on me. We're partners, right?"

Cash lifted her hands and kissed her knuckles. "I've said it from the beginning. But what if Anderson asks me to do something illegal? I can't say yes, but if I say no I'll be out."

"We've come this far. I won't let that happen to you."

"Are you sure you want to go out tonight?" Benjamin asked for the tenth time that day. He'd called her at home to check on her. Though she had only a minor scratch on her arm from diving off her chair at the restaurant, her leg wasn't fully healed. She'd been injured more on this job than in the violent-crime unit.

Lucia leaned closer to the mirror to apply her mascara. "Cash and I can do this. Cash's father was released from the hospital and he said we should come to the casino." She hadn't told Benjamin about Cash's concerns that Anderson would force Cash to do something illegal. She'd wait to see if his fears were justified.

She could hear Benjamin tapping a pen against his desk. "If you have the smallest inkling that this could go bad, I want you out of there."

"I understand. I'll text you the location if we go anywhere else tonight," Lucia said. She disconnected the call and slid her phone into her clutch bag.

Cash was waiting in the living room for her. This wasn't a date. And yet she was nervous. Not nervous about getting into the casino again or about the night she had ahead of her, but nervous about being alone with Cash.

Every hour they were together was a test of her control. Watching him with his father earlier that day had shown her the softer, caring side of him. It had been a raw and honest portrayal of the hurt Cash must feel.

Add to it that Cash had tried to save her life—again—and Lucia had completely let go of her initial dislike of him.

The casino hadn't moved, but it would shortly. It was Friday night and more crowded than it had been previously. Word was spreading and the more people who knew about its existence, the higher the probability of law enforcement busting it.

Cash took Lucia's hand in his. "Stay close to me. I don't want to lose track of you tonight."

Lucia remained at his side. Her eyes were wide open and taking in every face in the room. Any sign of Anderson and she'd alert Benjamin. They could close in on him tonight before Cash was pulled further into Anderson's criminal world.

Cash swore under his breath, breaking into her anticipation of a big win tonight.

Lucia nuzzled her face close to his. "What's the matter?"

"Audrey's here."

She followed his gaze and her heart fell. If Audrey spotted them and greeted them, they'd tangle her up in this op. Anderson would have questions for Audrey, putting her and their operation in jeopardy.

"Can we leave?" Lucia asked.

"Not without a good reason. Whoever's watching surveillance already knows we're here," Cash said.

They needed a plan B. "I could text her and tell her she needs to come home," Lucia said.

"Try it," Cash said.

Lucia typed her message, careful to conceal her screen. Video cameras could zoom into details human eyes could not.

Audrey didn't reach for her phone or touch her clutch. She either couldn't hear her phone or was ignoring it.

"We could have Benjamin raid the place," Cash said.

Lucia touched the side of Cash's face and drew him close. They were in a difficult spot, but they couldn't pull the plug yet. "We'll play this out. We'll meet with Anderson, then we'll zip out of here like we have somewhere to be."

Lucia smiled, gazing into Cash's eyes. They were supposed to be in love. Weren't dopey stares part of falling in love? "You were in prison for four years. You have a lot of sex to catch up on."

His eyes widened. "We can play that angle."

"I know what to do," Lucia said. "If I bend this way," she brushed her hip against his, "and that," she moved her hips the other way, "it's plausible this will lead to the bedroom."

Cash ran his hand down her back and cupped her bottom.

The action startled her as did the heat that zipped through her. She giggled. "Careful, we're in public."

Lucia felt the wall at her back. Somehow he had maneuvered her between a fake potted tree and a gold statue of a Roman bust. "What's your next move?"

"I need to make it clear where my mind is," he said.

Her thoughts rocketed to the idea of Cash naked. She couldn't help it. He had shaved that morning, but a day's worth of growth covered his jawline, giving him a rugged, roughened appearance. His suit fit well and his smile was seductive and warm. The combination was devastating to her control.

He moved his hips against hers and she felt the evidence of his excitement. Was he faking it? Could a man fake that?

"Impressive," she said.

"I aim to please," he said.

Now all she could think about was leaving. They were in the casino for an important reason, but that reason drifted further from her mind with every passing second.

"Why haven't we done this?" she asked.

He was moving slowly, but every inch of contact was causing friction in the right places.

"You keep stopping me," he said. He dropped his mouth to her neck and if his hands hadn't been at her hips and his lower body wasn't pinning her to the wall she would have crumpled to the floor.

She let her head fall to the side and his mouth grazed over her skin, just shy of rough. Though she was playing a part, there was nothing pretend about her body's reaction, urging her to find someplace private where she could do more of this. She would turn her body over to him, with undoubtedly fantastic and satisfying results.

She dipped her mouth low and caught his lips. His tongue swept inside hers in a slow, possessive gesture. The kiss was the right blend of desire and technique.

"Let's leave now," she said, hearing the pant in her voice and not caring how she sounded. "We can come back later for your meeting."

"Cash?"

Cash turned at the sound of his name and Lucia snapped to the present. She checked her green dress to be sure nothing had popped out during the last thirty seconds. Her mind felt fogged and her body hummed with unmet need.

Cash was speaking to a man she recognized from their file on of Anderson. Matt Mitchell, the fiancé of Kinsley Adams, a.k.a. Grace Tidings, and associate of Clifton Anderson.

"Why don't you two come to the VIP area? I'd like some privacy to talk with you," Mitchell said.

His words were spiked with a dangerous proposition: a private place with a known criminal.

Cash appeared to have no reservations about Mitchell's suggestion. He extended his arm to Lucia and she took it, following Cash and Matt.

Cash was patted down before being escorted into Mitchell's small, private office. The guard ran his hands down Lucia's sides, but her dress didn't make conceal-ment of a weapon an option.

Mitchell had a laptop open in front of him. Cash knew Mitchell's reputation, though he hadn't met him. He was cold, hard-working and had been the master-mind of several big scores. He wore a diamond earring in his right ear.

"Please have a seat," Mitchell said. "I'm sorry to hear that you and your father have had some trouble."

Was it trouble that Anderson had sent their way? "He's okay. Thankfully," Cash said. He hid his suspi-cion and anger under a lazy smile.

Lucia appeared bored. She inspected her nails.

"May I speak plainly?" Mitchell asked.

"I wish that you would," Cash said, knowing most of what Mitchell would tell him would be lies.

"You know who I work for. You know that he stays at the top of his game by being careful about who he allows into his circle."

Cash nodded. Anderson was being especially careful now, right before his grand exit. "My father has worked for him for years." Not that he believed much trust existed between thieves.

Mitchell nodded. "You didn't flip on anyone when you were arrested. That's good for you. Otherwise, you'd be dead. But you're on the FBI's payroll and that tracking device around your ankle could cause problems."

"It's the ankle monitor or jail." He'd wanted Benjamin to remove it for good behavior, but Benjamin seemed bent on keeping Cash under his thumb.

Mitchell set a device on the desktop. "Anderson went through a great deal of trouble to acquire a method of circumventing your leash. There are two pieces that snap apart. Set one in the location where you'd like the FBI to think you are and wrap the other around your device. It will broadcast your location as if from the first place."

Freedom and a way out from under the FBI's surveillance. He tried not to appear too eager, but it had been too long since he'd been a free man. "Impressive."

Mitchell grinned. "We know the right people."

Cash guessed the device was stolen, but he couldn't have guessed the source. The government? The mob? He could see uses for it in many scenarios. "I get this in exchange for what?" The price would be sky-high.

"Anderson is worried that someone is coming after

him," Mitchell said. "He's a wealthy man and he's been forced underground to protect himself and his wealth."

It wasn't *his* wealth. Anderson's money was stolen.

"We'd like you to look into what the FBI has on Anderson. Let us know if they are close to finding him," Mitchell said.

Cash rubbed his jaw. "I'm working my way into their trust. Getting to the right information might be possible. But I'd be taking a risk. I need something to compensate me for that risk."

Though the tracking concealment device was a valuable item, a con man didn't work for free. Cash was in character and he was behaving in a way he believed mirrored his father's actions.

Mitchell grinned. "You have a son."

Rage tore through him. If Mitchell tried to use Adrian to manipulate Cash, Cash would kill Mitchell before letting his son be hurt. These men were not getting near Adrian.

"I know you must want to see him. If you do this for Anderson, he'll make sure you're reunited with your son."

A muscle flexed in Cash's jaw. He didn't like the idea of anyone near Adrian, especially not Anderson. "Just the money. I want money." Adrian was not part of this.

Mitchell shook his head slowly in disbelief. "After what you did for your son, you're no longer interested in seeing him?"

Why would he want his son involved with Mitchell or Anderson or anyone like them?

"He's better off without me in his life. I did what I could and I'll send money when I can. But I don't want to see him. I'm not good for him."

Not exactly lies, they were thoughts he'd had about a reunion with his son, never sure if it was right for Adrian.

"I don't think that will be a problem. We want the information. You want money. Message received loud and clear." Mitchell slid a picture across the table. "But if you decide to betray Anderson, we can get to Adrian."

Cash picked up the picture and an array of emotions pummeled him. Happiness, sadness, a sharp protective instinct, but the strongest emotion was longing. It was the most recent picture he'd seen of Adrian. He was wearing a maroon hooded sweatshirt and carrying a backpack. He was talking to a girl about his age who had a pretty smile and long brown hair.

Cash was dying to know more about the picture, but he hid his interest for Adrian's sake.

"I don't want you near my son," Cash said. He'd been holding back his affection for his son, but a direct threat from Mitchell was serious.

Lucia touched Cash's arm, both a reminder and a comfort. She was there for him. She'd back him up if he needed it.

"Anderson has friends everywhere," Mitchell said.

If his son was hurt, Cash would see that Anderson and every member of his organization paid.

Mitchell pulled the picture away and slid it back into a folder. "Anderson wants one more action to prove your loyalty."

"I've proven my loyalty," Cash said. The threat against his son lingered and he had a hard time keeping a lid on his anger.

"Then let's call this an exercise to be sure you haven't lost your touch while you were in prison."

Cash knew he appeared angry and frustrated. The honesty of the emotions played well in the situation. "What is it that you want me to do? Because Anderson knows I have rules."

Mitchell laughed. "Right. Your code of honor. I can't understand your aversion to shows of strength, but it shouldn't interfere."

Shows of strength meant violence. Cash wouldn't maim or kill someone. That was not negotiable. Cash waited in silence.

Mitchell pulled out another picture and slid it across the desk. "Anderson wants a Copley painting, *Mrs. George Watson*. It would round out his collection of early American artwork."

Cash snorted. "And I want Picasso's *The Old Guitarist* because I like blue, but I'm over it."

Mitchell lifted a brow. "Are you saying you can't get it?"

The request was ridiculous.

"It's too much of a risk. Do you know what the price of a job like this would be on the street?" Cash asked.

Mitchell folded his hands on his desk. "This isn't the street. This is Anderson's private club. He wants that painting and he wants you to get it for him. If you deliver it by next Friday, then you'll be on Anderson's payroll."

Cash took the picture from Mitchell. The beginnings of an idea formed. A long shot. He'd need a series of lucky breaks to acquire the painting. He either had to take the job or they were done now. "I'll get it."

Mitchell smiled at him. "Right answer."

The right answer to Mitchell's request, but it opened

a slew of additional questions for Cash, one of them being how was he going to pull off the biggest theft of his career with the FBI at his back.

Chapter 7

"How exactly will we do this?" Lucia asked, pressing her mouth close to Cash's ear.

He had agreed to steal a painting from the Smithsonian American Art Museum. No one had ever managed to rob the museum, and with improvements to security every year it was unlikely he would succeed.

"I have a plan." Cash sat at the bar inside the casino and signaled for a drink. The bartender slid a glass of rum to him. He took a sip.

Lucia stepped between his legs. "The FBI won't sanction a theft." She tugged at his tie, implying she wanted to leave. She hoped her posture and body language made the reason clear to anyone watching.

"Let's talk about this in the car," Cash said.

Out of the corner of her eye, Lucia saw Audrey at one of the card tables. She had a drink in one hand and was laughing at something the dealer was saying.

Was Audrey caught up with Anderson? Lucia knew her friend wasn't naive. An underground casino reeked of illegal activity. Audrey liked the thrill of the forbidden and the exclusive.

Lucia set her hands on the tops of Cash's thighs. "Do you think this helps?"

"It makes it harder to think. It makes the blood rush out of my brain," Cash said. Her hands moved higher and her thumb brushed his erection through his pants.

As his hands traversed her dress, Lucia kissed his neck. He smelled good, clean, and the strength in his arms turned her on.

"Do you want this to happen here?" Cash asked.

She giggled. "I'm not a sex-in-public kind of woman. We have a perfectly serviceable car outside." She spoke the last part a little louder. The bartender glanced over at them, but Lucia kept her eyes on Cash.

Cash threw some cash on the bar. Thirty seconds later, they were in the backseat of the car the FBI had acquired for them. If anyone checked, it was registered to her alias, Lucy Harris.

Cash was on top of her and Lucia's heart was pounding. Could someone have bugged her car while she was inside? Would they have to see this through or pretend to have sex?

She moaned and Cash sent her an inquisitive look. "A bug," she mouthed.

He nodded. He slipped his hand from her knee to her thigh and stroked the inside of it. She shivered.

"Please, don't make me wait. I've been waiting all night." If they were putting on a show, she would put on a show.

"That's what I love about you, Luc. You're insatiable."

She giggled and Cash removed his jacket, rumpling it for sound effects. He pulled out his wallet and removed a condom. A condom? Why did he have that? He tore it open and then set it on the floor.

"Oh, Cash, that feels so good. Harder. More, please."

Cash swiveled his hips into hers. The car rocked rhythmically. "I want to make you feel good," he said, the roughened sound of his voice exciting her.

She moaned. "Oh, right there." This was supposed to be a show, but the sensations were real.

Cash had the moves. It was tight in the backseat of the car, but he made it work. How would she feel if he were making love to her?

He was giving her a preview and she liked what she saw and felt. "Don't stop," she said.

Then he kissed her. The touch of his lips to hers switched the situation from play-acting into the real thing. She was transported to a time when she was alone with Cash, not in the backseat of a car.

Emotions welled up inside her and her eyes filled with tears. Cash stopped. "Did I hurt you?" he asked. He went still and his body tensed.

"Everything feels so good."

She could fake her orgasm and be done. She had a feeling that if she let Cash continue, her emotions would wrap around this and him and she would fall for Cash, hard and completely.

With his thumb, he brushed at the tear that ran down her cheek. He sat and pulled her up with him, adjusting her to sit on his lap. Then he kissed her, long and sweet and slow.

She wasn't sure she understood the reason for the change. They'd been performing for anyone who might have been listening, but this was something else entirely. "What are you thinking about right now?" he asked.

"You and me in bed."

She could read the questions in his eyes. He'd sensed her shift in emotion and was trying to find a reason for it. If the car was bugged, they couldn't talk about it now, and even if it wasn't, how could she explain how she felt?

Nothing she was feeling was part of their plan.

She was falling for Cash. Her crush was developing into something stronger, deeper and more potent. She returned his kiss and sank into it, letting herself live in the moment, sure that she wouldn't find herself in this position again. It was too compromising.

She was an FBI agent. He was a criminal. The two did not meet on common ground.

Cash felt as though he was grappling for control. Lucia was in his arms, in his lap, kissing him, pressing her tight body against him. He wanted to grind into her, tear off her clothes and get inside her in a hurry.

They were being watched and this moment couldn't unfold the way he wanted it to unless he had privacy. He reached forward across the front seats and put the keys in the ignition, turned on the car and blasted the radio.

If anyone had been listening with the volume up to hear their dialogue, they'd gotten their eardrums blown. It would serve them right to have their ears ring for a few minutes.

Lucia let out a loud sigh and then a moan. He guessed she sounded nothing like that when she was having an orgasm. Then he wondered exactly what she sounded like. Breathless? Intense? Out of her mind?

"That was great, Luc," he said.

Lucia screwed up her mouth and he kissed her lips. "Round two at home?"

"I can always go another round with you."

She was breathing heavily and she sounded unsure. What was she thinking? Was she worried about this mission? Shy about having fake sex in a car? He couldn't read her emotions. They seemed to be bouncing all over the place. Reality and fantasy, real attraction and play acting, and in any given moment, he couldn't sort them.

They arrived at her home an hour later, after doubling back several times to ensure they weren't followed.

When she opened the door to her condo, he rushed her inside. Timing was everything and he believed in striking while the iron was hot. Something more was happening between them, and for the first time he sensed she was open to it. Really open. She wouldn't shut him down as she had so many times before and she knew what this was about. They were partners in the field. They were friends. And now maybe something more.

Was she ready to admit they had some great chemistry between them?

"Are we going to do this?" he asked. "Actually do this?" He rocked his pelvis against hers leaving no question what he was referring to.

She stammered a few moments before she spoke. "In the car, that was pretend."

He wouldn't let her emotionally pull away again. "Bull. You felt something."

She said nothing. Didn't deny it.

"You are so hot. You got me going in that car, but I can walk away if you tell me this isn't what you want," he said. It had been years since he'd had sex and he could do without it another night. But could he go another night without Lucia?

She remained silent.

"You have five more seconds and then I'm making a judgment call."

He made it to two and then he was kissing her. "I want to kiss you everywhere. I want to hear how you sound when you come. I want you to come with me inside you."

Lucia's eyes were half closed with desire. She tugged at his tie and threw it to the ground. "How do you manage to look this good? Don't you ever have an off day?"

He slid his hands under her butt and she jumped, wrapping her legs around his waist. He set her on the bar stool near the breakfast counter. She was the perfect height. He lifted her dress and bit back a groan.

She was wearing a thong. He pushed it to the side and slid his finger down her body and between her parted thighs. A brush of his fingers and he found her hot and wet. "Are you thinking about me? About what it will be like when I take you?"

Lucia nodded. "I've been thinking about it since that first kiss."

That long? "The anticipation will be worth it."

He pushed his fingers deeper inside her. She let her head fall back and a moan escaped. She was ready, but he wanted to draw this out and show her that he was more in her life than a quick screw.

He let his fingers build her into a frenzy. When she was gasping with need, he dropped to his knees and brought his mouth to her. Stroking, probing, she jerked against him. With one finger inside her and then another, he set a hard, fast pace. He kept one hand on her to keep her balanced on the stool.

"I love the sounds you make when you like how I'm touching you," he said.

She was on the brink of release. The bar stool knocked against the wall. He needed her to let go.

"Cash," she whispered.

His name and a surrender. Her body convulsed with pleasure and he gathered her close to him as her climax eased.

Cash lifted her and carried her to the bedroom. He set her on the bed.

She took the sides of her dress and pulled it over her head, flinging it to the ground. He didn't make a move to undress.

"Aren't you expecting a turnabout?" she asked.

He shook his head. "That isn't what this is about."

She rose to her knees and beckoned with her finger. "You were showing off, then."

He laughed and came to the bed. She unbuttoned his shirt and let it fall off his shoulders. Next came his belt and then she undid his pants. He shucked them off quickly and she rotated over him.

Her mattress was at his back and he waited, anticipation building. Without warning, she lowered herself and sucked him into her mouth.

Her tongue worked the head of his arousal and her

hands moved in sync with the up-and-down movement of her mouth. Everything she was doing felt great. She was strength and sexiness, and watching his arousal disappear into her mouth was an image he wouldn't forget. He came quick and hard.

Lucia moved beside him and rested her head on his chest.

Cash tried to process what had happened. He hadn't slept with a woman since his wife. Though thinking of Britney now felt strange, it was alarming that he didn't feel as if he'd betrayed her.

Cash had been attracted to Lucia from the start. She was his type with an edge. Classy, beautiful, sophisticated and charming, but tough as nails. An FBI agent was an improbable choice for a lover, but she was the complete package.

"Want to sleep over?" Lucia asked.

He was thrilled she hadn't made excuses or asked him to leave. He did. Very much. "Sleep? No. But I'll stay."

Lucia was stark naked next to him and it felt like the most natural thing in the world. She ran her fingers down his bare chest. "Tell me your brilliant plan for acquiring *Mrs. George Watson*."

"It relies on you," Cash said.

Lucia lifted her brow. "To do what?"

"Pull some strings. Pull every string you have. We'll have a replica made and have the museum curator switch out the authentic Copley for the fake. We'll stage an elaborate break-in and we'll steal the replica."

"Won't Anderson know when we give him a fake?" Lucia asked.

Possibly. "I have a friend who specializes in forgeries. If we can get him the right materials and for the right price, he'll create a copy of *Mrs. George Watson* that is almost perfect."

Lucia whistled. "We're on a tight timeline. If Anderson figures out we've passed him a fake, he'll kill you."

He knew the risks. "If the museum curator is the only person who knows the switch was made, an important piece of artwork being stolen will make headlines. The media attention will be convincing. Besides, I think Anderson has a lot going on. He's looking to get out of town with assets. He won't be able to confirm it's a fake, either because he won't have time or because the guy he uses is the guy who will paint the fake and confirm its authenticity. I happen to know that Anderson trusts one particular art expert. He'll go to him."

Anderson occasionally had Cash's father authenticate art, but given his relationship with Cash, Anderson would use Franco to be sure it was an impartial assessment.

Cash hoped that Anderson's relationship with Franco hadn't changed. If he was wrong, it was a grave miscalculation.

"How will you convince your art expert to lie to Anderson?"

"Money. We need to offer him ten times his normal fee. You think Benjamin will authorize it?"

"What's the normal fee?" Lucia asked.

When Cash named the price, Lucia's jaw slackened. "Are you serious? That's some big-time money for the FBI to pay a criminal."

"My contact is not a criminal. He is a legitimate businessman with a specialized skill. We're asking him to lie to one of the most dangerous men in the city. We need to compensate him for that."

"I'll call Benjamin, but this is a long shot."

Cash shifted and pulled Lucia closer. Every con— and relationship—was.

Cash strolled into Franco's studio, knowing the artist was likely sleeping, working or entertaining a woman. Or women. Given their history, Cash would take his chances walking in on any of those activities.

Franco was in his art room, a large open space with dark walls and various types of lighting pointed at canvases on easels. The room smelled of paint and paint thinner.

"Franco," Cash called at the door.

His friend didn't acknowledge him. Cash waited. The man was an artist. He was eccentric. His genius was legendary.

Lucia gave Cash an inquisitive look. Cash held up his hand and smiled. They'd wait. A few minutes later, Franco turned.

"Cash Stone. Out of lockup. Legally, I assume?" Franco asked.

"Probation. My release has conditions," he said, thinking of the GPS tracker around his ankle.

"If it helps, I thought you were done wrong," Franco said.

"Me and every other criminal in prison," Cash said.

"You had good reasons for what you did," Franco said. "That whole incident left a bad taste in my mouth. Police. Can't trust 'em."

Cash didn't want to discuss the con that had landed

him in prison in front of Lucia. He introduced her and then moved the conversation to the purpose of his visit.

"I need a copy of Copley's *Mrs. George Watson* dry and ready to go by Thursday."

Franco laughed. "Impossible. My work log is booked for months."

"I'll make it worth your while."

"My fees make every job worth my while," Franco said.

"Ten times your normal fee. Seventy-five percent up-front. The rest when it's finished to my liking. We'll supply whatever mediums you need. No mistakes."

Franco's eye glittered at the proposal. He enjoyed a challenge and likely the prospect of good, fast money. "I don't make mistakes. Having the oil dry and the work look authentic require highly specialized skills. But you're lucky. I have that skill. You're a big fan of Copley? Last I heard, you were more of a Renoir connoisseur."

Franco was digging around for Cash's reasons for wanting the piece. He kept it simple. "I need it for a job."

Franco looked at Lucia. "It goes without saying that my copies, as perfect as they are, are copies. I am not selling you canvases with the intention to mislead anyone by selling it as authentic. My work is for private enjoyment."

Cash laughed. "I don't need the disclaimer and neither does Lucy. You and I have known each other a long time. We're paying for your discretion and expertise in this matter. After you hand over the painting, I want you to say it's authentic."

Franco looked at him sideways. "You want me to

pretend it's the real thing? When? At your next dinner party?"

"If you are questioned, I want you to stand behind the skill of your work," Cash said.

"What are you playing at, Cash? I thought you got out of the game. The incident with your son was a one-off."

"What incident with your son?" Lucia asked.

Cash didn't want to bring his son anywhere near this. His son was safe and his son was staying out of this lifestyle. He ignored Lucia's question. "This is a job I need to do."

Franco returned to his canvas. He looked at it and then back at Cash. "I'll do it if you tell me more about who you're planning to con."

The word *con* smarted. It was a word he hated being associated with. "Clifton Anderson."

Franco whistled. "Wow. Just wow. Talk about going for the throat."

"You said you'd do it if I told you who it was." He wouldn't let Franco back out.

"What will I do when he figures it out and comes looking for me? Pretend I don't recognize my work?"

"He won't figure it out. You're his expert and when you tell him it's authentic, he'll believe you."

Franco rocked back on his heels. "I'll do it, but if he calls my bluff, I'm turning him loose on you."

Cash grinned. "When has anyone called your bluff? You're a one of a kind, Franco." Artist, genius, liar.

Franco brought his hand to his chest. "You flatter me, but I don't need flattery. I just need my paycheck."

"Do you know everyone in the art world?" Lucia asked, following Cash into the office of the chief curator of the Smithsonian American Art Museum. His connections were endless.

"Elizabeth and I go back to our high school days. She's an old friend. She was talented back then and I'm not even a little surprised how far she's come in her career."

Lucia wondered if Elizabeth was a criminal, but it didn't fit. The woman's résumé was long and robust, no hint of criminal activity. Would she be willing to help the FBI with a con of Clifton Anderson and the public?

Elizabeth Romano was waiting for Cash when they entered the office. The short, slim redhead greeted Cash with a hug and then clasped his hands, kissing each of his cheeks. Lucia picked up on something between Elizabeth and Cash immediately. Cash had a flirtatious manner with most women, but the look in Elizabeth's eyes made her intention clear. She liked Cash, maybe even as someone who wanted to date him.

"It's been too long," Elizabeth said. "I heard what happened to you and the whole thing sounded unfair."

Lucia wondered about Elizabeth's comment. She wasn't the first person to comment on the injustice of Cash's jail time. Lucia felt as if she was missing part of the story. She made a note to ask Cash about it later. Whenever she'd brought it up in the past, he'd hedged.

Lucia fell back a step, not wanting the intimacy she'd shared with Cash to seep into their work and put Elizabeth off. They needed her help and a huge favor. Lucia half expected Elizabeth to turn them down. Lucia was letting Cash take the lead on this for certain.

"Please tell me how I can help you. You said the matter was urgent," Elizabeth said.

Cash remained close to Elizabeth, his full attention

on her. "I need an enormous favor and what I'm about to ask you must stay between us."

Elizabeth took a deep breath. She held up her hand. "Before you say anything Cash, I need to tell you that I won't commit a crime to help you. I'll do almost anything else. But not that."

Cash winced. "I'm with the good guys."

Lucia took out her badge. "I'm with the FBI. This request is fully sanctioned by the United States Federal Bureau of Investigation."

Elizabeth's shoulders relaxed. "Wow, I must have sounded really presumptuous. I know with your father and the jail time, it's hard." She fluttered her hands as if waving away her thoughts. "Tell me what you need."

"I need you to replace Copley's *Mrs. George Watson* with a replica that we'll provide. Then I need you to help me break in to steal the replica."

Elizabeth looked at Lucia and Cash. "That makes no sense. Why do you want to steal a fake that you already have?"

"We need it to look like the original was taken," Lucia said. "We want the media to know and the staff to gossip about it. You'll be one of the few people who know that the real painting is safe and secure."

Elizabeth sat in her chair. "When that painting is stolen, if I pretend it's the real one, I'll be in the middle of a storm. The paperwork, the insurance and my bosses will be up in arms. There will be a thorough investigation and someone will figure out I was involved."

Lucia felt she was about to say no. "It will be for a short period of time. As soon as possible, we'll let everyone know the real painting has been recovered and we'll make any explanation we need for you," Lucia said.

"How long?" Elizabeth said. "I don't know how well I'll stand up to questioning."

Elizabeth was smart and talented, but she wasn't a natural liar. Her thoughts and emotions played out plain on her face.

"We will contact the secretary of the Smithsonian Institution to alert him to our plan. We can ask him to use whatever control he has over the investigation to keep you out of it. Maybe you can even stay busy with something else for a few weeks."

Elizabeth seemed to perk up at the idea. "I have some vacation time coming up. Maybe I could take a vacation."

It might come across as suspicious, but with any luck, the investigation would be wrapped up within a few weeks. Once Anderson was in custody, Elizabeth wouldn't need to keep up the charade or dodge questions.

"What are you wearing?" Cash asked.

Lucia looked down at her clothes. "Black."

She folded her arms across her chest. "I tried to pick an outfit that would blend. I figured this makes me disappear into the shadows better."

Cash gave her a long look up and down. "You look a little like an emo teenager."

"I thought I looked like an art student."

"Have you ever taken an art class?" he asked.

She shook her head. "I majored in psychology with a minor in criminal justice. No art classes."

She would be better in something more natural. "Just don't put on a black ski mask and we should be okay."

"Aren't we planning to hide our faces?" she asked.

"We sure are. But we'll wait until we're closer to the museum." If someone saw them walking on the street in ski masks, he'd expect the police would be called in a hurry.

Lucia took another clip from the counter and twisted her hair up, securing the ends. "Are you sure this will work?"

Cash nodded. "It has to work. Mitchell gave us a short deadline. If we fail, it will be in the news. Botched art theft." Anderson wouldn't give him another chance. Cash was already getting more than he expected based on his con of the senator's real estate company.

They parked several blocks from the museum. Before they got out of the car, Cash kissed her. "Good luck." If this worked, he'd get in the habit of kissing her more, whenever he needed luck. Or maybe even if he didn't. Kissing Lucia had enormous appeal.

"You, too." She touched her lips with her fingertips.

He might have caused a distraction. Was she thinking about the night they'd spent together in her bed? Maybe he shouldn't have kissed her, but adrenaline and anxiety were reverberating around his nerves.

They had their plan and timing was tight. Even with the inside information Elizabeth had provided, it was a two-person job with little room for obstacles or surprises. The theft had to go flawlessly.

The stakes were high with any con. This was his most risky.

When they were close to the museum, they pulled on their hats and masks. It would take Cash at least two minutes to disable the video monitoring and black out their movements to reach the Copley painting. It would take Lucia four minutes to get to the electrical box in the basement and turn off the electricity. When the museum's backup generators kicked on after seven minutes, Cash and Lucia would be long gone.

Using a fake employee ID card that Elizabeth had supplied and couldn't be traced to her, they entered the master PIN to unlock the entrance to the restoration area. The restoration area was closed to the public and had fewer video surveillance devices. It was dark and quiet.

They slipped inside the museum. They were unarmed. Cash had insisted the theft play out without weapons. He wouldn't carry a gun unless he had the intention of using it and he wouldn't kill a guard over a painting.

Cash took the stairs to the main lobby security desk and Lucia fled to the basement.

They would encounter anywhere from one to three night-shift guards. The museum mandated that one guard remain at the security desk and the other two patrol the galleries.

Cash stepped behind the desk. "Stand up, put your hands on your head. This is the DC police. I have a warrant for your arrest."

The guard half turned, but Cash put his hands on the smaller man's shoulders to prevent him from looking.

"I haven't done anything wrong! What warrant for my arrest?"

Few people jumped to the worst possible conclusion right away, in this case, that a robbery was in progress. Denial was a good defense mechanism. "Hands behind your back."

He didn't have handcuffs. He had duct tape. He wrapped the guard's hands behind his back and secured his legs. Then he covered his mouth so he couldn't call for help.

Cash laid the man on the ground. "This is a robbery. Don't do anything stupid and it will be over in three minutes."

The guard watched him, but made no noise.

Cash turned to the main console and used the credentials Elizabeth had supplied to disable the alarm in the gallery where the Copley was hung.

He looked at his watch. His first tasks were complete with three seconds to spare. The lights turned off and the video monitors went dark. Cash crawled under the desk and removed the cords running from the wireless receiver to the recording device that captured the feeds from the galleries' cameras.

By now, Lucia should be en route to the replica Copley that Elizabeth had swapped into place earlier that night.

When Cash arrived at the gallery, Lucia had it half out of the frame. Cash stepped in to help her. No alarms blared. No police sirens in the distance. No shouting for help. Silence was a good sign.

An alarm sounded and Lucia looked at Cash in panic. The alarm ringing meant one of the guards must have returned to the security desk. Had they reconnected the surveillance devices? Cash had memorized the blackout spots in the room, but keeping to them would cost time. The alarms would summon the police and they had a two-minute response time.

Cash removed the Copley and rolled it. He slid it into the case on his back and gestured for Lucia to follow him. Keeping to the dark, he pulled Lucia into the corner to wait for the sweep of the camera through the room.

The guards might not immediately notice the Copley missing from the frame. In the darkened room, shadows were hard to interpret.

"What now?" Lucia asked. She was pressed against him and breathing hard.

He hugged her, wanting to provide some comfort. "I'll get us out. Stay close to me. Do not leave my side."

Cash watched the camera in the room swivel away and then they ran. Darting down the hallway, through galleries, he could see the restoration area door ahead.

"Stop! Put your hands in air."

Cash turned to see one of the security guards pointing a Taser in his direction. "Go," he said to Lucia.

Another shouted a warning.

Cash would take his chances that the guard was a lousy shot. They fled into the restoration area and Cash locked the door.

He heard the guards calling after him, but he and Lucia raced outside before the guards opened the door.

Following their path, they ran and didn't stop until they'd reached the Dumpster where they removed a black trash bag they'd planted earlier, took their change of clothes from it and filled it with their masks and clothes. Cash opened the bottle of lighter fluid and dumped it inside the bag. He threw the bag into the mostly empty Dumpster and lit the bag on fire. They pulled on their new clothes.

Benjamin pulled up, and Cash and Lucia climbed into the car.

"Nice work," he said. "You had about fifteen seconds to spare. I heard over the police scanner that the five-oh are seconds away from surrounding the museum."

Cash breathed a sigh of relief. Lucia appeared in shock.

"I've never been on that end of a crime before. It was unsettling. Scary," Lucia said. Her hands were shaking as she jammed them through her hair.

"Glad to know you won't be switching sides anytime soon," Benjamin said. "We need you on ours."

Lucia reclined against the seat and Cash wished she would recline on him. But with Benjamin around, they had boundaries.

Another thought came to mind. Anytime someone else was around, he and Lucia would have boundaries. The only time they could be themselves was when they were alone.

The thought put a damper on his adrenaline high. He had finally met a woman who understood him, who challenged him and who he could really fall for, but he knew it would never work.

Chapter 8

Lucia handed Cash a glass of champagne. She hadn't seen the night sky so alive with stars and lights. The view from her balcony was extraordinary. "A toast. To new skills and new partners." She was trying to keep her thoughts on the case, but seeing Cash in a black robe with nothing beneath was titillating her senses.

Working a theft with him had been exciting. High-risk, adrenaline pumping and she had loved being his partner.

Cash slid his arms around her. "You know what I'm in the mood for now?"

"If you say pizza, I'll be disappointed."

"Pizza would be great. But after." He took a few steps away from the railing. "I want to have some fun with you." He kissed her, hard and deep, and walked her toward the open doors to her condo. "Take off all your clothes," he whispered.

"The door is open."

"No one can see us," Cash said, helping her with his request but lifting the hem of her shirt.

"I have a stalker, remember?"

Cash ran his nose along her jaw. "No one is watching us now. If your stalker could see us, he would take a shot at us."

"That's not comforting."

"Let me make it up to you." Cash banded his arms around her. "Your skin is soft and always smells so good. How do you do that?"

"One of my trade secrets as a woman."

"You want to know one of my secrets?" he asked.

"I guess you have many."

"That's correct. But this secret involves you."

Her body overreacted to his words and his touch. "Tell me," she said.

"When I first met you, I wanted to strip you naked and have you in the conference room."

No one had ever spoken to her this way and it turned her on. "We had friction when we met."

"What you call friction, I call heat."

She was naked in the doorway to her balcony and not concerned about it. Cash inspired that confidence. He was cool and relaxed and devastatingly sexy. He pulled her to the floor, reaching to the couch and grabbing a pillow for behind her head. "If this was a bearskin rug, I could make this a cliché."

"I don't want a cliché," she said. She didn't want red roses and chocolates. She desired something more. Could Cash provide her version of happiness? He wasn't a cookie cutter of the men she'd dated before. He had so many talents, some of his best related to the pleasure he was giving her.

He reached between her legs and his eyes shot from the apex of her thighs to her face. "You like this." He ran his finger slowly along her sensitive skin.

"Of course I do."

"Did you want to sleep with me when we met?" he asked.

"Most women probably think about having sex with you at some point."

"That's not answering my question," he said.

He ran his fingers up and down. When she lifted her hips, he pulled them away. "Tell me."

Coercion. "Yes, of course I did."

She was rewarded for her honesty. He plunged his fingers inside her and she cried out as a fierce orgasm ripped through her. "You must have liked the heist," he said.

She had. "I shouldn't have. I'm an FBI agent. I should find the idea repulsive."

"*Should* is a difficult word," Cash said.

He produced a condom from somewhere and slid it on. Without more foreplay, he slid inside her, one slow, smooth glide.

She opened her legs farther apart, making room for him. He slipped his hands under her, lifting her hips and seating himself deeper. "You make me feel things I haven't felt in a long time."

Lucia believed that most men said a lot of things during sex that they didn't mean. Not lies exactly, more like excited utterances. Cash was a con man. He might say things that were true in the moment and he might say things that would make this better for her. Could she believe him?

"Hey," he said. "Look at me."

She met his gaze.

He'd stopped moving. "You're thinking too much. You won't enjoy this if you can't let go. Do you want me to stop?"

She shook her head. "It's hard for my mind to keep up with my body."

He moved slowly. "I loved the noises you made when you came before. I want to hear that noise again while I'm inside you. Even if I have to work for it all night."

Lucia took the sides of his robe and pulled it off his shoulders. "I want to look at you." She had some demands of her own.

Cash swiveled his hips, rocking inside her. He had rhythm and style, and his body coaxed pleasure from hers.

He lowered his mouth to her nipples and sucked one, then the other.

She felt another orgasm just out of reach.

"When we were leaving the museum, I wished I would have had time to make love to you there. A beautiful woman among beautiful things."

Whether it was the words *make love* or the reminder of the excitement they'd shared earlier that night, her body tipped over the summit. Cash joined her, his body going tight a moment before he closed his eyes and his body pulsed inside hers.

They lay on the floor of her living room, in the least likely place she could think to have sex with someone. Cash rolled to his side, taking her with him.

"Are you feeling a little high?" Lucia asked.

"From the heist? Or sex?" he asked, then chuckled. "Never mind. The answer is the same. Yes to both."

Lucia rested her head on his chest. Cash wasn't jewelry and five-star restaurants. His affection came in a more humble package. A package that was real and honest, two words she wouldn't have thought would describe Cash so accurately.

Her phone vibrated. It could be Benjamin with a follow-up about the theft. Stifling a groan, Lucia untangled herself from Cash and checked it. She was stark naked and felt Cash watching her. She grabbed a blanket from the back of the couch and wrapped it around herself.

Benjamin had texted her and she relayed the message. "It's Benjamin. The news of the robbery already hit the media."

"That was fast," Cash said.

"We wanted fast. Do you think Anderson knows?"

"Most definitely. I told him to expect the delivery tomorrow at 6:00 a.m. I don't disappoint."

Lucia let her gaze wander down his naked body. He certainly didn't.

Lucia was wearing a short purple minidress as they walked toward their meeting with Mitchell. "I think this dress is riding up as I walk." She tugged at the hem, cursing the cheap fabric. Next time she had to play this role, she would splurge for her own clothes. Even if she only wore them once, at least she could control the hemline.

"As much as I'd like another eyeful of your bare rear end, I'm feeling a little more possessive now that we're in public. Would you like my jacket?" he asked.

"I'm supposed to be comfortable in my clothes and it's not cold enough to need your jacket," she said.

"Have you spoken to Audrey since we saw her at the casino?" Cash asked.

"I did. I asked her about what she had been up to the last couple of weeks, but she was evasive, which is strange. Normally, she's happy to share every detail about her nights out."

"Do you think she's involved with Anderson?" Cash asked.

Lucia wasn't sure what to think about seeing Audrey at the casino. The further they sank into Anderson's world, the more connected the players became. "Audrey isn't a criminal. She has no reason to be."

"Some people like the thrill of it, not the money," Cash said.

Lucia thought again of the previous night. During the theft, she had been in the zone in the same way she was during any operation and an element of excitement had pulled at her. "We'll see. When Anderson gets his painting, it will put us closer to finding the money."

Ten minutes later, Cash and Lucia were sitting in the back of an almost empty restaurant sipping coffee. Mitchell appeared and strode directly to them. He threw a newspaper on the table, almost knocking over Lucia's coffee. She snapped up the cup before the hot liquid spilled on her.

Granted, it would have ruined the dress. But it was borrowed from the FBI's closet and she planned to clean and return it. Plus, she thought Mitchell was rude. High ranking in Anderson's organization or not, he was a thug and it showed.

"You pulled it off," Mitchell said.

The front-page news was the theft at the American Art Museum. Lucia scanned the article. The security guard at the main desk had been interviewed and had claimed guns had been used to intimidate him. With nothing on their video or audio surveillance, the police had no evidence to prove otherwise.

Benjamin was keeping an eye on the investigation, trying to get an inside bead on anything the police were holding back from the media, such as the cameras had picked up a clue about the thieves.

"I told you I would." The Franco copy of the painting was sitting on the seat next to Cash. He didn't hold it up. Would Mitchell look at it right away? Would he know it was a fake?

Lucia took a sip of her coffee to have something to do with her hands. She didn't want to say anything. Cash was handling the transaction. She had to keep reminding herself she was the dim-witted girlfriend.

"Who was your second?" Mitchell asked.

"What makes you think I had an accomplice?" Cash asked.

Mitchell slanted him a look. "I know a job like this."

"I'm not giving away trade secrets. Considering how I landed in prison for the last con I pulled, you can understand that I'm keeping details close to my vest."

Mitchell waited a few beats before nodding. Maybe he figured Cash wouldn't give away anything else, but it didn't matter. "If this checks out, I'll let you know a time and place to meet. We've had to move from our previous location."

Why? Had the FBI or local police raided the casino? Anderson had to be feeling jumpy. One mistake and his empire would come crashing down.

"Let me know," Cash said. He stood up from the booth. Lucia did the same.

Mitchell tapped Cash's chest with the rolled-up canvas. "If this is a con, I'll kill you, I'll kill her, I'll kill your boy and I'll kill your dad."

Cash's lip lifted in distaste. "Easy. I gave you what you wanted. Threatening me isn't a good idea."

Lucia hadn't liked Mitchell before and she liked him even less now. But the painting was an expert copy. Given what they'd paid him, Franco should stand behind his work. But if Franco didn't validate the Copley as authentic, Cash would be marked for death.

"Do you mind if I drop you at the office and visit my dad?" Cash asked as they drove toward the office.

Lucia was behind on her caseload and her filing. Cash might want private time to talk to his father. They weren't certain how much his father knew about the Copley theft or Anderson's organization. The closer Cash became with his father, the more answers they'd have.

"I have lots of paperwork to do. And I need to change out of this dress."

"The look isn't growing on you?" Cash asked.

Lucia rolled her eyes. "Not even a little. Women who can pull this off deserve more credit. I feel like I'm on display and borderline indecent. And don't get me started on these shoes."

"Believe it or not, you look good and you're making it work." He reached across the console and squeezed her thigh.

Lucia wished they had time to stop at her condo, but with Cash on the GPS, Benjamin may wonder what they were doing and Lucia did not want to have that conversation with her boss. Now that she and Cash had crossed the line into having, at best, an inappropriate interoffice relationship, she'd need to be careful.

Twenty minutes later, Lucia felt more like herself in her navy suit. She hadn't finished one document when Benjamin called her into his office.

"Close the door please," he said.

Immediately feeling uneasy, Lucia followed his direction. "Something wrong?"

Benjamin laid a report in front of her. "These are the GPS locations of Cash's ankle monitor over the last several days. He's been spending the night at your place."

"That's right," Lucia said. It wasn't anything new. Even before she and Cash had slept together, Cash had stayed over with her and she had told Ben about it.

She wouldn't elaborate on the nature of their relationship on her personal time. Benjamin wouldn't approve. The FBI had policies on relationships with coworkers and she didn't need to give Benjamin a reason to write her up or fire her.

"I also have a copy of a report indicating that you and Cash seem intimate."

A report from Jonathan Wolfe? It was the closest Benjamin had come to admitting he'd had Lucia followed.

"We're in character and we're making progress toward finding Clifton Anderson."

"Is that it? Because I've noticed something, too," Benjamin said. "Something between you two. I won't jeopardize this case. If you can't be objective, then I need to find someone who can."

He wanted to pull her from the case and maybe even white collar. Lucia stayed calm. An overreaction on her part would make Benjamin's case for him. "I know the players. I've been with Cash inside the casino. If you switch me out, Mitchell will have questions."

"Can you be objective about Cash? If he flips on us, if he tries to con you, will you see through it?" Benjamin asked.

Question and doubts tumbled over her. Was Cash playing her? "What's going on, Benjamin? Do you know something about Cash that I need to be aware of?" Call him out on it. Make him justify his reasons for questioning her. When she had worked in violent crime, she had taken implications and rumors and accusations quietly. She wouldn't do the same now. She was a good, hardworking agent. She deserved the benefit of the doubt that she knew what she was doing.

Benjamin leaned forward. "I have reason to believe that Cash is planning to run."

Doubts pricked at her, but she checked her response. No impulsive emotional reactions. "Why would you think that?"

"He's reached out to his son."

Cash hadn't hidden that from her. He'd even asked to use her phone to call his son. "I need more than that to believe Cash wants to run. What parent wouldn't call and talk to their child when they could?"

"He's been looking into purchasing a plane ticket. One way. For himself to Bhutan. Bhutan, a country without extradition laws."

Cash had looked at these sites from work? How sloppy did Benjamin think Cash was? "If he was planning to run, he'd be careful. He wouldn't surf travel sites from work."

"He was careful. He used a computer at a public library."

She had questions, but wasn't ready to believe any of this. "If you believe Cash is planning to run, why haven't you returned him to prison?"

"We need him."

"I know what I'm doing. I'm being a friend to Cash," Lucia said. "He's better at his job when he isn't sleeping in a crack den."

Benjamin fixed his gaze on her. "You had better be right Lucia. I've had reasons to question your judgment, but I've given you some leeway."

What was he implying? "When have I exhibited poor judgment?"

"You were promoted out of violent crime, but it seemed like there was more to the story than a simple promotion. I heard rumors about problems with the team there."

Rumors? Problems? "I did my job in violent crime," she said. She was in a tough position. She had no facts to prove she had been moved because her former boss was a chauvinist and badmouthing him made her look bad. But if Benjamin wanted to question her about rumors, how could she defend herself?

"Just be aware that I'm watching you. Both you and Cash. Don't step out of line."

Cash opened the flimsy screen door and tapped on the wooden front door of his father's house. He heard his father moving around inside. He opened the door with a smile on his face.

"Cash." His father seemed genuinely pleased to see him.

"I wanted to check to see how you were feeling,"

Cash said. After the drive-by at the restaurant and his father's heart scare, Cash had been worried.

His father touched his rib cage. "Better every day. Where's your lady?"

"She had a nail appointment." He was impressed with his quick thinking.

"She's quite a woman."

Cash nodded.

"Different from Britney."

Wyatt hadn't spent much time with Cash's late wife. Britney hadn't liked Cash's father for the same reasons she hadn't liked her own.

Cash had turned away from his father because the life that Britney had offered was better than the life he'd grown up with. She was eleven years older than he was, and that age difference had made her seem wiser. Though she'd been living with her mother most of her life, she understood the world where Cash and his father lived. She had been a way out of something he'd never enjoyed. "Lucy's one of a kind."

"Does she know everything? Did you go on the level with her?" his father asked.

"She knows." About mostly everything.

"She wants you back in this game?" his father asked.

"She's okay with it."

His father said nothing for a long time. He walked unsteadily to the refrigerator. He took out two beers, pulled the caps and handed one to Cash. Cash wasn't in the mood to drink, but he took a swig.

"I've known Anderson for a long time. He and I go way back to the old neighborhood," his father said.

"I know."

"Keep that in mind when you hear what I have to

say. I don't want you involved with Anderson. I don't want you tied up in something that will land you back in prison." His father lowered his voice over the word *prison*.

"I'm not returning to prison. I'll be careful," Cash said.

His father touched his cheek. "Careful isn't enough. Anderson is looking for a big score. Anderson doesn't ever tell anyone his plans, but I hear things, you know? Good things, bad things. Mostly I hear that Anderson wants out of the game. When he leaves, he'll take his money with him and he won't care if the people around him take the fall for what he's done."

Cash sensed his father knew more. "Why would anyone need to take the fall? Anderson is careful."

Cash's father let out a burst of laughter. "He's shrewd. He doesn't put himself in the direct line of fire. He has plenty of people willing to do it for him. Why do you want in, anyway? I thought you turned your back on this life."

He had. Though the life of a con man was exciting and could be lucrative, he wasn't interested in being a criminal. His only interest was his son. "I don't have any other way to make a living." The admission burned because it was true.

Cash didn't have a college degree or skills. When he was married to Britney, he'd had a job working at a hardware store, stocking shelves overnight. It had left him free during the day to stay with Adrian. He'd been tired many days, but it had been worth it to spend so much time with his son.

"You're a smart man. You're a people person. People like you. Why don't you use that?"

"To do what? What pays as well as this?"

His father frowned and his shoulders sagged. "I couldn't figure it out. I've done this for so long I don't know how to get out."

Did his father want out? He had always seemed to enjoy running cons. He was good at it. "Do you want to retire?"

His father drummed his fingers against the countertop. "I can't."

"Can't or won't?"

His father smashed a fist against the counter, rattling some dishes that were sitting unwashed next to the sink. "Can't. But Cash, I was never more proud of you than when you walked away from this."

Proud? His father had been furious. "It didn't seem that way."

"I was hurt that you'd turned away from family. But I didn't want you back into this."

"It's a tough life to quit," Cash said.

"Sometimes, it's the only option," his father said. "But Lucy might change her mind. She might want a family and stability."

"I can give her whatever she needs," Cash said.

"This life is not what anyone needs," Wyatt said.

"Tell me what I can do to help you."

"Will you let me see my grandson?" his father asked.

Cash's heart squeezed. Adrian. Cash did not want Adrian involved in this situation. Britney had been adamant that his father not be near Adrian, but Cash didn't have the same feelings. Not anymore. "That's a logistical problem."

His father took a sip of his beer and looked away.

"Britney's mom has custody of Adrian. They live

on the other side of the country. He isn't interested in seeing me. I am not planning to pursue him." Did his father hear the lie?

If he did, he didn't call Cash out. "I understand. It's a conversation for another day."

Searching for a single one-way plane ticket was damning evidence.

Had Cash lied to her about his son? Had he been conning her? If he was, what was he conning her into doing?

Arguing with herself and considering the angles was making her crazy. Lucia took the stairs to her condo feeling grumpy and unpleasant. The old townhouse should have been outfitted with an elevator.

Audrey stepped out of her place. "Have time for a visit?"

Lucia had time, but she wasn't in the mood. "I've had a long day."

"Following a long night?" Audrey asked.

For a moment, Lucia feared that Audrey knew she and Cash had been involved in the break-in at the art museum. Based on the look in Audrey's eyes, she was referring to Cash. "Not enough sleep."

Audrey smiled. "Best kind of nonsleep."

"It's complicated."

"Always is," Audrey said.

"It shouldn't be," Lucia said.

"When it's easy, it's boring. Cash is not a boring man. I would use a lot of words to describe him, but not that one."

Boring described Lucia's past relationships. Revisiting those relationships, especially the disastrous ones, would send her mood on a downward spiral. "I don't know what I want."

"I think it's clear you don't want a safe, normal relationship," Audrey said.

"What makes you say that?" Safe and normal wouldn't have problems involving criminals and extradition laws.

Audrey threw up her hands. "I've met Bradley. I've met the kind of men your mom loves to force on you. You reject them and you don't look back."

"I didn't reject Bradley." It had been the other way around.

Audrey rolled her eyes. "Didn't you? Were you heartbroken when he left you?"

Yes. No. A little. "I was hurt."

"Your *pride* was hurt. You were fine. You were happy to throw off those old chains and do what you wanted."

Party girl turned therapist. "I was pissed off at my sister's wedding to Bradley. I made a drunken spectacle of myself."

"I was pissed off at your sister and Bradley's wedding, too. It was so dull, I fell asleep twice. You did not make a spectacle. You got drunk. Big deal. A spectacle would have been if you'd jumped her and ripped off her veil, then stolen her bouquet and beaten Bradley with it."

Lucia laughed, the picture Audrey painted making her feel better. That was something else she liked about Audrey. She said what was on her mind. "Well, now I'm in a nonboring relationship-type situation and it feels…"

"Nauseating?"

"No." She tried to find the right word. "Cash makes me feel afraid."

"Because he's the real deal."

If only Audrey knew the truth. He was a con man. And he might be conning her. "He's intense."

"Intensely sexy. Smart. Handsome. Can't hold his liquor, but we can fix that."

"He isn't looking for commitment."

"Did he say that?"

They hadn't talked about the future of their relationship. How could they when Cash's future was uncertain? "He hasn't said anything."

"Why do you assume he doesn't want you, then? Why do you assume the worst?" Audrey asked.

Cash not wanting her wasn't the worst scenario. The worst scenario was that their entire relationship was a long con.

"I can't see him wanting to be with me." The words were pathetic but honest.

"I can see it. Easily. You're a phenomenal woman and it's about time a man sees it," Audrey said.

"Thanks, Audrey. That makes me feel better."

Audrey rolled her eyes. "I'm not saying things just to make you feel better. I'm being honest. You sell yourself short and I don't know why. Maybe it's because your family is bent on making you something you're not or maybe it's because you don't toot your own horn and so people overlook you, but stop expecting people to reject you. Maybe they won't."

Lucia was upset about something. Cash was good at reading people. This job depended on it. It was part of how he'd survived jail. She wasn't upset about the case.

She was too cool and calm on the job. She was upset with him. It was personal, and if they didn't clear the air Matt Mitchell might pick up on it, too. They were meeting with him at Franco's place in a few minutes and they needed to pull it together.

"Tell me what I did so I can apologize."

Lucia stopped and whirled on him. "If I tell you what's wrong, then what's the point of the apology? Aren't you supposed to realize it on your own?"

"Then it's something personal." At least he'd read her right.

She glared at him. "We'll talk about it later. We're working."

"We can spare three minutes," he said.

"Three minutes? You want to give me three minutes?"

"It's more complicated than that?" If it took her more than three minutes to explain the problem, the resolution would be a great deal longer than that.

Lucia threw up her hands. "Just forget it. The case. That's what we're doing now."

Cash shook off his worry and focused on their meeting. They were paying Franco well for his assistance, but Cash wasn't a stranger to being crossed. Anderson paid Franco well, too.

This could be an ambush. He knew Lucia had her gun in her purse, but Cash wasn't carrying a weapon. A gun could go off in a split second. The FBI was waiting outside and covering exits, but once he was dead, why would he care if his killer was caught?

They did a quick check of their earpieces and microphones before going inside Franco's apartment. Lucia's microphone was hidden in a pair of large, yellow earrings that were the same shade as the dress she was wearing. He knew she hated the clothes she wore, but he liked them. They had a certain party-girl, sexy and flirty vibe that he enjoyed. Knowing she was already annoyed at him, he didn't voice his opinion. It would only serve to aggravate her further.

When they entered Franco's apartment, Mitchell was inside, talking to Franco. The tension in the air made it difficult for Cash to tell if Franco had sold them out. He was standing in front of the fake Copley painting, holding a glass of wine and swirling it in his right hand.

He turned when Cash entered, his face unreadable.

"What's the good news?" Cash asked, feigning confidence he didn't feel.

Mitchell stared at him and glanced at Lucia. "Franco is finishing his assessment."

"I don't like to be rushed," Franco said over his shoulder. "Great artwork deserves time and a thorough review."

Cash didn't react to anything Franco said. Mitchell must've known that he and Franco were acquaintances, but he wouldn't know that Cash had the resources to pay him off to suit his purposes.

"Look at the lines, the brush strokes and the shading. Copley had many works of art, but this is one of my favorites. I know it well," Franco said. He circled the canvas on the easel, looking behind it.

"Then it's authentic?" Mitchell asked.

Franco made a sound like he wasn't sure. Out of the corner of his eye, Cash noticed Lucia's eye twitch and her fingers slide toward the opening of her handbag. The FBI was listening, likely poised to spring if Franco revealed them as liars.

After a long pause, Franco turned and smiled. "Yes. It's authentic."

"You're sure?" Mitchell asked.

Franco appeared incensed. He was keeping that part of his personality true to form. He did not like being questioned. He considered himself an art authority, absolutely beyond reproach. "I am sure. Don't bring me a hot item and put me in jeopardy and then question my assessment. It's insulting."

"What about the painting makes you think it's hot?" Mitchell asked.

Franco smirked and strolled to his liquor bar. "First, I read. Second, I know my artwork."

He winked at Cash when Mitchell's back was to him.

"Are we done here?" Cash asked.

Mitchell nodded. "We have another stop tonight. We'll take my car. Leave the lady."

Lucia made a sound of disapproval.

Mitchell glared at her. "What are you, his shadow?"

"We're soul mates," she said, in a voice that was almost believable. Had Cash not been in character, he would have laughed.

"I'm taking your *soul mate* on a drive. I'll return him later."

"Lucy, baby, I'll be fine. I'll make it up to you tomorrow."

Lucia cuddled up to Cash, pressing into his side, her breasts nearly popping out the top of her dress. "Make it up to me tonight."

Cash took a long look at her cleavage, both to play the part and because he was a man who found Lucia wildly attractive. Even Mitchell seemed entranced for a moment. Lucia had given Cash a good excuse for not lingering in whatever hotbed of illegal activity Mitchell was taking him to.

With luck, Cash would return to her place alive.

Chapter 9

"What's going on with you and Lucy?" Mitchell asked.

Why was everyone suddenly obsessed with asking him about Lucia? Guys didn't talk about relationships. Life couldn't have changed that much while he was in prison. "What do you mean?"

"She seemed upset."

Mitchell was fishing to find out if Lucia's emotions would have any blowback on him or Anderson, such as a bitter ex-girlfriend running to the cops about what she knew about a secret underground casino or newsworthy art theft.

"She's fine. I'll make it up to her," Cash said.

"Make what up to her?"

Nothing to do with Anderson or the art theft. He needed a reason for Lucia to be angry with him, but not angry enough that the relationship was doomed to fail. "She wants to get married. I'm not ready."

Mitchell snorted. "Why do women think marriage is the only endgame?"

"No idea. The diamond. The dress. The party. Who knows?"

"My fiancée has been riding me about setting a date for our wedding. Isn't it enough she has the ring?"

"For some women, they need that gold band," Cash said.

"You've been married before," Mitchell said.

Cash had been married to Anderson's estranged daughter and it wasn't a secret. "Yes."

"What made you pull the trigger?"

And interesting choice of words, as if marriage equaled death. "My wife was someone special. I needed her in my life. She made me happy."

"Anderson will be pleased to know that," Mitchell said.

Anderson and Cash hadn't discussed Britney. It was a sore subject for Anderson. While Cash had tried to convince Britney that keeping her father out of her life was extreme, she hadn't yielded. "Why don't you tell me what you need from me? I've proven my loyalty. I want to work."

"Eager," Mitchell said.

"To make some money? Of course," Cash said.

"Get us the FBI file on Anderson," Mitchell said.

Demanding. Cash laughed. "Do you think they'll hand it over to me? I don't have an all-access pass. I'm a convict."

"Anderson and I have talked about that. Is the FBI using you to get close to Anderson?"

Cash knew this moment would decide it he lived or died. However he answered, whatever his facial expression or tone, Mitchell would use it against him. Anderson wasn't an idiot. He was smart enough to suspect this was a setup. "No. They're using my hacking skills to close off vulnerabilities in their computer systems."

"Use those computer skills and get the files we need."

Cash could communicate the request to Lucia and Benjamin, and they could create a fake file on Anderson for Mitchell, but Cash couldn't be too enthusiastic or Mitchell would know something was off. "I'll need a few days."

"Get the file. Get it quickly. We have more work to do."

Cash called Lucia from the Hideaway. He hated sleeping in the small, dirty room, but he sensed she needed space and he had not wanted to lead Mitchell to her place. Cash had gotten used to staying with her. It wasn't difficult to become accustomed to soft sheets and the scents that wafted up from the chef's condo below hers.

"Lucia, it's me."

"Are you okay? My caller ID shows this number as the Hideaway. Are you home?" Despite the late hour, she sounded wide-awake.

"I'm at the Hideaway and I'm fine. Mitchell wanted to talk shop for a while."

"Your microphone cut out about ten minutes after you left Franco's loft. We couldn't get a bead on your GPS device. We've had dead silence over here."

"They must have had a signal blocker somewhere in the building. I couldn't hear anything from you, either."

"We were worried," Lucia said.

We? "You're with the team?" he asked.

"Yes."

So much for discussing anything personal with Lucia. He was glad he hadn't led with asking about how she was feeling or attempting to open the conversation about why she was angry with him.

"Hold on. Switching the call to speaker," Lucia said.

"Cash? You okay?" Benjamin asked.

"I'm fine. I need to get Anderson's FBI file for Mitchell."

The shuffling of papers. "We can do that," Lucia said.

"It needs to take a few days," Cash said. "I told Mitchell I'd need to hack in and steal it. Do you want me to come in to the office tonight?"

"Yes," Lucia said.

"No, it's late," Benjamin said. "We'll get an early start tomorrow. Cash, write some notes on what you heard and saw tonight. Be ready to talk about it to the team tomorrow."

"Will do."

He disconnected the call. He was too wound up to sleep, but it was after midnight. He sat on the bed. He didn't have anything else to do, but he had plenty of places he'd rather be.

Somehow Mitchell must have prevented his GPS signal from being broadcast. Lucia had taken the signal-disrupting device he'd given Cash. Could Cash find a device on the black market that worked similarly?

He wanted to believe that the work he was doing now would lead to a reunion with his son. What if he was wrong? He needed a backup plan. Nothing could stand between him and his son.

Cash must have fallen asleep because he awoke to a light tap on his door. He rolled to his feet and looked through the peephole. Lucia? What was she doing in this part of town? He opened the door and pulled her inside his room before she caught the attention of the wrong people. "You should not be here."

She lifted a brow. "Why's that? You come to my place all the time."

"This place is a dump and it's dangerous. I think I've heard four fistfights and a gunshot already tonight. The police have been here twice."

Lucia sighed. "I'm an FBI agent. I carry a weapon."

"Someone could still hurt you."

"I didn't know you cared."

Something in that comment struck him. What had he done to make her believe he didn't care about her? It was shocking to him how much he did care for her. He had set out to win her over, but what had unfolded between them had nothing to do with a con or any plans he'd made. "I do care. Of course I do."

Lucia handed him a file. "While you were on radio silence, I had time to do my homework."

"What's this?" Cash asked, opening the file folder.

It was his file. Cash went ramrod straight. "Why do you have this?" He assumed she'd had access to his file from the time he had joined the team, but why bring it to him now? Did it contain something that upset her?

"I wanted to know if your story checked out."

His blood ran cold. "What story is that?"

"About Adrian."

His Achilles heel. "You better be careful about what

you say next." If she threatened his son or implied anything untoward about him, he wasn't sure he could control himself. Master of control that he was, Adrian was his everything. He'd wanted to kill Mitchell for making a threat against his son. Only knowing that Mitchell was just one man on a crew of many had stopped Cash.

"His birth certificate does not list you as his father."

Anger seared him. He was Adrian's father regardless of what Britney had or had not written on the hospital's paperwork. "I am his father."

"Care to explain why it's blank?"

Cash resented her question. It was not her business. Britney and his marriage had been rocky when she'd given birth to Adrian. But Cash had been with her, in the delivery room and in her post-recovery room. He had been there for Adrian's first bath and he'd changed his first diaper. He was Adrian's father. "I do not owe you an explanation."

Lucia lifted her chin. "If you want me to believe your story, you do."

Anger turned to rage, an emotion Cash rarely let himself feel. Lucia could push all his buttons, the good ones and the bad ones. "Would you question someone else like this? I am not a criminal in an interview room. I'm a man you're sleeping with."

Lucia snatched the folder back from him. "You can understand, given your history, that I should be wary that history will repeat itself. You've been secretive about Adrian. I want to know why."

Did she really need an explanation? What kind of pathetic father dragged his son into a world filled with criminals? "I don't want him pulled into this sick, twisted game that Anderson is playing. I would die to protect Adrian. I do not like to talk about Adrian because every time I do it just reinforces that I'm a failure as a father."

Lucia recoiled and he read shame in her reaction. She had crossed a line and she knew it.

"Get out," he said. He didn't want to see her. He didn't want to talk about this any further.

"Cash," she started.

"Get out. Get out now."

Lucia left, closing the door behind her.

Cash scarcely looked at Lucia at their team's morning meeting. He answered every question politely, but he was distant. If anyone else noticed, they didn't say anything. Maybe they chalked it up to the late night, but no one knew Cash the way she did.

Lucia didn't know why she had pressed him about his son. It was wrong on so many levels. It was a betrayal of his trust, his privacy and his confidence. She could blame the past, Bradley and her sister's betrayal, but it wasn't an excuse for her behavior.

After the meeting, she waited until he returned to his desk before approaching him. "Cash?"

He was reviewing the report he had written with the details about the night before.

He spun to face her. "What do you want?"

She deserved his rudeness. "I want to apologize. I'm sorry, Cash."

"For what?" he asked.

He knew, but he wanted her to say it. Here in the office where others could hear her. "For not believing you. For invading your privacy." She lowered her voice. "For using something you told me in confidence against you."

He nodded. "Okay."

"Okay, what?"

"I accept your apology."

"That's it? That simple?"

"I want something in return."

Was this part of the con? She felt bad for even thinking it. "Know that I have limits to what I am allowed to do." She couldn't remove his tracker. She couldn't approve movements outside the city.

"I want you to host your family for brunch at your place and invite me."

She paused for a moment. "You want to meet my family?"

"Yes."

"Why?"

Cash reclined in his chair and she was struck again by how handsome he was. It was that much harder to say no to him when he looked at her. "I want you to trust me."

Her family was difficult on a good day. "How is meeting my family proving I trust you?" Gatherings with her family were stressful. Add a convict to it and she was sure her parents would not approve. Though her mother would hide her feelings, Lucia knew her father would be frank about his dislike.

"If you want to be involved in my personal life, then let me into yours."

Lucia sensed that if she didn't agree it would change her relationship with Cash irrevocably. He didn't want to be treated like a criminal. "I'll make the arrangements."

"What time?" He asked as if it were set in stone.

Lucia had never invited her family to her place. With the exception of the day her father had given it to her and a few visits from her parents, it wasn't a spot where the family gathered.

"Nine," she said, still thinking about the cleaning and preparation that would need to go into the brunch. But if it's what it took to made amends with Cash, she would do it.

Cash arrived an hour early to help her prepare for brunch with her family. He hadn't slept at her place since she'd gone to the Hideaway with the intent of catching him in a con.

He said he'd forgiven her for her intrusive questions about Adrian, but he was still upset. She had broken his trust. Strangely, she hadn't thought about earning his trust. She had only been worried about whether or not she could trust him. It was a two-way street.

Lucia had missed him. She'd grown accustomed to having him around and felt strangely lost without him. Lonely. Her quiet solitude bored her. Her condo felt too large for one person.

"The food is being delivered in an hour, but I need to prepare drinks. Mimosas, heavy on the alcohol," she said. If she could dull her family's senses, maybe they'd go easy on her.

"Before Britney died, our relationship was not in a good place. We were separated and she wanted a divorce."

Lucia turned. The words were unexpected. Lucia put down the glass pitcher and faced Cash. "I'm sorry to hear that."

"That information wouldn't be in my FBI file. Britney was a vivacious and exciting woman, but our relationship had its ups and downs. She didn't write my name on Adrian's birth certificate because she hoped if our marriage went sour, I wouldn't take Adrian with me. She knew how much I loved him."

"That's not how it works. Just because your name isn't on paper doesn't mean you're not his father," Lucia said.

"I know that," Cash said.

Lucia shouldn't have questioned him about Adrian. "Again, I'm sorry I interrogated you about your personal life and your son."

"I wasn't fishing for another apology. I thought you might like to know why Adrian's birth certificate is incomplete. I was too angry to talk about it the other day. But I know why you looked into my history. You still don't trust me."

"I trust you," Lucia said. How could she prove to him that she did? She offered up the one piece of information that was most difficult for her to share. "I wasn't moved to white collar because I was owed a promotion. I was moved because violent crime wanted to get rid of me."

Cash tilted his head. "Special Agent Wolfe's apology. That's what he meant?"

She nodded. It was embarrassing and difficult to speak about this. "I was the only woman on the team and I couldn't hack it."

Cash stood straighter. "Couldn't hack it or didn't have the right equipment?" He gestured down her body.

She laughed. She had to. Only Cash would see right to the heart of the issue. He hadn't accused her of doing anything wrong and she appreciated it. "I didn't have the right equipment. I wasn't invited to their happy hours or to their sports games or to their birthday parties. The harder I worked, the more they made me feel like I'd done something wrong and didn't deserve a spot on their team."

Cash put his arm around her. "I'm sorry, Lucia. I knew something had happened, but I didn't know it was that bad for you."

She wiped at the tears that came to her eyes. "It's not just that. I don't fit in with my family. I don't fit in at work. I don't fit in anywhere."

He made a sympathetic noise and hugged her to him. "Here. You fit right here."

The words were balm on a raw part of her soul. Of all the partners she'd had, the boyfriends, the friends and the colleagues, she felt most like herself with Cash. "I could not have been more wrong about you," she said.

"I'm trying to be a good man," Cash said. "It's hard. Sometimes I think about running away from my problems, buying a plane ticket to some tropical island and losing myself in the anonymity of a resort town. A fresh start. A new life. People who won't know I'm a convict."

Like researching a one-way plane ticket to Bhutan? "Why don't you?" Lucia asked, wondering if that was the explanation for the library internet search that Benjamin had told her about.

"My life is here. Adrian needs me. Sounds like you need me. Running away is for cowards. My mom left my father and me, and I never forgave her. I can't do that to the people I love."

Love. Was he including her in that word?

Her doorbell rang and Lucia tensed. She raced to answer the door. It was the caterer, dropping off trays of food.

After Lucia inspected everything, she paid the caterer and fixed herself a drink. She took one sip and her doorbell rang again. This time, it was her family. Her entire family, arriving all at once.

After making the introductions, Cash fixed drinks while she helped her family with their plates.

"Is he your boyfriend?" Meg asked.

Lucia shook her head. "We work together."

"Well, then let me say, I should have asked you to set me up with your eligible coworkers. My God, he is cute."

"You're married," Lucia said, annoyed at her sister's comment. Meg had Bradley. That was enough. Lucia suddenly felt territorial and wished she had said Cash was more than a colleague. Would that have made her sister more interested? Lucia's relationship with Bradley hadn't stopped Meg from sleeping with him.

Meg waved her hand. "I know. It doesn't hurt to window-shop." Her sister walked away and Lucia shook off her irritation. She wouldn't enter into a debate with her family over Cash. It didn't matter what her sister said about him. He wouldn't be interested in Meg.

When her family was seated at the table, her father's attention went to Cash.

"Tell me what you do," her father said.

"He works with me," Lucia said, not wanting Cash to have to explain his situation.

Her father held up his hand. "I was asking Cash."

"I'm a consultant for the FBI."

"What kind of consulting?" her mother asked.

"On special cases," Cash said.

"That's an unusual name. Cash. A family name?" her father asked.

"It's a nickname," Cash said.

"Do you work in finances?" Bradley asked.

Now they were getting into the thick of it. At any minute, her family would figure out Cash was a convict and it was over. Why had Cash wanted this?

"I have an ability to make money in difficult situations," Cash said.

Her father's eyes narrowed. "What does that mean?"

Cash glanced at Lucia. He didn't appear upset at her family's interrogation. "It means that I grew up running cons to take people's money. I was good at it. I quit when I was old enough to make my own decisions, but the name stuck."

Her family stared at him. Why had he told them about being a con man? Why couldn't he have kept his explanation to the present? FBI consultant, the end.

"My daughter knows you're a thief?" her mother asked.

"Talk about a rebellion. Come on, Lucia, are you serious with this?" Bradley asked, gesturing at Cash. The condescension in his voice set her on edge.

"As I explained, Cash is my coworker. Just because he has a different background than we do doesn't mean we need to be rude." She hoped her tone conveyed her disappointment. Couldn't her family lower their noses for a few minutes to look at Cash, really look at him, and see that he was a good man?

"Everyone knows you're sleeping with him," Meg said.

Lucia rose to her feet. "That is no one's business."

"I don't see you denying it," Chloe said.

Fury and embarrassment welled up inside her. Why did her family have to behave this way? "I don't owe you an explanation. Is this how you speak to people at the country club? Of course not! But because it's me and my friend, you think you can act like uppity, snot-nosed brats."

Cash remained silent.

"Lucia, you're making a scene and embarrassing yourself," her mother said.

She was the embarrassing one? "Am I? I don't feel embarrassed. I feel pissed off. I'm the only one who's on the receiving end of this scrutiny. Nothing I do is good enough. My sister can sleep with my fiancé and everyone applauds her when she gets engaged to him. But I invite you to meet a perfectly nice man, and you insult him and rudely pry into our relationship."

Tears welled in her eyes and Lucia blinked them back. Everyone was staring at her open-mouthed. Only Cash looked amused, as if he was glad she had finally spoken her mind. There was nothing passive-aggressive about her words this time. They were fighting words.

"I am so sorry I invited you over today. I shouldn't have bothered. Please, enjoy the meal. Lock the door on your way out." She grabbed her coat and her hand-bag and fled her condo.

She heard footsteps on the stairs above her. She didn't stop walking.

Cash caught up to her on the sidewalk, taking her arm. "Wait up, Lucia. Talk to me."

"Sorry to have left you in the den of rudeness," she said.

"Not the den of rudeness. They're worried about you. Protective. Although that shot at your sister was well deserved."

Lucia laughed. "For a second, I wiped that smug, satisfied look off her face."

"Why do you care if they call me a thief or know we're sleeping together?"

Because they were using both as reasons why Lucia was making a mistake. "It's not their business."

"Because I embarrass you," Cash said.

"You don't." It wasn't *his* behavior that had made her feel terrible.

Cash stared over her shoulder. "You looked like you wanted to jump out of your skin at brunch. Your family could sense something was wrong. They went in for the kill because you let them."

Lucia threw up her hands. "I don't understand why you wanted to meet them in the first place."

"This might be hard for you to understand, but I'm tired of people treating me like a tool to be used and discarded."

"I do not treat you like a tool," she said.

"I was brought onto the team for my skills and my connections. But I am still a person. You wouldn't know it from how I'm tracked and questioned and investigated."

Lucia opened her mouth to deny it, but she couldn't. His movements were tracked, she questioned him often enough and Benjamin had him under investigation. "You're a criminal," she said.

Cash's face turned stony. "Is that how you see me? A criminal?"

"Not just a criminal." But it was an explanation for why he was not allowed to do whatever he wanted and go wherever he wanted.

"Then what I am to you, Lucia? I thought you and I

had something, but I'm starting to think you only see me as a con man who's good in bed."

Lucia shifted. What could she say? They had slept together and it had been great. They worked well together as a team. But what else could she expect from him and the situation? It would end with each of them moving on to their next assignment. "You're my colleague." It wasn't what she wanted to say. He was more than that. But she didn't have the right words to describe their relationship.

"A colleague," he repeated, his voice flat.

She could see in his eyes she'd hurt him.

He turned to walk away and she grabbed the sleeve of his coat. "Wait, Cash."

Cash's phone rang. He pulled it from his pocket and glanced at the display. "It's a blocked number."

Likely someone from Anderson's crew. She gestured for him to answer it.

Cash leaned close so she could hear the call.

"Cash, it's Mitchell."

"What can I do for you?" Cash asked.

"Glad you asked. We're having a staff meeting tonight. Seven o'clock. I'll text you the location later today."

"Happy to be getting to work," Cash said.

"Don't bring your lady," Mitchell said.

"No problem. She can stay busy without me."

"Don't be late. I have big plans for your first job," Mitchell said.

Lucia didn't like the sound of that.

Cash said goodbye and disconnected the call.

"You can't go alone," Lucia said.

"What did you want me to say? Argue with him?

We're lucky he's let you tag along at all up until now," Cash said.

Lucia narrowed her gaze on him. "It could be a trap. I read in your report that he asked you point-blank about the FBI using you to find Anderson. Are you certain he believed you? He could kill you and I won't be there to help you."

Cash didn't appear alarmed. "He believed me. This is the chance we'll have to take."

Lucia grabbed his hand. "I don't want to take chances with your life."

She wasn't sure where she stood with Cash. Sometimes, she felt they had everything they needed in each other. Other times, she felt as though the world would do everything it could to keep them apart.

Without Lucia or the FBI at his back, Cash felt both more like himself and more on edge. He wouldn't need to worry about Lucia, but if anything went wrong, he'd have to rely on himself to get out of it.

Which hadn't been a problem in the past. But in the past, he hadn't been lying to a ruthless criminal and his thugs.

"Don't let him trick you into doing anything illegal," Lucia had said to him as he'd left her place that evening.

Illegal defined nearly everything Anderson had his hands in. How was Cash supposed to avoid it?

He arrived at the location Mitchell had texted him, an abandoned car dealership on the other side of DC from where the casino had been running. Cash was driving the car that was registered to Lucy Harris.

He parked it a few blocks away and walked. First, he wanted his getaway car to be inconspicuous. And second, a car parked in the lot of an abandoned building could bring the police. A seasoned con man wouldn't make such a rookie mistake.

He entered the dealership and waited for someone to approach him. It was quiet, but Mitchell would know he'd arrived. Sure enough, after a few minutes, Mitchell walked through one of the doorways across from the entry.

"First things first," Mitchell said, waving to Cash to follow him. "We need to get rid of your tracker."

"I've got the signal blocker on it and broadcasting from the Hideaway." Lucia had put it on his monitor before he'd left, but he had not activated it. If his tracker wasn't sending his signal, the FBI wouldn't know where he was to provide backup if he needed it. "If you cut it off, the FBI come running and I go back to jail."

Mitchell grinned at him and held up a key. "This came into my possession yesterday. I can remove your tracker without anyone being the wiser."

Cash propped his foot on the railing and Mitchell used his key to remove the device.

Though it was temporary, Cash felt lighter and freer than he had since before he'd been in prison. He could run. Get a good head start on the FBI before they knew he'd fled DC. He could make it to Seattle, find his son and start a new life.

Except it would be a life of running, of looking over his shoulder for the FBI to find him. Adrian deserved better.

And what about Lucia? Could he run away without saying goodbye to her? She had made it clear that his role in her life was fleeting and she didn't consider him more than a colleague. Why did that bother him?

"Feel better?" Mitchell asked.

"Can I keep the key?" Cash asked.

Mitchell shook his head. "We'll keep that as a secret between us when I have a need for you to be off the grid. Leave your tracker here. You can retrieve it when you're done."

"Done what?" Cash asked.

"We have a special project for you," Mitchell said.

The FBI would have no idea where he was going with Mitchell. Cash rolled with it. He would find a way to contact Lucia if he could.

"You need to meet the rest of the crew. I'll fill you in then," Mitchell said.

Lucia had an ominous feeling about Cash's meeting with Mitchell. Cash would have his tracking device, the signal blocker Mitchell had given him with him but disabled. Lucia needed to know where Cash was. She didn't trust Mitchell.

Her ominous feeling turned into dread when she received a call that Cash's ankle monitor had been removed and was sitting on the floor of an abandoned car dealership. Benjamin had sent someone to follow Cash and while they'd lost his trail, they'd found the monitor.

Mitchell could kill Cash and they wouldn't find his body.

Lucia's phone rang and she answered, hoping it was Cash.

It was her mother.

"You were very rude to us at brunch," her mother said.

Lucia closed her eyes. She didn't need this now. On top of everything else, family drama was too much. Maybe her mom and her sisters had time to fight and argue. Lucia didn't. "It was rude of me to leave, but that doesn't mean your behavior was any better."

Her mother gasped. "What has gotten into you lately? You are so mouthy."

"I am not being mouthy. I am being honest." Something she should have done years before. Instead of biting her tongue and checking her words, she should have let her family know how much they had hurt her. How much they did hurt her. "Mom, you've caught me at a bad time."

"Every time is a bad time for you."

"I'm busy," Lucia said.

"I'm busy, too. I have obligations and responsibilities and I still make time for my family."

Lucia's worry over Cash was cutting short her patience with her mother. "Mom, you do not have any pressing obligations. You have lunches at the country club and social events and shopping for those lunches and social events. Right now, I am working. I am waiting to hear from Cash because something bad has happened."

"That's why your father and I don't understand why you'd want a job like that. Whenever we've spoken to you about your work, something bad has happened or is about to happen. How can you live that way? Wouldn't you rather be like your sisters?"

Like her sisters? Directionless and totally dependent on another person? No. Not even a little. "Obviously you'd prefer that. You might love me, but you've never liked who I am. You've made me feel like I don't fit in and like I've done something wrong by being who I am." Now that the words were flowing, she couldn't stop them. "To add insult to injury, when Bradley cheated on me with Meg and then married her, you acted like I was the one in the wrong."

Her mother was quiet and Lucia wondered if she'd hung up. Lucia looked at her phone. Still connected.

"I don't like to start problems. I thought you were okay with Bradley marrying Meg."

Lucia said nothing. She was fine with it now. It would have been nice to have her parents' support when it had happened.

"You didn't love him. Your father and I both knew it. We knew he wouldn't make you happy. We didn't say anything because it would have made you more insistent on being with him."

"You didn't say anything to me about it even after," Lucia said.

"What could I say? Your sister needs someone like Bradley, someone to take care of her and provide for her. You've never needed that. You've never needed us. You do your own thing."

"What's wrong with that?" Lucia asked.

"Nothing, except we don't know how to fit into your life."

Lucia took a moment to digest her mother's words. "The way you fit into my life is to support my choices even when they are not your choices. I don't need you to do anything for me. I need you to be my family."

"We are your family, Lucia. We want you to be happy and we don't see how what you're doing will lead to that," her mother said. "I've known women like you and they regret being alone when they're older."

Her mother was trying to protect her from a life she feared. "Then don't chase off someone I care about."

"Are you in love with that crim—" Her mother cleared her throat. "With Cash?"

Lucia wasn't certain how to answer. "We're not there yet." He made her feel safe and they had fun together, but what future did they have?

Mitchell had assembled a crew to break into the headquarters of Holmes and White, access their safe in the basement and steal the contents.

Illegal. Absolutely. No gray area.

What made matters worse was that Cash's father was on the crew. Why was his father doing this? He'd implied he couldn't get away from Anderson. What did Anderson have on him?

If Cash backed out, he'd be blacklisted from Anderson's organization, useless to the FBI and sent back to prison. If he went through with it, he risked being caught and returning to prison.

Cash weighed his options. If he managed to acquire something of use to the FBI, as long as no one was hurt or killed, wasn't that the call that Lucia would make? Cash didn't have a way to contact her to discuss it without someone overhearing. He had not been alone for a moment.

"What is it that we need inside the box?" Cash asked.

"That is not your concern," Mitchell said. "Just get it and get out. Don't get caught."

He handed the crew their masks and rubber gloves. They each had an earpiece with a thin microphone attached that were linked together so they could be in constant communication. Mitchell would be handling the robbery from outside, the safest location, as the self-proclaimed mastermind.

Cash's expertise was cons. This wasn't a con. It was a robbery.

Mitchell handed Wyatt a small black bag. "This is the equipment you need to access the vault and the equipment to open the safe."

His father was adept at safe cracking. He had passed on some of his knowledge to Cash, but it had been a decade since Cash had broken into a safe, much less a safe in a financial services company that was likely new and up-to-date.

"Some advanced notice would have been good," Wyatt said.

"Are you saying you can't do it?" Mitchell asked.

"I can do it. But I could do it faster with practice," Wyatt said.

"You have seven minutes to complete this job. That's plenty of time," Mitchell said.

Right. Plenty of time, enough time to run a mile. Heat up a TV dinner. Not for robbing a safe with no advanced planning and little information about what they might encounter inside.

Cash liked Mitchell less and less. Anderson had always been methodical and careful. Mitchell seemed like a loose cannon. Did Anderson know what Mitchell was doing?

Hadn't Anderson robbed Holmes and White? What else did he need from them? Evidence that he'd left behind? If Holmes and White had evidence, why hadn't they handed it over to the FBI? The person overseeing the internal investigation could be on the take and keeping evidence pointing to others as insurance.

One of the men on the crew would disable the alarm, the other would spray paint over the cameras in a clear path to the vault and Cash and his father would break into it.

The chances for something to go wrong were high. If Cash intentionally bungled the operation, Mitchell's crew would be caught. The police would have a reason to look at the contents of the safe and maybe it would provide the evidence the FBI had been looking for to track down Anderson and the money he'd stolen.

But if Cash let this operation fail, he and his father were facing jail time. His father had avoided prison all his life. Prison terrified him.

A month ago, Cash would have let his father take the fall. Now, he couldn't.

Cash waited for the beep to signal the alarm was disabled, then the man with the can of spray paint broke open the door. He paved the way to the vault. Cash and his father followed, staying around corners until the path was hidden from video surveillance.

Once they reached the basement vault, the trailblazer fled.

Cash was alone with his father. His father opened his bag and removed the tools.

Cash worked beside him, holding tools and assisting like it was old times. Worse times.

It took Cash and his father less than thirty seconds to open the vault's door. To his surprise, the lock wasn't elaborate or complex.

Before relief took hold, a wave of fear hit him. There was a secondary alarm inside the vault, a silent alarm that would call the security guards on duty and the police. A red light above the door double flashed. They'd triggered it.

"There's a second alarm," Cash said.

"Get to the safe," Mitchell said over their comm device. "You have time before security responds."

His father was already working on opening the safe. Cash assisted his father, remaining quiet, knowing his father needed to listen, but also wondering if being caught was worth this.

He thought of the people who had lost their money to Anderson. Bowing out now would mean that money would disappear with Anderson. Lives had been ruined after Anderson's theft. He couldn't let the man get away with it.

Cash's father swore. "No time," he said under his breath.

Cash laid a hand on his father's shoulder. "I'm here. We'll do this together."

His father gave him a swift nod and started again. Slowly, step by step, they finessed the safe open.

But it was empty.

"The safe is empty," Wyatt said.

Mitchell swore and Cash feared the anger in Mitchell's voice. Would he kill them after this botched job? To come so far and then fail was unacceptable.

Cash reached into the safe and felt around until his fingers brushed a small ridge along the floor. He lifted the fake bottom. Another door.

"There's another lock," Cash said.

By this point, security would be en route to the basement.

"Dad, go. I can do this alone." Cash was already working the second lock.

His father shook his head. "I'm not letting you take the fall for us."

He had taken the fall for a failed Anderson con before. He would do it again. He'd made the choice to come into this basement and he would accept the consequences of that decision.

His father remained with him. It was the first time Cash felt his father had put his son's needs before his own.

Working together, they popped the second lock. This time, they were rewarded with a bundle of papers. Cash shoved the papers in the backpack full of tools and threw it over his shoulders.

They ran, the sounds of footsteps and sirens approaching. They turned a corner to hear shouts about the open vault. A second slower and they would have been seen.

He and his father raced out of the building to Mitchell's waiting vehicle.

The moment they pulled away from the building, Mitchell reached for the backpack at the same time Cash took the papers from the bag and tried to hand them to Mitchell. Their fingers collided, which sent the stolen paperwork across the floor of the van.

"Watch what you're doing!" Mitchell said, scooping up the papers.

As he helped Mitchell gather them, Cash scanned them, looking for a reason that Anderson wanted these documents.

Then he found it. The documents were a handwritten list of employees' names with number amounts next to their names, people who had likely been paid off to assist in the fraud.

Whose handwriting was it? Who knew about the

payoffs? Were they being kept on the premises to black-mail those involved into silence? Why did Anderson want the papers?

Chapter 10

"Based on your actions, you must love your cot in prison more than Lucia's bed," Benjamin said.

Cash didn't hide the shock in his eyes. It was an outrageously inappropriate statement. He expected pushback from the choices he'd made at Holmes and White tonight, but he did not expect Benjamin to drag Lucia into this.

"I did what I thought was best for the investigation," Cash said.

"That wasn't your call to make," Benjamin said, his anger evident.

"He removed my tracker. I didn't have you for backup. I made the best choice I could," Cash said.

Benjamin rubbed his temples. "Tell me again what you saw in that safe and on the papers."

He was watching Cash closely, no doubt searching for hints of a lie. Cash wouldn't tell Benjamin that his father had been involved in the theft. He couldn't. He had plenty of anger for his father, but selling him out to the FBI wouldn't make him feel better. Besides, the FBI wanted to find Anderson, not his dad.

Cash repeated his story, keeping the details vague. He'd once heard someone say that the trick to a convincing lie was details. Cash thought the trick to a convincing lie was consistency. He would repeat his story exactly, until he was almost one with the lie and the lie was embedded in his head as truth.

Benjamin rubbed his chin. "What will we do about you robbing Holmes and White? Nothing you saw is admissible in court."

Cash was aware. "I know. It's a tough situation."

Benjamin's eyes narrowed. "Made tougher by the fact that you committed a crime after we warned you that you had to stay within the law at all times. All times. Not only when it suited you."

"It was a judgment call. If I had bailed, I wouldn't be helping the investigation."

"Or yourself."

Cash nodded once. He was looking out for himself. No one else was, so why not?

"You could go back to jail for this."

The threat was held over his head constantly. "I'm aware." He didn't like being reminded of it as if it could slip his mind.

"We thought Holmes and White had insiders."

"Now we've confirmed it," Cash said.

"Most of their staff is gone. Tracking them down one by one to question them is manpower we don't have," Benjamin said.

"I could mention a few names I saw with higher numbers next to them to give you a place to start. You've already questioned employees, what's a few more?" Cash said.

Benjamin appeared interested. "A few names? Tell me."

Cash was surprised that Benjamin was even considering the idea. "Kinsley Adams was on the list. So was Leonard Young." He named a few others he wasn't familiar with.

Benjamin rubbed his chin. "Young is involved."

"He was on the list."

"Someone at Holmes and White knows about that list," Benjamin said. He let out a grunt of frustration. "If we had gotten the document in a legal way, then we could have used it to put pressure on those people involved. Someone knows where Anderson is keeping his money. But who?"

"Perhaps Lucia and I can have another look at the list while we're undercover. If we steal one of the pages, you can run a handwriting analysis," Cash said.

As if knowing he had spoken her name, Lucia opened the door to Benjamin's office. "Cash, are you all right?"

She looked beautiful with her hair loose around her shoulders. Her jacket was unbuttoned, revealing a soft, clingy shirt beneath. Cash's mouth felt dry and he wished that he was alone with Lucia. His adrenaline was pumping just as it had been after the theft of the Copley that had led to fantastic sex.

He didn't miss the concern in her voice and neither did Benjamin. Cash watched Benjamin's face and he appeared angry at Lucia. It was a brief flash that lasted only a moment. Was Benjamin jealous of Lucia's concern for Cash? Angry that Cash had broken the rules and Lucia was more concerned about him than the law?

"We're wrapping up here. Cash, I'll email you my report. Please add your notes to the file by nine tomorrow. We'll have a status meeting in the morning to fill in the rest of the team."

Benjamin left the room, leaving Cash and Lucia alone.

Lucia watched Benjamin's retreating back. The tightness of Benjamin's shoulders and the crispness in his stride told Cash this incident wasn't over. Benjamin might not be sure what to do, but he wouldn't let Cash get away with breaking the law.

"What happened? Are you okay?"

Cash weighed how much to tell Lucia. He didn't want to drag her into the middle of his decisions. "The case isn't going as planned."

"When does it ever?" Lucia touched his sleeve and he felt the touch on another level.

Somehow, with the distance between them in every area of their lives, they found common ground when they were alone.

"In my experience, life is as likely to kick me in the teeth as it is to give me something wonderful. You'll read the details in the report tomorrow."

Lucia motioned to him to follow her. They were alone in their office building. Without the sun coming in through the window and the office chatter and the lights from computer monitors, it was still and dark. The quiet was nice and Cash was glad to have these moments with Lucia. They wouldn't have many more.

"We need to go back undercover and look for something."

Lucia nodded. "Are we taking another trip to the FBI's closet?" She screwed up her face.

"I know you hate those clothes, but you look good."

"I understand. Lots of leg. Leave nothing to the imagination."

Cash shook his head. "You leave many things to my imagination. You make me think about the ways I want to make love with you. You make me think about finding some way to pull you away from this job, to get you alone and do unspeakably pleasurable things to you."

Confusion marred her expression. "I thought you were mad at me. For what happened with my family."

He'd been hurt. But his life was filled with hurt. When she was with him it was easier for him to forgive than carry the anger. She could be taken from him at any time: if he was thrown in prison, if the case was solved, if she changed departments, if Cash found some way to get closer to Adrian.

"I am not angry."

She shot him a sideways look. "Something else?"

"Nothing else. I don't want anything but to spend the night with you." He slipped his arm around her waist and anchored her to him. "I would ask you to come home with me, but I don't want you anywhere near the Hideaway."

"My place?" she asked.

Her breath was coming faster, her chest rising and falling. Her place. Yes.

He scooped her into his arms and carried her to the elevator. She swatted at his chest. "Someone will see us."

"Do you care? Your reaction to me in Benjamin's office was almost as overt as this."

She wiggled out of his grasp once they were in the elevator. "I promise to let you hold me however you'd like when we're alone. But here, we're colleagues. In my place, we can be anything and do anything."

"Anything?" he asked, waggling his eyebrows at her.

The corners of her mouth lifted playfully. "Sure, I trust you."

The playful tone of their conversation turned on a dime. *Trust.* That word that was so hard for both of them to give to others. "If that's the case, I will be careful with your trust."

When they arrived at her car, Lucia threw him the keys. "You drive."

She climbed in the passenger seat and the moment they pulled away from the building, she stretched her seat belt to be close to him. She kissed his earlobe and his neck.

"Do you want your car to survive the drive home?" he asked. "If you keep doing that, I'll hit something."

She laughed and continued her assault on his senses. Everything in him burned for her. And then she slid her hand to the inside of his thigh and his brain could only focus on one thing: Lucia.

"I can see you're enjoying this."

"If we're pulled over because I'm driving erratically, what will we tell the police?"

"You're driving fine. You have spectacular control."

In this space, he felt out of control. He wanted to pull the car to the side of the road and have sex with her, fast and hot and hard. He stopped himself because her words of trust lingered in his mind. Trust was a big deal to him. Growing up with a father who was a liar, a father who still was a liar, and learning that lying was part of life had warped Cash's perception of a relationship. It was his wife who had taught him honesty, and now with Lucia he wanted to prove he was that honest,

better man. Not the man his father had raised to trick
and manipulate people and take what he wanted without regard to others.

When they arrived at her condo, they were barely inside the door before they were throwing their clothes to
the floor. He heard fabric tearing and didn't care. What
did a few seams and buttons matter?

Lucia was all he had left in his life that was good and
honest and pure. He needed her. And he needed to be
inside her. Though she had initiated this in the car, he
took control. He carried her to her bedroom and both
naked, they fell onto the bed.

Cash could have worshipped her body all night. He
took a moment to drink in the sight of her. She was
beautiful and strong. Having her in his life had been
the greatest stroke of luck he'd had in years.

"Change your mind?" she asked, as she lifted her
knees and spread her thighs in invitation.

"How could I change my mind?" He covered her
body with his and pushed inside her.

When he filled her completely they both groaned.
As he moved, she lifted her hips hard into his. He loved
that she wasn't passive as they made love.

She came apart in his arms and he crashed with her.
In the languor of the aftermath of their lovemaking, he
felt truly relaxed and happy.

She threaded her fingers through his. "I trust you,
Cash. I trust you at work, I trust you in the bedroom
and I trust you as the man in my life."

Benjamin handed Cash the document they'd doctored
to give to Mitchell about Anderson. He threw Cash's
GPS tracker on top of it.

The rest of the team watched the exchange. No one spoke.

"You forgot to put this on," Benjamin said. "Luckily, I knew where you were last night." He looked directly at Lucia who held his gaze without flinching. She refused to let her face turn red or hide under her desk.

If the team wanted to gossip about her and Cash, fine. She wouldn't apologize for having a relationship.

Cash's phone rang. "It's Mitchell."

"Answer it," Benjamin said.

Cash answered the phone. Lucia leaned in to listen to the exchange.

"Hey," Cash said.

"I need to speak with you immediately."

"I'm at work," Cash said.

Something in Mitchell's voice shook Lucia. He sounded…angry? He should be happy. Cash and the crew Mitchell had assembled had successfully broken into the safe at Holmes and White and had stolen important documents. They'd met their objective.

"Tell your boss you don't feel well. This is important. And bring Lucy."

That set Lucia's heart racing. Why would Mitchell need to speak with her? She was nothing to their operation. Mitchell had insisted that Lucia stay away during the previous night.

"I'll call her," Cash said.

"Do it. Move fast," Mitchell said and disconnected.

Cash set the phone on the table in front of him.

"It could be a trap," Lucia said. "Maybe he figured out the painting isn't real. Or your cover's blown."

"It's possible," Cash said.

"We can't meet with Mitchell until we know what

he wants," Lucia said. "We don't have time to plan this and set up proper backup."

"I'll tell him you were busy and couldn't come," Cash said.

Benjamin looked between the two of them. "Lucia stays with us. Cash, you go."

Lucia stood, slamming her hands on top of the table. "No. You can't send Cash in. If he were an FBI agent, would you tell him to go into an uncertain situation without backup and unarmed?"

"We'll be listening. Cash can take in a service weapon if he chooses."

Lucia could not believe the words coming from Benjamin's mouth. How could he consider letting Cash go without her? He wasn't trained. "I'm going with him. I'll be armed."

"We've got a serious problem," Mitchell said. He stood from behind the desk and cracked his knuckles. "I need to know how you know her and what you were doing with her," Mitchell said. He threw a picture of Audrey onto Cash's lap.

Cash was careful to hide any reaction. "Are you having me followed?" Did he know Lucia was an FBI agent?

"I've been watching you. You went into her condo building last night and stayed all night. What were you doing?"

Lucia turned to look at him, her eyes wide. "You weren't working last night? You told me you were working."

Lucia's hand inched to the gun at her thigh. She'd have it out and trained on Mitchell in seconds.

Cash wasn't sure if it was too late to salvage this operation, but he'd try. "Luc, I was working."

Mitchell folded his arms over his chest and smirked as if enjoying what he was seeing.

"With her?" Lucia asked, gesturing to the picture of Audrey.

If Mitchell was tracking Cash's movements, he knew Cash was in Audrey and Lucia's condo building. He had made the wrong assumption about who Cash was visiting. Lucia's condo could be in her father's name and perhaps he'd excluded the other residents based on who they were.

"She's a mark. A wealthy mark," Cash said. Would Mitchell buy that he was conning Audrey? Did Lucia catch his game?

"I thought you said you were done with all that," Lucia said. "You're working for him now." She gestured at Mitchell.

"It was an easy score," Cash said.

Lucia narrowed her eyes. "I've seen her before. She looks really familiar." She feigned surprise and looked between Mitchell and Cash. "I saw this woman at the casino. Who is she? Did you invite her when you knew I'd be with you?"

"I did not invite her anywhere. Her name is Audrey," Cash said slowly. "She's a wealthy heiress."

Lucia glared at him and let out an angry growl. "You said you'd changed."

"I have changed," Cash said.

Mitchell took the picture from Cash.

"Did you sleep with her?" Lucia asked.

"No!" Cash said. Even if Mitchell didn't believe him, he had to react the way a lying boyfriend would.

"I have another surprise for you two. I'm not a trusting man. Neither is Anderson. He's been worried about his godson."

Cash inwardly flinched, but said nothing. Anderson was his godfather, a fact that existed in the files of a church, but had no other meaning.

Mitchell handed Cash another folder. He opened it. It was a file on Lucia. Mitchell had blown a hole in her false identity. Lucy Harris didn't have an employment history or tax records. Cash didn't read anything in the file about her being an FBI agent. How much did Mitchell know and how much more could he find out? It might be too soon to hit the panic button, but Cash was flailing.

He quickly decided on a plan and hoped Lucia caught onto it. "So what? Her name isn't really Lucy Harris. I knew that."

"You did?" Mitchell asked.

Cash guessed he'd been expecting a different reaction from Cash. Panic or fear, but Cash wouldn't lose it. He'd given up the life of conning people, but his ability to control his emotions and his reactions were what had made him a good liar. It was a rough truth to admit, but a useful skill.

Cash reached for Lucia's hand. "I knew who she was when I met her. She knew who I was. What's your point?"

"I need to know the people I'm dealing with," Mitchell said.

Lucia pulled her hand away from Cash. "You slept with another woman."

Cash gave her points for fixating on the part of the story that would upset her most if they were a couple.

"I did not sleep with Audrey. I'm trying to build a better life for us. I love you. I want our future to be happy. I want people to see us as more than an ex-con and an ex-addict."

"Tell me what's going on," Mitchell said. "I don't like being the last to know."

"I need to tell him," Cash said.

Lucia appeared miserable. "It's not part of my life that I'm proud of." She was speaking in a whisper.

Cash patted her hand. "We have to tell him, Luc." He faced Mitchell, leaving his hand covering Lucia's. "Lucy was an addict. She's five years clean, but her past has a way of following her. She uses a pseudonym so she can have a fresh start and a fair chance."

Mitchell didn't look as if he believed their cover story. Even if he did, the threads of uncertainty were loose. The more he looked into Cash and Lucia, the more likely he'd stumble onto something that would give them away.

"I don't like that you lied about who you were," Mitchell said.

Lucia narrowed her gaze at Mitchell enough to come across as defensive, but not aggressive. "You've never needed a fresh start? You've never made a mistake that you've had to pay for all your life? I was too young and too rich and I spent too much time doing nothing. I got into trouble and in over my head. Now, I'm clean. I'm sober. I like it. I won't apologize for being a better person and trying to do better with my life."

Mitchell held up his hands. "I'll pass this along to Anderson. We'll be watching you both."

And monitoring him. Cash's immediate concern was

for Lucia, but now he was worried about Audrey, too. She'd need to be warned to stay away from the casino.

As Lucia and Cash were leaving Mitchell's office, they caught a glimpse of Kinsley Adams. She was leaning against one of the blackjack tables. She had a drink in one hand and was laughing at something being said to her.

Cash was caught for a moment, wondering about her and Mitchell. Was she happy? Did it matter?

Then the sound of gunfire peppered the air.

Cash grabbed Lucia and pulled her back into the hallway leading to Mitchell's office.

He peered around the corner and scanned for the source of the gunshots. It couldn't be a police or FBI raid. Their FBI team was outside, but they wouldn't storm inside the building and start shooting without warning with two of their own inside.

It took Cash a moment to process the scene.

Preston Hammer was holding a gun and waving it in the air. The man's body language was telling a violent and dangerous story. He was stressed out to a breaking point, he was possibly high and he was on the edge of snapping. Threatening the people in the casino was a suicide mission. If it wasn't for the off-hours appearance, Cash guessed one of Anderson's men would have gunned Hammer down where he stood.

Hammer leveled his gun at Kinsley and strode toward her. Cash weighed his options. If he stepped out from the hallway and Hammer saw him, it would blow his cover. Mitchell and Anderson knew Cash was working for the FBI, but they didn't know he was working the Holmes and White case. If they did, it wouldn't take them long to realize they had been right and Cash had inserted himself into their organization to dig for information about the stolen money.

Could Cash con Hammer into believing he was on his side? Hammer was swearing at Kinsley and when he moved close enough, he'd kill her. He might even turn the gun on himself.

Cash started into the casino and Lucia grabbed his arm. "I've already texted Benjamin. Wait here for help to arrive."

They couldn't wait. Hammer was on a hair trigger. If no one intervened, Kinsley's life was at stake.

"Trust me." He kissed Lucia's cheek and stepped away from her.

"Hey, man," Cash called. As long as he wasn't too friendly with Hammer, he could play off the interaction as if he was a stranger interceding. "I'm Cash Stone. Tell me what's going on here."

Cash took a drink from a slack-jawed waitress staring at Hammer.

Hammer turned, swinging the gun in Cash's direction and Cash prayed Hammer's trigger finger was steady and not poised to twitch at the slightest disturbance.

He'd get Hammer talking and do what he could to diffuse Hammer's intent.

Cash didn't want anyone to die today and that went double for him and Lucia.

Hammer narrowed his eyes in confusion. He was trying to place Cash. Cash knew the moment he did because annoyance screwed up his features. "What do you want?"

"I'm wondering if we can take a break for a second."

He gestured to the gun. "Maybe you forgot where you were, but believe me, that will get us killed."

It was too soon to make a play for the gun. Cash was close, but not close enough. He intentionally slurred his words and tried to appear as calm and nonthreatening as possible.

"This doesn't involve you," Hammer said. He looked around nervously. "Did you call the police?"

Cash waved his hand dismissively, grateful Hammer had said police and not FBI. "The last people I'd want to see are the police. I don't have a good explanation for what this is or why I'm here." He laughed softly and lowered his voice. "And as a convicted felon, my word is the last one they'd believe."

Hammer twisted his lips in thought, perhaps trying to remember what Cash had said about himself the first time they'd met. Hammer had been drunk then and was on something now. Cash was using his confusion to lead the conversation where he wanted it to go, to protect Hammer's life and maintain his and Lucia's cover. "I have something to finish here," Hammer said, pivoting to where Kinsley had been standing.

When Hammer realized she was gone, he let out a howl of frustration and a litany of curses. "I need to talk to her. She left me. She took everything from me and then she wouldn't even return my calls."

Cash didn't have to feign sympathy. The wrong woman could turn a man's world upside down, shake it and slam it back down shattered and broken. "I know, man. I've been there."

Hammer lowered his gun. "You?"

"Every man has. I could tell you how I landed in prison, and you'd hear all about how a woman played a vital role in getting me there." A lie. Britney had had nothing to do with the scam he'd run to get the money for Adrian's treatments. But Cash needed Hammer to see him as a friend and someone who could sympathize with him.

"This is the wrong way to do this," Cash said. "There are cameras here. There are people who would kill us, not because they care about protecting some woman, but because this place is run by businessmen serious about making a profit and they won't let anyone stand in the way."

Hammer scratched his head. "I know."

His arm lowered a few inches.

"Let's grab a drink. Not here. Somewhere we can talk in private," Cash said.

For a moment, he thought he had Hammer. He thought the man had given up on this murder-suicide mission. Then Hammer's face switched from relaxed to angry. He lifted the gun. "This ends now. I can't do this for another day. I can't wake up and know I've lost everything. Everything."

"It's not everything that's lost. You have family. Friends." Cash couldn't show too much familiarity or Mitchell would want an explanation for how Cash knew Preston Hammer.

Hammer looked around. "I'm dead. I came here with a gun and I knew I wouldn't make it out alive."

Cash heard the conviction in his voice. The next few seconds were critical. He needed to stop Hammer from making a huge mistake. People around them were backing away but Hammer didn't seem to see anything except the small space around him. His world was closing in and Cash knew he'd end it. "I've been where you are. I'll walk you out of here. No one will shoot us."

"Hammer, we told you to stay away." Cash heard Mitchell's voice behind him.

Cash looked over his shoulder at Mitchell who was pointing a gun at Hammer. Now two guns were in play and Cash was standing between them. He took a step out of the line of fire.

"He and I are heading out," Cash said.

Both Hammer and Mitchell answered in the negative.

"He stole her from me," Hammer said, glaring at Mitchell with rage in his eyes.

"Stole? I didn't steal her. She was working with you because I asked her to. Because we needed someone inside to keep you distracted. Turns out, it was easier than we expected," Mitchell said.

Cash inwardly cringed at the condescension in his voice. Belittling Hammer was a mistake and would add to his fury.

"I figured out what Anderson was doing," Hammer said, sounding defensive.

Mitchell nodded. "You did and you agreed to shut your mouth for the right payday."

"Which I never got!" Hammer screamed.

"You should have walked away and forgotten about the money and about Grace," Mitchell said. He fired at Hammer. His aim was off, but in the split second it took for Mitchell to realize that, Hammer returned the shot.

Hammer might have been a man with a death wish, but he was a good shot. Or a lucky one.

Mitchell stumbled back and lifted his gun again. Cash dove to the ground. Mitchell shot wildly in Hammer's direction.

Hammer finally fell to the ground and the shooting stopped. Lucia appeared, pressing her hand over Mitchell's chest. She was shouting something, but Cash couldn't hear her over the screaming around him.

Cash wasn't hit. At least he didn't think so. Hammer was on the ground bleeding from a head wound.

Horror washed over him. He'd failed to stop either of them from shooting. He'd needed the right moment to redirect the situation and it hadn't come.

Cash checked Hammer for a pulse and couldn't find one. He fumbled in his pockets for his phone. Forget the operation. The money Anderson had stolen was nothing compared to someone's life.

Before he could dial any numbers, paramedics and the police burst through the doors.

"We need to run," Lucia said into Cash's ear, pulling him away from the scene.

"What?" he turned to her.

He couldn't take his eyes off Hammer and Mitchell. They were both unmoving on stretchers and being loaded into an ambulance.

"The police will question people. We won't be able to explain to Anderson why we weren't arrested. We have to flee."

Cash closed his eyes. "Isn't this over?" The mission had to be over. How could they keep going? Someone had died. He wasn't naive. He knew that violence and death were part of Anderson's life, but Cash had thought he could somehow avoid it. That he could prevent anyone from being hurt or killed.

Lucia shook her head. "Of course not. Do you want it to be over?"

Cash had been involved with criminals from the time he was a teenager. He'd been involved with them his entire life, but it had taken him that long to understand that the lives his father's associates led were not on the up-and-up. His friends' parents had had jobs where they went to an office or a store and clocked in for the day. Not his father.

Cash hadn't saved Hammer. He hadn't saved Mitchell. He had intervened and gotten in over his head, and now two people were dead.

He let Lucia lead him away because he didn't have the strength to stop her. They got into her car and drove for several minutes before either of them spoke.

"Can you turn here?" Cash asked, pointing to the next right turn.

Lucia did as he asked. She didn't question him.

"You did everything you could," Lucia said.

"It wasn't enough." It was starting to feel as though it never was. When it came time to make critical life decisions, he almost always chose wrong.

"Cash, I'm sorry," Lucia said, slipping her hand into his.

He pointed to another road and she turned, following his directions.

"Can you let me out here?" he asked.

Lucia glanced at him. "The last time I let you out of the car, it exploded."

There was nothing humorous in her tone, but Cash understood the warning. They were being watched and followed. Whether it was the FBI or Anderson's crew or someone who was targeting Lucia, they were not safe.

He hadn't been certain of where he was going while they were driving, but now that he was here, he got it.

Death had a way of dragging him to the darkest place in his heart. The graveyard where Britney was buried was acres of headstones, open fields and quiet.

"We're safe here. We'll see someone coming." At least he hoped they would. He'd seen enough death.

"Is this where your wife is buried?" Lucia asked, getting out of the car after him.

"Yes." He knew the exact location, even if every grave marker looked alike.

The metal vase next to her headstone held a bouquet of pink roses. Cash was happy to know someone remembered Britney and her favorite flowers fondly.

Lucia stood a few steps away.

"I didn't plan to come here," he said.

"Do you want some privacy?"

"No." He wanted Lucia with him. He wanted her to understand a part of him that no one else did. He extended his hand to her and she joined him, slipping her arm around his waist and laying her head on his shoulder.

"My marriage to Britney would have ended in divorce. I know that. It makes me feel guilty. She was angry at how I had tried to help our son."

"What does that mean?" Lucia asked.

Cash hadn't wanted Lucia to know about Adrian or how screwed up the entire situation was. Talking about the scam that had landed him in prison made him feel worthless and pathetic. It had been the one thing he knew how to do, and when the stakes were highest, he hadn't been able to do it right. "My son was diagnosed with a rare form of cancer. The doctors we consulted told me it was untreatable. I refused to accept that." He couldn't let his little boy die. He had done everything he could to prevent that from happening. "I found a doctor who was running an experimental procedure on adults with a similar type of cancer. I convinced him to treat Adrian, but I needed money."

Lucia inhaled sharply. "So you scammed the senator's real estate company for the money."

"Yes."

"Your son lived," Lucia said.

"Yes. But Britney refused to trust me after that. I told her I was finished conning people and then I went back into that world."

"What did she want to do instead for Adrian?" Lucia asked.

Cash rubbed the back of his neck. "She thought we could try other treatments even though the doctors said it would have been useless and would have caused Adrian more pain. Radiation. Chemotherapy. Surgeries. I couldn't put Adrian through that, through round after round of hell. He was so small. I stole the money and then Adrian and I lived in Europe for six months while he was treated. Afterward, we returned to the United States. The experimental treatment had ravaged his body. I stayed home with Adrian, helping him grow stronger, but the police were unraveling my scam. Britney and I fought all the time and she filed for separation."

His life had fallen apart quickly after that. He was convicted of fraud and robbery. He'd only been in prison for a week when Britney was killed in a car accident on her way to work after she'd dropped off Adrian at daycare.

"After Britney died, her mother flew in to take custody of Adrian. Helen didn't want Anderson to have guardianship." Helen and Anderson hadn't spoken in years. Britney had been the result of a brief affair they'd had years before and Helen's hate for Anderson fueled Britney's anger for her biological father.

"I'm so sorry, Cash," Lucia said. "After all you did to save your son, you still aren't together."

The lost years were killing him, but he wouldn't give up. "I will find a way to make him part of my life. I can still earn his love. I can still show him that I am a good man."

Lucia put her arms around Cash's waist. "You are a good man. You should have told me this sooner."

"I don't like talking about it. It didn't help at my trial."

"I'm so sorry, Cash."

For a moment he felt the impulse to push her away. He didn't want anyone feeling sorry for him. But he met Lucia's gaze and something clicked. Britney was part of his past and Lucia was his bridge to the future. A future that didn't include scams or lying or fraud.

But could that future include both Lucia and Adrian?

Lucia's stress level was through the roof.

Benjamin was smoothing things over with the police. Having an FBI special agent and a consultant undercover was enough to keep the police from sending out an APB for them. He'd also sent a team of agents to take Audrey somewhere safer. Mitchell had been too interested in Cash's relationship with her and they didn't trust that someone in Anderson's organization wouldn't come looking for her to confirm Cash's story.

After leaving the graveyard, Lucia witnessed a change in Cash. Maybe it was the shock of seeing two men killed or perhaps he'd gotten some closure unburdening his soul to her, but Cash seemed freer, which was a strange thing to think about a man in his position.

Lucia had to hold herself back from mounting a full-scale campaign to help Cash find justice. He had broken the law. He'd had a trial. He was serving his time. It still didn't seem right that he wasn't with his son. He had done the wrong thing for the right reasons.

When they'd returned to her condo, she'd convinced Cash to lie down with her for a few minutes and he'd fallen asleep. Though whirling thoughts had kept her awake longer, the heat of his body and the comfort in his embrace had lured her to sleep, as well.

Lucia's eyes popped open when a creak interrupted her sleep. Was someone on her balcony? Lurking in the hallway? Attempting to break in? Or had she dreamed the noise?

Lucia rose from the bed and her leg muscles tightened and twitched. Her gun in hand, she left the lights off to keep the element of surprise. Checking her condo, she found each room empty. She peered out the two sets of French doors that opened to the balcony. The lights atop the cement pillars surrounding the balcony didn't leave many shadows. Watching for several minutes, she felt content no one was outside. She checked the hallway and then returned her gun to its place inside her bedside table.

Cash's phone rang and Lucia reached for it, wanting to silence it before it woke him. If their team needed him, it could wait a few minutes. He'd been through a lot that day.

It was a blocked number. Wondering if it could be

Adrian, Lucia hesitated and then decided to answer. "Hello?"

"Who's this?" A male voice.

Lucia was momentarily taken aback by the rude question. Then she realized he could be someone from Anderson's group. "It's Lucy. Who's this?"

"Cash around?"

No answer to her question. She couldn't be sure, but Lucia had a strong sensation she was speaking to Clifton Anderson.

Chapter 11

Cash took the phone from Lucia, clearing his head and focusing. Images of Britney and Adrian and Mitchell and Hammer and Lucia spun through his mind.

"This is Cash," he said.

"Cash, my long-lost son-in-law," Anderson said. "I saw you at Britney's grave today."

Anderson had been at the graveyard. It confirmed the FBI's hope that Anderson was still in the United States. "It was a bad day." He hadn't spoken to Anderson in years. His father-in-law had helped with Britney's funeral plans. Cash had allowed it, knowing that despite Britney's feelings toward her father he'd needed closure, too. By then, Cash had been incarcerated and could not attend the funeral.

"You brought your girlfriend," Anderson said.

"Yes." If Anderson had seen him, there was no point

in denying it. "I tried to stop Hammer." He wanted to explain to Anderson, who undoubtedly knew about the shooting inside the casino, to make him understand that what had happened to Mitchell wasn't his fault.

"I know that. I've reviewed the security footage," Anderson said.

"What can I do to help you?" Cash asked.

"Plenty. But I want to ask you a few things. Are you in a place where you can talk?" Anderson said.

"I'm not at work. I can talk." He and Lucia had been more careful to be sure no one was following them.

"I was surprised that you came to see me," Anderson said.

Cash heard the unasked question. Why? Why had he returned to Anderson after being in jail? Why return to the life that had cost him his marriage, time with his son and his freedom? "I need the money."

"Why not finish your time with the FBI and then work something that gives you benefits and a regular paycheck?"

Was this a trick? Was he trying to convince him to walk away? Their relationship was complex. They'd been close while Cash was growing up. After a chance meeting with Britney at her grandfather's funeral, Cash had fallen for her instantly. Britney had been eleven years older, and wiser, and Cash had been looking for something that had been missing in his life. The strength of his feelings for Britney and her anger for her father had created a wedge in Cash's relationship with Anderson.

"Life is too short to live paycheck to paycheck." Or to live in a dump that's better suited for rats. Or to repeat mistakes.

Anderson made a sound of agreement. "Why don't we meet for a drink?"

In person? Anderson was willing to meet Cash? Should Cash pretend to know that Anderson was staying underground? "Are you sure it's safe?" He didn't want to appear too eager.

"I have a few places left that are safe. You'll need to black out your tracker. Do you have the device?"

"Of course," Cash said.

"Bring your new woman. I want to meet her." Anderson gave him an address and told him to come within the hour.

Lucia was shaking her head as Cash hung up the phone. "Something's off," she said.

"Like?"

"Why would someone in hiding invite you to meet him and tell you to bring me?"

"He's my father-in-law. He's my son's grandfather."

Lucia's lips slightly parted. "That means nothing."

"We stole a priceless work of art for him."

"Unless he's figured out the Copley is a fake."

"I tried to stop Hammer from shooting Mitchell. He saw it on the casino's video surveillance," Cash said.

"Is that enough to bring you into his circle of trust especially when he suspected you were working against him for the FBI?"

"I was never out of the circle of trust, as you call it. I was in prison. I screwed up by getting caught. I wasn't disloyal to Anderson." At least, not that Anderson knew about.

Lucia rubbed her temples. "I don't like this. My gut tells me something is not right. We'll go. But we're bringing backup."

"He'll know it."

Lucia threw up her hands. "Then what's the play? Show up and walk into his circus and hope he's not conning you?"

"He's not conning me."

"Would you know it if he was?"

"One con man to another, yes, I'd sense it."

"We're talking about Clifton Anderson. One of the most skilled liars of this century."

"I'm a good liar." She had pointed it out to him many times before.

Lucia balled her fists at her sides. She looked hot when she was angry. "I hate to break this to you, Cash, but you're one of the good guys now and that means you're not as good a liar as you think. Besides, you're off your game. You saw a man gunned down. I know what that can do to someone. Even hardened agents get shaken when someone dies in the field. It's difficult."

He wasn't sure whether to be hurt that she didn't think he knew the difference or pleased she considered him a good guy. "That's quite the assessment from a woman who wanted me back in jail."

"I don't want you in jail," she said softly. "When you ran into the casino to speak to Hammer, I almost lost it. I realized something important in that moment."

He said nothing.

"You. You're important to me."

He couldn't have expressed what that meant to him. Her genuine caring touched him deeply, but fresh wounds reminded him to be cautious. "Important to you or to the case?"

"To me. This case isn't anywhere near as important as you are."

Proving herself to the FBI had seemed to drive Lucia, and now she was telling him he ranked above that. He was humbled by her words. "If I don't solve this case, I'll be put in jail."

"Right. That," Lucia said. She bit her lip. Lucia was holding something back.

"Tell me," he said. "You know something I don't."

Lucia sighed. "I didn't want this to come from me. I didn't want your hopes up too high but I called a friend I went through training with at Quantico. He works in a field office in Washington state. I explained the situation and he said if I could get Benjamin on board, he'd take you under his wing for the remainder of your time with the FBI."

Cash felt dizzy for a moment. It was the outcome he'd been hoping for and while he hadn't found a way to con Lucia into it, she'd done it just the same. He hadn't had to lie to her and it made the victory that much sweeter. He swallowed the lump of emotion in his throat.

Winning Adrian over would be so much easier if they were closer. Cash could drive to see him. He could build a better life. Baby steps, but baby steps were miles apart from his current gridlock situation. "Thank you, Lucia. Thank you for doing this. Why? Why would you do that for me?"

Lucia's eyes watered and she cleared her throat. "I think it's obvious. We don't need to say the words."

She loved him. He knew it. In that instant, the impact of knowing she loved him blew him away. He couldn't put his arms around the emotion she evoked. "Lucia, I can't thank you enough—"

She waved her hand and moved away from him. "It's no guarantee. I wanted you to have a chance at something real with your son. But it's moot if we don't catch Anderson. Benjamin doesn't grant boons easily. He'll want his man and his glory. He's been angling for a promotion, and capturing Anderson would be a sweet win to put on his résumé."

"If you think it's too dangerous, let me go alone to meet Anderson."

She snorted. "Please. We're partners. We have been from the start. Let's finish this together."

"An abandoned private airstrip?" Lucia asked. "I don't like this. He's planning to run." The accounts the FBI were monitoring hadn't be accessed recently. What was Anderson planning? Cash was not himself. The shooting had shaken him. If it wasn't for that, he'd see this for what it was: a setup.

Except Lucia had prepared for it. She had her team standing by. She wanted Anderson to come at her. She'd bring him in and prove she was a good agent and had earned her place on Benjamin's team. The past wouldn't haunt her. Questions about her time with the violent-crime division would disappear. Cash would be transferred closer to his son. Though she would lose him, she would give him happiness.

Lucia got out of the car and stayed close to Cash.

Anderson met them on the tarmac. "Greetings, Cash. You look well."

Lucia's heart fell when she saw Wyatt behind Anderson. How was Cash's father tied up in this? Would Anderson use him to manipulate Cash?

"Please, come with me. We have much work to be done," Anderson said.

What work? Lucia stayed close. Benjamin and the

rest of the team were monitoring the situation, but they'd needed to stay out of sight. Anderson was leading them off the airstrip toward a small forest where a black van was parked. Behind the van was a small tent.

Was some of the money in that van? In the tent? Lucia stayed alert and braced herself for whatever was to follow.

"First, let me welcome you both. To my godson, thank God you got out of that place," Anderson said. "It's been fortuitous for me that you've come back to the team. When Hammer killed Mitchell, I lost my money man."

His money man and Mitchell's ability to move money, too, Lucia guessed.

"That's where you can help me," Anderson said.

"Tell me what you need," Cash said.

"I need you to move some money from some accounts into others," Anderson said.

He made it sound simple. By asking Cash to break the law, he would be held responsible as an accomplice. Anderson had a knack for getting the people around him as dirty as possible.

"I can do that," Cash said. "For a fee."

"I can offer you something we both want in exchange," Anderson said.

Cash lifted his chin. "You know what I want. Money. A better life."

"What about a life with your son?" Anderson asked. "I've missed having my grandson in my life."

Cash didn't move. "He's living with Helen and he's best staying with her. I send money when I can."

Anderson laughed. "I don't believe that. I've known you since you were a little boy. You can pretend you don't want Adrian with you, but I see through that lie. I have an offer you'll love. You move the money for me and we flee with Adrian."

A muscle worked in Cash's jaw. He didn't want Anderson near Adrian. "No."

"No? You went to jail trying to save your son. Now you don't want anything to do with him?" Anderson asked.

"I'm not good for him. A life on the run, a life of lying isn't good for him," Cash said.

Cash's father flinched. Perhaps he knew the truth behind Cash's words.

"He should be with you. With me. Living a life that he could only dream about before now. Everything he could ever want will be his," Anderson said.

"I never thought about that before. What do you think, Lucy? A fresh start? A new life?"

Anderson *tsked*. "You misunderstand me. It would be the four of us, Adrian, his dad and his grandfathers. No room for girlfriends."

Anderson withdrew his gun and Lucia reached for hers at the same time, removing it from the thigh harness under her skirt and pointing it at Anderson's heart.

"I hope that clarifies any doubts you had," Anderson said over his shoulder to Wyatt.

Cash looked between Lucia and Anderson. "What doubts? What's going on? Lucy always carries a gun."

Anderson looked at Cash and frowned. "She carries a gun because she's an FBI agent."

Shock registered on Cash's face. Maybe she had underestimated how good a liar he was. "She isn't," he said. "She's like me. I told Mitchell she is a recovering addict. She's built a new life for herself, a life she deserves." If he was striving for blindsided and in denial, he was hitting it right.

"Son, I'm sorry. When Anderson came to me about her, I didn't believe it either," Wyatt said.

"There has to be a mistake," Cash said.

"Tell her, Lucy," Anderson said.

Boots climbed out of the van and trained his gun on Lucia.

Lucia had to stay calm. She and Cash were in this together. They'd find a way out.

"Tell him," Anderson said, shooting at her. The shot caught her in the arm and it burned like flames, but Lucia didn't return fire. If she used her weapon, she'd need to kill Anderson and Boots. If she killed Anderson, the FBI might not recover the money he'd stolen.

Her arm was killing her, but she held steady. "My name is Lucia Huntington and I'm with the FBI. Put your weapon on the ground and put your hands in the air." Her cover was blown. Was her team hearing this and moving in?

Cash's reaction could have been an award-winning performance. Anger darkened his face and rage distorted his features. Anderson and Wyatt were watching him.

He called her a word she hadn't heard him speak before. Then a demand. "Give me your gun," he said to Lucia.

He glanced at the wound on her arm, and only a trace of worry crossed his face.

"You're going to kill me with my gun?" Lucia asked. Where was her backup?

Cash appeared unsure. "I'm not sure what I'll do."

"Cash, stay calm. I'll clean this up. I need your help

with something. Boots will take care of her and we'll go," Anderson said.

"No," Cash said, rage hot in his voice. "I take care of my messes. I'll clean this up." He tore the gun from Lucia's hand. She let him take it, trusting he had a plan.

"What are you planning to do?" Lucia asked. "Backup will be on their way."

"Sorry, Special Agent, but you're sadly mistaken. I'm blocking every network signal in a half-mile radius except the one I need to move my money," Anderson said.

Cash narrowed his eyes. "Give me thirty minutes with her. I won't let another woman screw up my life and I won't let someone else take the fall for my mistakes."

Anderson gestured to Boots and Cash's father. "Go with him. Clean it up. Report back here."

"I have a plan," Cash said. Not a good one, but one that would get Lucia away from Anderson. Her arm was bleeding and Cash didn't like the paleness of her face.

If he could move outside Anderson's half-mile radius, his GPS tracker would broadcast his location and he could contact Benjamin and get help.

At the car, Cash opened the back door. "I don't want any blood on the seats. No evidence left behind." A good reason for why he cared about treating her injury. He removed his belt and wrapped it tight around her arm to slow the bleeding. She winced and Cash put his mouth close to hers as he put her in the back of the car as gently as he could. "I'm sorry, Luc, I'll get you out of this."

"Don't worry about the blood. We'll burn the car," Boots said.

Cash glared at him. "Do you realize the FBI can find DNA traces even after it's been burned?" A lie, but it sounded good.

Cash made sure his father rode in the backseat with Lucia. He wasn't sure he trusted him, but he didn't trust Boot for a split second. He was a hired gun and Anderson was promising him more money than Cash could. He didn't want Lucia roughed up and Cash's father didn't do violence. He and his father had that in common.

As they drove, Cash kept looking at Lucia in the rearview mirror and checking his phone for a signal. Lucia's eyes were closed.

He needed her to stay awake. He hit the steering wheel with his fist. If he was a man with a broken heart who'd been lied to, he'd be a little out of his mind. Crazy could work, enough to set his father and Boots off balance and give him space to stash Lucia somewhere safe.

"Lucy, why did you do it? Why? I gave you everything!" Cash shouted.

She didn't answer. Panic gripped him.

"Dad, wake her up," Cash said, unable to hide the terror in his voice. How much blood could someone lose and survive?

His thoughts flashed to Britney. Help had not arrived in time. She'd been pronounced dead at the hospital following her accident.

Not again. He wouldn't lose a woman he loved again.

Love. That word, an emotion that could wreak absolute havoc on him. Love for his son had turned him into a criminal and love for Lucia was turning him into a desperate man. She had to be okay. He shoved away the fear and fog and tried to think of the best play.

Cash drove faster to escape Anderson's network black hole. Finally, his phone signal bars lit up. Cash dialed Benjamin and then slipped the phone into his pocket. He hoped Benjamin could hear everything and send help.

His father slapped Lucia's cheeks. "Wha...?"

She was alive. The sound of her voice was heavenly. "Why did you do it?" he asked her again.

"To catch him," Lucia said. "They said I had to watch you to make sure you were doing your work. When you made contact with Anderson, we decided to use that."

"I love you. I love you and you did this," he said.

"I love you, too," Lucia said.

He knew the words were the truth. Did she know his words were true, as well?

"What's your plan, Cash?" his father asked.

"I told you. To get rid of her. Anderson gave me thirty minutes. I'll use the covered bridge and we'll burn the car at the airstrip," Cash said.

They arrived at a location he used to visit with his father to fish, an abandoned railway bridge. It was eerily beautiful and secluded, plenty of places for the FBI to lie in wait and then rush in to help Lucia.

He couldn't risk driving around looking for a better place. Lucia needed medical attention.

He glanced at his phone. He had an open connection to Benjamin. The FBI had to be sending help. If he wasn't following Cash by his tracker, he could find his cell phone signal. "You remember this place, dad? I used to love thinking about the trains that used to drive through here. That was when I thought I'd be a conductor." Did that help Benjamin track the location?

His father's face softened. "I remember."

He and his father lifted Lucia out of the car. Cash slipped one arm under her shoulders and the other under her knees.

"Give us a minute," he said, telling his father and Boots to stay back.

He carried Lucia inside the covered bridge and set her on the ground. It was dark, with rays of sunlight peeking through places where rust had eaten the metal. "Hang in with me, Lucia. Help is coming."

"Cash, please. He will use you and then kill you." She sounded so tired.

"I have to go back. He'll go after Adrian if I don't stop him. He'll kill Helen."

Lucia groaned. "You have my gun. Kill him. Backup will come."

"I'm counting on it. Lucia, I only have a few seconds. I'll shoot above your head. Slump on the ground and don't move until Benjamin arrives, okay?"

Lucia shook her head. "I can help you."

"You're losing too much blood. Listen to me. We'll get through this because we're partners. I can't lose you. I meant what I said. I love you."

She smiled. "Now you tell me."

Cash heard his father and Boot's voices drifting toward them. Were they coming to investigate?

"I'm the master of timing," he said. He kissed her softly and raised her gun. For the benefit of his father and Boots, he shouted a few curses at her and then, praying the bullets pierced the rusted metal and didn't ricochet anywhere near her, he shot four times. It might be overkill, but he wanted to sell this. He didn't want his father or Boots anywhere near Lucia.

"I love you. Stay strong," he whispered. He left his

phone next to Lucia and took hers. Brushing his hand across her cheek, he ran to meet his father. "Let's go."

"You sure she's dead?" Boots asked, looking around him. "She's with the FBI. She can identify us. You have to be sure she's dead."

"She's dead," Cash said.

"Anderson sent me along to confirm," Boots said.

Panic sliced through him. He couldn't let this man anywhere near Lucia. He would know Cash hadn't shot her. "I don't want to linger at the scene. Someone could have heard the shots."

"I'll check," his father said. "Anderson trusts me."

Cash sent his father a pleading look he wasn't sure he caught. His father was gone fifteen seconds and returned. "Nice work, son. She won't be identifying anyone." He winked at Cash and relief tumbled through him.

His father was on his side. Somehow, for some reason, his father knew Lucia was alive and wasn't selling him out.

"It isn't helping matters that I have a gun on me," Cash said.

Since leaving the covered bridge, Boots had had his gun to Cash's head. They were sealed inside the tent. Easy cleanup of blood spatter after Boots killed him? His father was standing inside the tent watching.

Anderson had a laptop and an internet connection and he wanted Cash to work miracles. Cash was very good at what he did. He was good at cons and he was good at moving money, but he'd grossly exaggerated his skills and confidence in his ability to do what Anderson had asked. Without the right information, honoring Anderson's request was impossible.

Lucia's face flashed to mind. Had Benjamin found her? Was she safe?

As he typed, trying to buy time, Cash went for broke. "Give me the list of accounts. The full list. I can upload it to a temp database and try to simultaneously move as much of the money as I can before flags go up and the transactions are shut down."

Anderson snorted. "Talk about sending up red flags around the world."

Cash turned from the computer. "I know what I'm doing. We'll have at least fifteen seconds before any of those flags warrants a human response and someone stops the money from moving. Do you know how much money I can move in fifteen seconds from across all the accounts you have? Once the transaction starts and I authenticate to the server, we'll have sub-second response time. Even if we move only ten percent of the money you took from Holmes and White, that's a big slice of the pie."

Anderson licked his lips as if hungry. Had Cash sold it? Did he have enough confidence in his lie to convince the greatest con man of their generation that he was telling the truth?

"Fine, do it. This is our only shot. I have to get out of the country today. The shooting at the casino brought the cops sniffing around. Once they have their warrant, they'll tear the place up. They'll find something. Don't screw this up." He handed Cash a USB drive.

Anderson dialed his phone and spoke to someone, saying to "start the engines."

The sound of a plane engine engaging filled the air.

"Hurry up, boy. I'll give you sixty seconds and then I cut my losses."

Cash needed an out. He had Lucia's gun, but he couldn't blast his way out of this. He didn't want his father killed as collateral damage.

"What's the delay?" Anderson said, resting his gun on Cash's shoulder. How subtle.

"I'm working on it. A little heads-up would have gone a long way," Cash said.

"Enough with the backtalk. Get it done or I'm cleaning house. I'll grab whatever I can get my hands on."

Cash had no doubt he was setting off alarms with Interpol and the CIA and the NSA and whoever else was watching Anderson. He set up a fake screen to make it appear as though the money was moving.

"Thanks, Cash. Good work. I'll give your best to Adrian," Anderson said.

Cash rose to his feet, whirled and leveled Lucia's gun at Anderson. "You aren't taking my son."

"Sure I am. I told Britney she couldn't keep my grandson from me forever and I'm always right. I always win." He turned to Boots. "Kill them."

Cash moved in front of his father. "We've done everything you asked. We've broken the law for you. We won't go to the police."

Anderson laughed. "This is my grand finale, the final act of my play. I can't trust your instincts and you'll bring me down. You were caught running a simple con on some drunk senator and then you fell in love with an FBI agent. Terrible, terrible."

"Let us leave. You'll be somewhere with your millions. We don't matter," Cash said.

"You won't stop looking for me. You went to prison

for your son. You won't give up on me that easily," Anderson said.

Anderson turned and left the small tent. The sound of the airplane engines grew louder.

"Boots, don't do this," Cash said.

Boots cocked his gun. "I'm hired to do what Anderson tells me. This isn't personal."

"Forget Anderson. Walk away from this. Don't you think there will be backlash when the FBI figures out one of their own was killed? With me alive, the full weight of their retribution comes down on me. If you kill me, they'll let you hang for her death. Anderson is leaving the country. He won't and can't protect you."

Boots blinked at him and lowered his gun. "Forget this. Not worth it. I'm not running and hiding for the rest of my life."

Relief tumbled through Cash. He was alive. But Anderson was free and going after Adrian. Lucia was bleeding in some rusted-out abandoned bridge. He'd saved his life, but how could he save the woman he loved and his son?

Lucia had never been so angry. Her arm was bleeding and she'd waited almost eight minutes before Benjamin and the team picked her up.

"Cash is with Anderson. Anderson will kill him."

Benjamin wrapped her arm with cloth, trying to stop the bleeding. "We need to take you to the hospital. I'll call for SWAT to help Cash."

Even in her dizzy, weakened state, she knew that was a bad idea. Their SWAT team was some of the faster responders in the city, but explaining the logistics would take time. "We'll go to the scene and we'll call SWAT on the way. Come on, Ben. This is for your promotion."

Benjamin sighed and then pointed to the two other cars. "We're going to the airstrip. Approach with caution. Wait for my instructions. Lucia, you're with me."

She climbed into the passenger side of the car, in pain, but more worried about Cash than she was about herself. She would survive an arm injury. Cash wouldn't survive a bullet in his head.

Benjamin waited for the other two cars to pull away. Then he started the car. "You've been a real pain in my neck, Lucia."

Lucia stilled. Benjamin's voice dripped with hostility. He was not joking with her.

"You should have backed away when I warned you," Benjamin said.

"Backed away? You don't want people on your team to back away."

"I didn't want you on my team at all," Benjamin said. "That was the unit chief's decision. Violent crime wanted to get rid of you, but you wouldn't make a big enough mistake for them to kick you out. They had to give you a promotion and put you in my way. I had to get a Goody Two-shoes."

"I've done everything you asked."

"That's part of the problem! The paperwork was supposed to keep you busy and the unit chief wouldn't let me bench you to keep you out of the field. I like having control of my team and you have something to prove. I can't control you. That was what violent crime hated about you. Always needing to play by the rules and do things by the book."

Lucia had missed something crucial. Benjamin

wasn't the clean agent he pretended. He was dirty. But how dirty? Was he working with Anderson? "Why did you get Cash out of prison if you didn't want Anderson caught?"

"Again, not my choice. Someone above my pay grade took an interest in Cash after finding out that he'd been given a raw deal and realizing he had a connection to Anderson."

Lucia had given Cash her gun. Could she grab Benjamin's gun before he did? Her right arm was useless, but she had her left. "You're working with Anderson."

"Not true. He paid me to take care of a few details," Benjamin said.

"Like killing me."

"When the car bomb didn't take you out, I changed my methods. I wanted you to back off and request a transfer elsewhere. If I'd wanted you dead, you'd be dead," Benjamin said.

He'd wanted her to walk away from the case. He'd let her believe that a team of trained killers was stalking her. He'd let her believe he was investigating the person following her. He'd manipulated FBI resources for his purposes.

"But that's changed. Now I want you dead," Benjamin said. "I'll clean this mess up quickly. You'll rush to see Cash, your emotions overtaking your good sense and training, and sadly, you'll be caught in the crossfire."

"There will be an investigation," Lucia said. "You won't get your promotion if I'm killed by friendly fire."

"You underestimate me," Benjamin said. "I have Jonathan Wolfe and his team looking out for you. I've done everything to protect you. I can't protect you from yourself."

"They're reporting to you so you could circumvent any plans they had to keep me safe."

"You're not as dumb as you look. Spoiled rich girl has some sense," Benjamin said.

Lucia's anger sharpened. "You didn't tell Anderson I was undercover as Lucy," she said.

"I played my cards close. I told him I would lead my special agents in a circle around him, but not close in. I had to tell him last night you were undercover. You were too close. Cash had already found a list of the people Anderson paid off at Holmes and White, and if you started digging, you might find the list of everyone on Anderson's payroll and that would include me."

"Why, Benjamin? Why would you do this? Everyone respects you." Respected. Lucia had nothing but disgust for him now.

"I'm tired of playing the game and getting nowhere. I deserve a little fun money. I deserve a break from the job. As long as the criminals are caught, what's the harm?"

"Anderson will kill Cash and his father and then he'll flee the country," Lucia said.

Benjamin laughed. "News flash, Lucia. Cash and his father are criminals, too."

It wasn't black and white. There were so many shades of gray when dealing with Cash, with love and with life.

Lucia looked out the window and caught a glimpse of an ice scraper tucked in the pocket of the door. It was spring, so it had likely been forgotten. She reached for it, her arm burning and throbbing. Her fingers brushed the plastic and then she carefully pulled it into her hand.

She waited until Benjamin was focused on the traffic, paying little attention to her.

She let her head fall back against the seat. "I won't make it."

"You were shot in the arm. You're fine."

She lifted her left hand, pretending to grab at her wound and switched the ice scraper to her left hand. Then she whipped it across the seat at Benjamin and lunged for his gun.

In a flurry of swinging and grappling for the gun, the car veered off the road. It crashed into something, stopping the car and Lucia sailed forward into the dashboard.

Lucia recovered and put her hand on Benjamin's gun. She pulled it into both hands and pointed it at him. "Get out of the car."

Benjamin held up his hands. "Careful, Lucia. You don't want to shoot me. Your word against mine. You'll look unstable. Being in a relationship with a criminal and trying to protect him by killing me after I realized he was working for Anderson. Think about how I can spin this to destroy your life."

Lucia waved the gun at him, ignoring his threat. "Hurry up. I don't have time for this!" Cash was at Anderson's mercy. She had to help him.

She forced Benjamin out of the car and had him use his handcuffs to secure himself to a nearby iron bike rack. With onlookers watching, she pointed at a man who'd come out of a used book store. "Call the police. Please!"

"I'm an FBI agent! Help me!" Benjamin said.

"He's lying," Lucia said. "He tried to kidnap me. He shot me." She gestured to her arm as proof.

She took Benjamin's FBI identification and his handcuff keys and climbed back into the car, grateful when it started. She threw the car into Reverse and then drove. Cash needed her.

According to dispatch, the SWAT team was one minute away. Lucia dragged herself out of the banged-up FBI vehicle. Her team was positioned at the places Benjamin had asked them to be, but she didn't wait for them, unsure if they were compromised, as well. She didn't know if she was too late, but the sight of a small airplane on the runway, propellers whirling, told her she had seconds to stop whatever was happening.

She held up Benjamin's ID and demanded the plane stop. The pilot ignored her. The plane started forward. Was Cash on that plane?

"Lucia!"

She turned. Cash, his father and Boots were walking toward her. Lucia ran to him, Benjamin's words echoing in her head. This was what he'd wanted, except he wasn't here to put a bullet in her back.

Could she trust the rest of the team?

The sound of sirens approached.

She hugged Cash with everything in her, throwing herself into his arms and wrapping her legs around him. She was so happy he was alive.

"Anderson is going after Adrian." Cash sounded panicked.

He set her down and she turned. A line of SWAT cars were racing up the tarmac.

The sight was imposing and terrifying.

Though one woman waving a gun and a badge hadn't stopped the pilot, an army of SWAT cars did.

The engines on the plane died and the SWAT team surrounded it.

"The unit chief approved your transfer," Lucia said. She should be thrilled for Cash. He would be working at the field office in Seattle and be near his son. It was everything he'd wanted.

Cash looked up from his desk. "I didn't know what to say when she told me."

Not caring that the team was watching them, Lucia sat on Cash's desk. "Why didn't you say anything as soon as you heard?"

Cash stood, putting himself between her thighs. Not appropriate behavior for the recently promoted special agent in charge, but Lucia didn't care. The unit chief knew about her relationship with Cash and he couldn't work with her anymore. Too much liability for the Bureau to take on and they had their hands full sorting out the mess Benjamin had made.

"I'm not going, so it doesn't matter. I'm not leaving you," Cash said.

Lucia shook her head. "You have to go. Your son needs you."

"He does. But Helen agreed to bring Adrian here. For a visit, at first. But if it goes well, maybe more."

"How? What made Helen change her mind?" Lucia asked.

"The unit chief called her and Adrian." Cash's eyes misted. "She told my son I was a hero. She told him why I ran a con and that while what I did was wrong, I did it because I love him."

Lucia took his face in her hands. "I'm so happy for you, Cash."

"But I could use a favor. I have enough money saved to move to a better place. A place more suitable for my son and Helen. I was thinking you and I could move to a new place together. We could be a family. A strange, patched-together family, but a family. It fits, don't you think?"

Happiness filled her heart. "Are you asking me to live with you?"

He groaned. "You make it sound so unromantic, but yes, I can't imagine another night without you sleeping beside me."

"Is there a reason we can't live together at my place? Isn't it big enough?" she asked.

Cash laughed. "Your place is big enough for five families. But I can't ask you to let us live there. I want to do my part and I can't afford your place."

Lucia stroked the side of Cash's face. "Money isn't something I'll allow to come between us. Not having too much of it or not having enough. I grew up in a house with plenty of money and it didn't mean that anyone was happy because of it. I want you and me and Adrian and Helen to be together where we're comfortable and happy."

"I'll feel like a kept man," Cash said, his eyes sparkling.

Lucia rolled her eyes. "Then we can move wherever you want. But I'm partial to my view of the sky."

Cash gathered her close and she felt the heat and excitement of his arousal against her.

"What will your family say about us?" he asked.

"Who cares? It took me meeting you to realize I don't care about their approval. I know what I want."

"And what do you want?" Cash asked.

"You. Just you."

She pressed a kiss to his lips and Cash kissed her back fiercely.

The dozen special agents around them and the unit chief let out catcalls and whoops of delight.

A man in a cowboy costume was leading a horse across her parents' lawn.

"Mom, please, you need to tone it down," Lucia said. "This is not necessary. You promised you would make Adrian feel comfortable."

Her mother sniffed. "Helen and I agreed this was best. Adrian is my first grandchild and I have already missed too many birthdays. He's having this birthday party, it will be fabulous and he will know we adore him."

Adrian already knew that. Her family, even Bradley, had gone out of their way to include and welcome Adrian and Helen. Lucia hugged her mother. "Thank you, Mom."

"For what?" her mother asked.

She knew what Lucia meant, but Lucia would tell her again. "For accepting Cash, his son and Helen. For accepting me as I am."

Her mother turned her, arm still around her. "You picked a good man. Look at them."

Cash, Wyatt, her father and Adrian were running around her parents' basketball court, playing some variation of the game that made them laugh.

Wyatt had been given community service for the

theft of the documents from Holmes and White. Because he had saved an FBI agent's life by lying to Boots at the abandoned covered bridge, the judge had gone easy on him. He was part of their lives, and with Adrian living in DC and without Anderson blackmailing him, he'd quit his criminal lifestyle.

Leonard Young and a host of other Holmes and White employees had been arrested as part of the embezzlement scandal. Boots and Kinsley Adams joined him in prison for their parts in the scheme.

Anderson was given no leniency. He was serving a triple life sentence in prison.

With the list of accounts that Anderson had given to Cash, ninety percent of the stolen money had been returned to its rightful owners.

Much to Elizabeth Romano's relief, the original Copley was rehung in the art museum. Audrey was allowed to return to her home with a stern warning to be careful with whom she made associations.

Elizabeth and Lucia returned the fake Copley to Franco, and Franco had immediately asked Elizabeth on a date to discuss art. Lucia had warned Elizabeth about Franco, but she swore her interest in him was purely professional curiosity.

And Cash. Cash had been given a position on another team in the white-collar unit. They wouldn't be working together day-to-day, but they spent every night together in their home.

When they noticed Lucia watching, Adrian and Cash waved.

Lucia and her mother approached them.

"Don't let her in here. I don't want the baby to get hit," Adrian said.

Lucia touched her stomach. She was only two months pregnant. They had told Adrian and Helen, but not her parents yet.

Her mom's and dad's faces had matching looks of joy and surprise.

Cash circled the court enclosure and took Lucia in his arms.

"Guess the secret's out," he said.

A smile played on her lips. "We're not a keeping-secrets kind of family. The truth tends to find its way out."

Cash laughed. "And I couldn't be happier to be part of it."

* * * * *

If you loved this novel, don't miss these other sexy, suspenseful stories from C.J. Miller:

UNDER THE SHEIK'S PROTECTION
TRAITOROUS ATTRACTION
PROTECTING HIS PRINCESS
SHIELDING THE SUSPECT

Available now from
Harlequin Romantic Suspense!

REQUEST YOUR FREE BOOKS!
2 FREE NOVELS PLUS 2 FREE GIFTS!

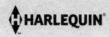

ROMANTIC suspense

Sparked by danger, fueled by passion

YES! Please send me 2 FREE Harlequin® Romantic Suspense novels and my 2 FREE gifts (gifts are worth about $10). After receiving them, if I don't wish to receive any more books, I can return the shipping statement marked "cancel." If I don't cancel, I will receive 4 brand-new novels every month and be billed just $4.74 per book in the U.S. or $5.24 per book in Canada. That's a savings of at least 14% off the cover price! It's quite a bargain! Shipping and handling is just 50¢ per book in the U.S. and 75¢ per book in Canada.* I understand that accepting the 2 free books and gifts places me under no obligation to buy anything. I can always return a shipment and cancel at any time. Even if I never buy another book, the two free books and gifts are mine to keep forever.

240/340 HDN F45N

Name	(PLEASE PRINT)	
Address		Apt. #
City	State/Prov.	Zip/Postal Code

Signature (if under 18, a parent or guardian must sign)

Mail to the **Harlequin® Reader Service:**
IN U.S.A.: P.O. Box 1867, Buffalo, NY 14240-1867
IN CANADA: P.O. Box 609, Fort Erie, Ontario L2A 5X3

Want to try two free books from another line?
Call 1-800-873-8635 or visit www.ReaderService.com.

* Terms and prices subject to change without notice. Prices do not include applicable taxes. Sales tax applicable in N.Y. Canadian residents will be charged applicable taxes. Offer not valid in Quebec. This offer is limited to one order per household. Not valid for current subscribers to Harlequin Romantic Suspense books. All orders subject to credit approval. Credit or debit balances in a customer's account(s) may be offset by any other outstanding balance owed by or to the customer. Please allow 4 to 6 weeks for delivery. Offer available while quantities last.

Your Privacy—The Harlequin® Reader Service is committed to protecting your privacy. Our Privacy Policy is available online at www.ReaderService.com or upon request from the Harlequin Reader Service.

We make a portion of our mailing list available to reputable third parties that offer products we believe may interest you. If you prefer that we not exchange your name with third parties, or if you wish to clarify or modify your communication preferences, please visit us at www.ReaderService.com/consumerchoice or write to us at Harlequin Reader Service Preference Service, P.O. Box 9062, Buffalo, NY 14269. Include your complete name and address.

HRS13R

He stepped outside and looked around. "What are you
doing out here all by yourself in the dark?"

"You told my son that cowboys only bathe once a
week, and now Sammy won't get into the bathtub."

By the light of the room spilling out where they stood,
she saw his amusement curve his lips upward. "Is that
a fact?" he replied. "Sounds like a personal problem to
me."

"It's all your fault," she said, at the same time trying
not to notice the wonder of his broad shoulders, the slim
hips that wore his jeans so well.

He raised a dark eyebrow. "The way I see it, you started
it."

This time the heat that filled her cheeks was a new
wave of pure embarrassment. "Look, I'm sorry. When I
told my son those things, I'd never really met a cowboy
before. The only cowboy I've ever even seen in my entire

ife is the naked singing cowboy in Times Square. I
now have a little boy who refuses to take a bath. Can
you please come back to the house with me and tell him
differently?"

Amusement once again danced in his eyes as he gave
her a smile that made her feel just a little bit breathless.
"Basically you've come to say you're sorry about your
preconceived notions about cowboys, because I think it
would be nice if you apologized before asking for my
help about anything."

"You're right. I am sorry," she replied, wondering if
he wanted her to get down on her knees before him and
grovel, as well.

"Okay, then, let's go." He pulled the door of his unit
closed behind him and fell into step next to her.

"A naked singing cowboy…and you New Yorkers
think we're strange." He laughed, a low, deep rumble that
she found far too pleasant.

She realized at that moment that she wasn't afraid of
cows or horses, that she wasn't worried about falling into
the mud or getting her hands dirty.

The real danger came from the attraction she felt for
the man who walked next to her, a man whose laughter
warmed her and who smelled like spring wind and leather.

Don't miss A REAL COWBOY by Carla Cassidy,
available March 2015
wherever Harlequin® Romantic Suspense
books and ebooks are sold.

www.Harlequin.com

Love the Harlequin book you just read?

Your opinion matters.

Review this book on your favorite book site, review site, blog or your own social media properties and share your opinion with other readers!

JUST CAN'T GET ENOUGH
ROMANCE
Looking for more?

Harlequin has everything from contemporary, passionate and heartwarming to suspenseful and inspirational stories.

Whatever your mood,
we have a romance just for you!

Connect with us to find your next great read,
special offers and more.

Facebook.com/HarlequinBooks
Twitter.com/HarlequinBooks
HarlequinBlog.com
Harlequin.com/Newsletters